# LEGACY REJECTED

## NUTFIELD SAGA
## BOOK 6

## ROBIN PATCHEN

JDO PUBLISHING

Print ISBN: 978-1079507355

Large Print ISBN: 979-8841012382


Cover by Lynnette Bonner.

*For Mom.*
*Your encouragement has fueled my achievements.*

# ACKNOWLEDGMENTS

No story comes together easily. This one was harder than most. I couldn't have done it without the brainstorming help of Susan Crawford, Regina Jennings, and my brilliant and insightful husband, Eddie, who knows much more about the workings of the criminal underworld than I'd ever imagined.

Once again to my my critique partners, Normandie Fischer, Kara Hunt, Jericha Kingston, Candice Sue Patterson, Sharon Srock, Pegg Thomas, and Terri Weldon—you make me look good. I couldn't do this without you.

Misty Beller, your marketing advice is invaluable, as is your friendship.

Thank you, Ray Rhamey, for your excellent editing.

Sara Jo Odom—whom I'm lucky enough to call Mom—thank you for all your support—and your proofreading skills as well.

Eddie, Nick, Lexi, and Jacob, your encouragement means more than I can express. It's an odd person who makes up fictional characters for a living and a special family that will encourage the dream.

Finally and most importantly, thank you, Lord, for the story idea and the ability to bring it together. I owe this book, everything I do, and everything I am to You.

# CHAPTER ONE

Ginny Lamont stepped onto her front porch and breathed in the sunshine. She loved everything about her new home. Even the cold New Hampshire winter had felt cozy and homey here. She'd built fires in her fireplace on particularly chilly nights. And it didn't hurt that when the roads were slick, she could bundle up and walk to the office and all the little shops and restaurants in downtown Nutfield.

Winter had tried to nudge its way back in more than once this April, but spring in New England knew how to nudge right back. Today, warmth won the battle, and the birds were celebrating with song from the beautiful old maple in her front yard.

She slid behind the wheel of her Toyota. It was too nice a day to stay inside, though the work there beckoned—painting and updating her house took up most of her spare time. But she needed a little family time. And she wasn't going to think about the way her mother had shoved her out the door the previous summer and told her never to return. She wasn't going to think about Kathryn's cold welcome when she'd relocated to Nutfield. Ginny had come here to be close to her sister. She'd gotten to know her brother-in-law, and she'd fallen in love with the kids.

Kathryn hadn't invited Ginny over in weeks. Not that she invited her very often. In fact, no matter how hard Ginny tried, she and her sister still hadn't rekindled the sisterly relationship they'd had as kids. But today, Ginny was going to take a chance and stop by. It was simply too glorious a day not to share it with people she loved. Maybe today would be the day she'd break through Kathryn's hard shell.

Ginny picked up lunch at KFC, including a box of cookies for the kids. Kathryn would give her that look of disappointment—the one Ginny had seen so often during their childhood—but the kids' excitement over the treats would soften the blow of her sister's disapproval.

When Ginny turned onto their street, she had to maneuver around a giant moving truck in front of Kathryn's house. Were the neighbors moving?

She parked on the street behind a big silver Mercedes, grabbed the bag filled with lunch, and climbed out of the car.

When she rounded the huge moving truck, she froze.

The movers weren't at the neighbor's house. They were at Kathryn's.

Her sister directed traffic outside. "Did you get the lawn chairs?" she asked one of the movers.

"We got it all."

"Good," Kathryn said. "Then it looks like we're about finished."

The man passed Kathryn and headed for the truck.

Kathryn called into the house, "Matthew, are you ready?"

Ginny stood at the edge of the yard and watched. She couldn't seem to make her feet move. Maybe it was all a nightmare, a terrible nightmare.

*Come on, Ginny. Wake up.* This couldn't be happening. Not again.

The moving truck's rear door slammed shut. The sound reverberated like a gunshot.

Kathryn turned at the noise and saw Ginny. Her eyes widened, and she glanced at the front door as if she might run.

And then, she approached. "What are you doing here?"

Ginny lifted the meal. "I missed you. I haven't seen you in..." A long time. She hadn't been invited over in weeks, and now she knew why. Kathryn had been packing.

Kathryn crossed her arms. "We're leaving."

Ginny set the sack of food on the sidewalk. "I thought you loved New Hampshire."

"We do." Kathryn's scowl slipped a little, and behind it, Ginny saw the sister she'd once known. The sister who'd once loved her back. "We did. We made a home here. Our kids were happy here."

"Then why?" Ginny scanned the front yard of the giant Colonial. There was no *For Sale* sign in the yard. Apparently, it had been a private sale.

A secret sale.

But why?

Kathryn shook her head. "You're either monumentally stupid or you think I am."

Ginny opened her mouth but couldn't come up with a suitable answer. Finally, she said, "Since we both know you've always been the smart one, I guess I'm the stupid one."

"You really don't understand what your coming here has done?"

"I came here to be near you. Since Dad died and Mom sent me away, you're the only family I have left."

A door closed, and they turned to see Matthew chase their two-year-old daughter out of the gaping garage. He snatched her, carried her to the far side of their SUV, opened the door, and wrangled her into the car seat.

Ginny had found herself surrounded by this big, chaotic family of six. She'd been invited for Thanksgiving and Christmas and New Year's and Easter. She'd babysat and played with the kids and enjoyed the family time, so different from her own growing-up years. And if her sister had been cold to her, her brother-in-law standoffish, at least the kids had made her feel welcome. The boys with their toy guns and crazy antics, the girls with their giggles and hugs. She'd fallen in love with them.

Tears burned, and she didn't bother to brush them away. "I don't understand."

Kathryn inhaled a deep sigh, blew it out through her nose in her signature *You're too stupid to live* move. And as always, Kathryn was right. Ginny was ten steps behind.

Then, Kathryn touched Ginny's hand. The lightest touch, a gesture of... what? Kindness, maybe? Sympathy? "You should leave, too. And don't tell anyone where you're going."

"I don't understand."

"It's just a matter of time before they come after you."

*They?* She had no idea what her sister was talking about, but her heartbeat raced anyway. "Who?"

Behind them, Matthew spoke in quiet tones to the movers. A moment later, the truck pulled away.

When the noise died, Ginny asked, "Who am I supposed to be running from?"

Kathryn rolled her eyes, an adolescent gesture that brought a pang of memories. "Mom and Dad's associates. Seriously, open your eyes. You're in danger. You need to leave, and don't look back. Change your name. Get new ID. Do whatever you have to do. But hide."

"You haven't been hiding."

"That was before you led them here, before Dad's accident."

Behind them, Matthew called, "It's time to go."

Kathryn nodded at her husband, then stepped forward and pulled Ginny into a tight embrace. Into her ear, she said, "They're here, Ginny. I don't know why, and I don't know what they want. You have to run." Kathryn stepped back, swiped a tear from her eyes.

"Who did you see?"

She glanced at Matthew, who nodded, before she faced Ginny again. "I spotted a man in town a couple of weeks ago. He was at Dad's funeral. I didn't know his name, and when I asked Mom about him, she was evasive. She seemed scared."

"Mom's never scared."

"I know," Kathryn said. "It can't be a coincidence that he's here."

"Why didn't you tell me?"

Kathryn sighed, shook her head. "I can't be responsible for you anymore. I have my own family now."

"This guy, what does he—?"

"I have no idea!"

Ginny wanted to demand more information, but if Kathryn knew anything else, she wasn't sharing. Ginny swallowed all her questions. If she had to leave Nutfield to stay with her sister, she would. "I'll just come—"

"No." The word was harsh, and any tenderness Ginny might have seen in Kathryn's eyes vanished. "You stay away from me and my family. Don't try to find us. If you love us at all, stay far away."

"But—"

"Good bye, Ginny."

Kathryn marched to the SUV and slid in the passenger seat.

Matthew followed. Just before he climbed in, he turned and met Ginny's eyes. "God bless you. Be safe."

The only family she had left in the world drove down the street and out of sight.

Ginny stared at the empty road long after they'd disappeared.

The neighborhood was quiet. As far as Ginny could see, nobody had witnessed her latest shame.

As usual, she was alone.

Ginny had known her sister wasn't thrilled when she'd arrived in Nutfield the previous summer, but Kathryn seemed to come to terms with it. Had that all been a lie?

Stupid question. Ginny was standing in the driveway of an empty house, nothing but the lingering scents of exhaust and cooling fried chicken to show anybody else had been there at all. Tears streamed from her eyes, and she grabbed a napkin from the bag and wiped them.

Sunlight glinted off her sedan. The Mercedes was still there. She had no idea whose it was. She glanced at the lunch she'd brought to surprise them.

The surprise had been hers.

If she hadn't shown up, her sister would have disappeared without a word.

She should leave, but she couldn't seem to make her feet move. It made no sense. Why would Kathryn do this?

That question brought back another. Why had Ginny's mother sent her away the day of her father's memorial? That had been one of the strangest, most heartbreaking moments of her life. The duffel bag Mom had shoved into her hand just before she pushed Ginny out the door had been filled with cash—her first clue that her parents' business wasn't legitimate.

But she cared nothing about that. She hadn't touched the money. Hadn't wanted to. She'd stuck it in a safe deposit box and left it, figuring Mom would call to collect it eventually.

Ginny didn't need money. She needed family.

The breeze kicked up. She snatched the sack of food. She should go. There was nothing left for her here.

She was mustering the energy to walk to her car when a man stepped from the house onto the front porch steps. He smiled and lifted a hand in greeting.

She froze. It was Kade Powers, real estate developer and entrepreneur.

He started toward her. "I hate to break it to you, but you're too late to get this listing. It's already..." His words trailed as he approached. "What happened? Are you all right?"

Right. She must be a mess. Just her luck she'd run into the most attractive single man in town when she was bawling like a baby. She turned away and sniffed and wiped the tears with the damp napkin. Not that it would do any good. With a sigh, she turned back to him. "Just got a bit of bad news."

His lips turned down at the corners. "Anything I can do?"

She shook her head, wiped her eyes again. "Why are you here?"

"I just bought this house. The owners insisted we keep it quiet, so I didn't say anything at the meeting the other day." The real estate meeting. She also knew him from Rotary Club and the food bank, where they both volunteered.

Kathryn had sure been thorough, hadn't she? No way was her little sister going to get wind of her plan to skip town.

Kade stepped forward and placed his hand on her elbow. "I'm sorry about your bad news. You want to talk about it?"

"It doesn't matter."

"Were you here looking for Kathryn Jacobs? They just left."

"I talked to her. Did they tell you where they were going?"

Maybe Kathryn had been more honest with this practical stranger than she'd been with Ginny.

"Sorry." Kade let his hand drop "Like I said, all very hush-hush. How did you know her?"

"She's my sister."

He blinked once, twice. "Wait... You don't know where—?"

"I'm the reason it was all very hush-hush." She couldn't keep the sadness from her voice.

"Wow." His normally cheerful demeanor shifted to pity. "That's... harsh."

Ginny shrugged. "Whatever." Her bid for nonchalance failed when her voice cracked.

He glanced at his watch. "I have a meeting this afternoon, but I have time for lunch... or coffee... if you need to talk."

He was trying to be nice, to take care of the pathetic loser whose own sister wanted nothing to do with her. She didn't need his pity. Or maybe she did, but she sure as heck wasn't going to take it.

She pushed her shoulders back and tried to arrange her lips into a smile. "I brought lunch. I was going to share with Kathryn, but she had to rush out. Thanks, anyway."

His warm eyes held hers. "Okay, if you're—"

"Congrats on the house." She broke the eye contact. The way he was looking at her, the sadness and concern, made her want to cry all over again. "I'm sure you'll be very happy here."

"I'm not going to live here. I plan to resell it. They sold it for..." His words trailed.

"Right. Probably practically gave it away. Who knew I was so repulsive?"

He touched her arm. "I'm sure it had nothing to do with you."

Ginny forced a laugh. "Now you're just making stuff up." She turned and headed for her car, calling over her shoulder, "See you at the food bank."

He said nothing else, but when Ginny slid into her car, she peeked, and sure enough, he was still standing there, watching her go.

Excellent. It wasn't humiliating enough that her sister had schemed to get away without telling her, but now her embarrassment was public.

No wonder Ginny had always been alone. Even when she was a kid, Ginny had been on the outside looking in. Her biggest mistake was believing that might change.

She pulled onto the street, careful not to hit the Mercedes, which must have belonged to Kade. She didn't have any appointments that day. In fact, she didn't have anything to do at all. The lunch she'd purchased in town filled the car with delicious scents, but they turned her stomach now. She'd find a dumpster and toss the entire bag. Then...

Then she'd have to decide what to do. Because Kathryn seemed to think she was in danger in Nutfield. But Ginny had nowhere else to go.

## CHAPTER TWO

That had gone well.

If he'd been hoping to alienate and embarrass the attractive real estate agent, he'd call it a win-win.

Kade Powers stepped back inside his latest acquisition and wandered through the rooms, barely seeing anything. He'd gone outside because he'd seen movement in the driveway and assumed the cleaners had arrived. He'd been shocked to see Ginny Lamont.

What kind of person was Kathryn, a woman planning to move away without telling her own sister? He'd never heard of such a thing. His own family was supportive and generous. His folks had retired to Florida a few years back, but his older brothers and sister still lived in New Hampshire. He saw them often. So maybe they were a little nosy about his life, always offering *helpful* advice on every subject from his growing development business to his romantic relationships—or lack thereof. Ten minutes ago, he'd have complained about his siblings. Having seen the other side...

The sadness in Ginny's eyes made all the joy about this quick acquisition leach away.

He wandered into the kitchen. The house was in good shape. Maybe if it didn't sell right away, he'd have Ginny list it for him. Would he be willing to lose a huge percentage of profit just to have an excuse to call her?

Probably.

Because he'd been looking for an excuse. Ever since he'd met her at the Chamber of Commerce meeting a few months ago, he'd been thinking of asking her out. He probably would have that first day if his big brother hadn't been there. He loved Darren and his wife. But Darren seemed to think Kade wasn't capable of managing his own dating life. After his fourth suggestion, whispered while the speaker droned on, that Kade ask Ginny out—each with helpful hints on how to approach her, where to take her on a date, how to make a good impression—Kade had decided there was no way he was going to do it then. He didn't need his big brother's dating advice. He sure didn't need Darren taking credit for it if she accepted.

Then, he and Ginny had settled into a friendly but distant relationship, business acquaintances. They saw each other often, chatted about the real estate market and the weather. And while he had a profound attraction to her, it seemed she felt nothing for him but mild friendship. For months he'd been trying to figure out how to breach the wall of the friend zone and kicking himself for the stupid pride that had kept him from asking her out that first day.

If Darren had just kept his mouth shut...

At least his brother cared.

Ginny was new to the area and had only moved here to be near her sister. She'd shared that much with him during a conversation at the food bank during a lull in clients.

Ginny'd probably give anything for a pushy older brother.

The doorbell rang, and Kade let the cleaners in. He'd worked with them often enough that he didn't need to give them instructions. They knew what to do. The house would be advertised in tomorrow's newspaper at a price below market value, which should guarantee him a quick sale. It would yield him a nice profit.

Now that he knew what this meant for Ginny, the triumph felt hollow.

Heading to his car, he tried to focus on what this would mean for him. More money to invest in the development he was trying to get off the ground. But even the thought of building a country club and high-end housing on the far side of Clearwater Lake couldn't improve his mood.

He'd blown his chance with Ginny before he'd ever mustered the nerve to ask her out.

~

WITH HIS LEATHER portfolio tucked under his arm, Kade stepped inside the Nutfield town offices. The building was one of the oldest in town, and the underlying scent of mildew hit him as soon as the door closed. The black and white tile floors were scuffed, and the painted walls and hardwood doors leading off the wide hallway showed years of wear. The structure was solid, but it could use a facelift. New floors, fresh paint, updated light fixtures. The glass in the windows that flanked the entrance was so old, it barely let in any of the late afternoon April sun. Nutfield was a growing, dynamic community, but nobody would know that based on the state of the city offices.

That he noticed was an occupational hazard.

At the far end of the building, the corridor opened to a reception area. Clerks worked on the town's day-to-day business behind a long counter. People waited in line to pay traffic tickets or renew their car registrations or for any number of other reasons. Before Kade could run into anybody he knew, he climbed the ancient staircase to the second floor and made his way down another hallway—this one carpeted—to a door that read *Town Manager.* He stepped inside.

Seated at the receptionist desk was a woman whose age rivaled that of the building. Thinning white hair, skin lined like a crumpled piece of paper, hands darkened with age spots, Penny welcomed him with a wide smile. "Ah, Kade." Her voice came out stronger than anybody her age should be able to manage. "I'm afraid you've come at a bad time."

"He's not in?"

"He's in all right." Her eyes twinkled, and she lowered her

voice. "He just found out the jewelry repair shop on the corner sold out to a fellow who wants to open an upscale coffee shop."

Kade shook his head. "Heaven forbid people should be able to buy coffee."

She cackled, then slapped her hand over her mouth. "Not just coffee, but"—she made air quotes—"fancy frou-frou wussy coffee." She dropped her hands. "He and change get along like the Bruins and the Canadiens in the playoffs."

Kade chuckled, but the underlying issue wasn't so funny. Since Bruce Collier was the town manager, every change in Nutfield had to go through him.

"Maybe you should come back on Monday," Penny said.

Not an option, and Bruce's mood probably wouldn't make a difference. "If you can just get me on the agenda for the board meeting—"

"No can do, hon. You gotta get Bruce's approval."

"In this town, you have to get Bruce's approval to sneeze without a cotton handkerchief."

"If he could, he'd start a petition against Kleenex." She deepened her voice and offered a fair impersonation of her boss. "All these young people's obsession with the environment, and they go through tissues like water."

How Penny kept her spirits so high working for a curmudgeon like Bruce, Kade would never understand. She'd worked for every town manager since parachute pants were in style, and she'd probably stay long past this one.

The door to the inner sanctum was yanked open. "What the devil is all the racket about?" Bruce Collier stepped out. Though in his seventies, he stood tall and straight. He had gray hair cropped short and beady brown eyes. When he saw Kade, he smiled, though Kade knew it was forced. "What brings you by?"

"Need to get on the agenda for next week's meeting."

The old man exhaled a long breath. "Come on in, then." He turned to Penny. "You finish typing that agenda yet? If it's done, then it's too late."

"Thanks to this fancy-shmancy computer, I can make changes in a jiffy. Don't you worry about me."

Bruce huffed and marched into his office.

Kade followed, offering Penny a wink before he closed the door.

He could give Bruce credit for one thing—the man didn't have a double standard. His office was as old and dingy as the rest of the building. The desk could have been built during the War for Independence, and though it had attractive lines, it was desperate for a refinishing job. The upholstered furniture was faded, and when Kade sat in the chair across from Bruce's desk, he sank into it as if the stuffing had long since retired.

Bruce sat, folded his hands on his desk, and gave Kade a look intended to intimidate.

Kade wasn't so easily scared. He tapped his portfolio on his lap. Inside were numbers and studies and artists' renderings of the development he was planning, but he doubted Bruce would want to see any of it. The guy'd already made up his mind. "Last time I met with the zoning board about my development project, I was told to have an environmental impact study completed. It was also suggested to me that the board wouldn't waste its time"—as if it wasn't their job—"looking at my plans until I had the funding—"

"Don't waste *my* time telling me what I already know. Get to the point."

"The study is ready, and I've put together a group of investors willing to take on the project. We're nearly fully funded."

A small, triumphant smile crossed the man's lips. "Nearly, you say? But not fully. We can't go forward—"

"Until the project is approved, many investors won't even look at it. I need to get approval. Then, the rest of the investors will fall into place."

"So you say."

"It's a vote, Bruce. A debate and a vote, nothing more. As a longtime citizen of this community and the owner of a number of properties, including a large parcel of valuable land, I have the right to bring items before the board."

"That you do. But I have the right to require certain things. Until you can confirm the project will be fully funded, I'm not wasting the board's time."

Kade stood and paced to the far side of the room, frustration churning like the spring wind outside the window. The zoning board only met every quarter. If he didn't get on their agenda now, it would be late summer before he could get approval, and by then, it would be too late to break ground before winter. Another year would pass without his having accomplished anything of substance.

He turned back to Bruce. "I need to get on the agenda."

Bruce didn't even fight his triumphant smile. "Then you have some work to do, don't you?"

"Fine." He strode out, slamming the door behind him.

Outside, Kade stormed down the sidewalk. Some of his investors wouldn't wait another year to get the project started. It had been too long already. His father had given Kade the parcel of land on Clearwater Lake five years before. Each of the kids had gotten something from their Dad to use to build their futures.

Andrea, the oldest, had invested her allotment of their parents' wealth in a number of businesses, which had succeeded beyond anyone's wildest dreams. Now, she focused on her kids and oversaw her businesses from home.

Rich, the second child, had used his allotment to go to law school. He'd graduated debt-free from Harvard and now was a partner in a big Boston law firm.

Darren, the one closest in age to Kade and the only one who lived in town, had bought a gas station franchise. Today, he owned multiple stores in southern New Hampshire, all of which were doing well.

Instead of cash, Kade's parents had given him a huge parcel of land on the shores of Clearwater Lake. He'd always wanted to be a real estate developer, and he'd been working to develop that property for years. But lack of vision, then lack of funds, had kept him from doing anything with it. He was thirty-two, older than his older siblings had been by the time they'd achieved their dreams. He was the baby of the family, dubbed a late bloomer. A straggler.

Never mind that few people in the world achieved their dreams by the time they were thirty. In the Powers family, success was expected.

Which meant Kade needed more investors. Fast.

He pushed into McNeal's. The restaurant was about half-full, not bad for four o'clock in the afternoon. Bonnie, the older woman who'd been managing the place as long as he could remember, led him to a booth near the window and promised to bring him a Coke. He could have gone home, but he got more done in public places. He liked the energy at McNeal's. The atmosphere, the conversation going on around him, fueled him when he was discouraged.

He pulled out his phone and set his portfolio on the table. He had a list of investors who'd shown interest in the development. Though he hated to do it without new information, he started calling them one by one.

Thirty minutes later, he had no more promised money and much less enthusiasm. Sure, the investors were still interested, but until Kade got the plans approved by the town, they weren't willing to commit. Considering others had only promised to invest if he could get the project underway this quarter, Kade was in trouble.

And out of good options. If he wanted the development to get approved and started before summer, he was going to have to do something he'd sworn he'd never do. He was going to have to ask his family to invest.

Either that or admit defeat for another year.

Before he had to decide, a familiar figure stepped into the diner. Ginny was alone and looked to be in no better spirits than she had been earlier in the day. She spoke to Bonnie, then propped herself against the far wall and crossed her arms.

He waved to get her attention.

She caught his eye and headed toward him. "Meeting someone for dinner?"

"Trying to get some work done."

"Well, I won't keep—"

"Actually, I was finished." Not true, but he'd happily put off his impossible decision in order to have another conversation with Ginny. Just looking at that nearly black hair and those sparkling blue eyes lifted his spirits. "If you'd like to join me..."

"Maybe for a second." She perched on the seat across from him without taking off her jacket. "I was picking up a to-go order."

"You could always stay and eat with me."

"I'm not really up for company tonight." Her glance flicked to the window, to the floor. Her eyes were red-rimmed and swollen, and her sadness seemed as heavy as the wool coat she wore.

"What can I do?"

"I'll be fine."

It was all so odd, the way her sister had left. He'd love to know more about it. About Ginny.

Bonnie set a paper bag on the table in front of Ginny. "I threw in a cookie for good measure."

Ginny attempted a smile, though the effort seemed painful. "Thank you." After Bonnie left, Ginny stood and focused on him. "Good to see you again."

"Um... How about lunch? Tomorrow?"

"Don't worry about me. I have plenty to keep me busy."

"I have no doubt." Kade stood. "But I'd still like to have lunch with you." Months he'd wanted to ask her. It was probably a bad idea to do it now, but the words had popped out without his permission.

"Oh." She offered the first genuine smile he'd seen on her that day. "I guess, if you don't have anything better to do."

"I'll call you in the morning."

"My number—"

"It's in the club directory, right?"

"Oh, right." Her cheeks turned a beautiful shade of pink.

"Good." He nodded toward her take-out bag. "You're still welcome to join me."

"No. Thanks. I'll talk to you tomorrow."

She turned toward the exit. At the same time, a man seated at a neighboring table stood and stepped into her path.

She crashed into him. She kept a hold of the bag, but her purse slipped and clattered to the floor. "Oh! I'm sorry."

"Entirely my fault." The man crouched, lifted her purse, and held it out it to her.

She nodded her thanks, tossed a "see you tomorrow" to Kade over her shoulder, and rushed out.

The man watched her leave before turning to Kade. "I was lost in thought." He had an accent—maybe Russian? "I do that sometimes. I hope I didn't hurt her."

Kade turned his focus to the stranger. He wanted to dress the man down for his behavior, but the guy seemed genuinely sorry. "I think she's okay."

He had the look of someone who'd lifted a lot of weights in his younger years. Not flabby but no longer at his peak. Aside from a little fuzz over his ears, he was bald, and a pair of reading glasses was perched low on his nose. He wore a suit and tie and was nearly as tall as Kade, over six feet.

"I was going to make a phone call," the man said, "but I also wanted to talk to you."

Kade took a step back. He'd never seen this guy before in his life. "Why?"

"I will explain. It concerns the investment opportunity you've been making calls about. But first"—he held up his cell phone—"I'll be right back."

With that, the man disappeared out the door.

Kade sipped his drink and tried to think of other investors he could call. He'd written down the names of three people he could approach again about investing before the stranger stepped back inside the cafe. Kade stood as he walked toward the table and held out his hand. "My name is Mike Sokolov."

Kade shook it. "Kade Powers."

"Mind if I sit?"

"Help yourself."

Sokolov shrugged off his suit jacket, and both men slid into the booth. He was polite and refined, but there was something about him that made his mannerisms seem forced. Or maybe it was just that he was so big—and he'd nearly knocked Ginny over—that his manners felt out of place.

"I overheard you talking on the phone before your friend came in." The man shifted his sizable weight on the bench seat and spread his arms along the back. "I may be able to help you."

"How?"

"You are from this town, right?"

"All my life."

The man nodded. "You seem very invested in it."

Kade resisted the urge to check his watch. He had no idea what this guy wanted, but he wished he'd get to the point. Any minute now, the guy would start a sales spiel. Insurance, cleaning supplies, energy drinks... Whatever he was selling, Kade wasn't buying. When Sokolov said nothing else, Kade added, "Nutfield is my home. It's important to me."

"I like that." Sokolov's small eyes studied him, appraised him. "You seem sincere."

What was he supposed to say to that?

"Tell me about your project."

"May I ask why you're interested?"

The man smiled, showing crooked, yellowing teeth. "I have a big family. Big." He reached into his suit jacket, which was folded on the seat beside him, pulled a wallet from the inside pocket, and opened it to reveal a photo of a large family. Surrounding Sokolov were a woman who looked to be about his age and a number of other adults—his kids, Kade assumed. There were children, too. Some standing, some in the arms of an adult. There had to be fifteen, maybe twenty people in the photo, all smiling at the camera.

"Good looking family," Kade said.

"My wife"—he pointed to the woman beside him in the picture

—"thinks we need a vacation home, one large enough for all of us. She wants a house by a lake, but me..." He flipped the wallet closed. "I was raised near the shore of the Black Sea. There's something raw about the sea, don't you think? I want to share it with my kids."

The Black Sea. So the guy was likely Russian or Ukrainian. That tracked with the accent.

Sokolov returned the wallet to its pocket. "The grandkids, I think they would like the boardwalk on Hampton Beach, which isn't too far from here, and my kids would be happy with a quiet place where they can relax, someplace the kids can play and be safe. We all need a place we can get to easily from the Boston area. So I'm looking for a home that will make everyone happy. We visited Nutfield years ago and liked it. When I was doing research, I decided to check it out."

"Have you found anything?"

"Nothing suitable. Along the lake, there are many homes, but nothing large enough to accommodate my family."

Didn't Kade know it. It was one of the reasons he knew his development would be not only a great investment for him and his partners but good for the community. "There are lots of small homes, three or four bedrooms at most. There may be some with converted basements, attic rooms, or other spaces that could make it work for a larger family. I have a friend who manages many of the properties around the lake. I'd be happy to ask him if he knows of anything."

"They are old," Sokolov said, "or, if they aren't old, they are surrounded by old houses. I'm looking for something new, something to suit my wife's taste."

"More upscale?"

"Exactly." Sokolov rested his forearms on the table and leaned on them. "I overheard you on the phone say that you're working on a housing development."

"We won't break ground for months. The homes won't be ready until late summer at best."

Sokolov was nodding. "Tell me your plans."

Kade didn't have time to chit-chat with this guy, but getting a promise to buy one of the properties might help spur reluctant investors into finally committing the money he needed to get the project off the ground.

"The land I own stretches across the far, undeveloped side of Clearwater Lake. An environmental impact study has already been done, and there's nothing to keep us from developing it. There are a few marshy areas we'll have to develop around, but we'll be able to protect those." He skimmed through his portfolio and pulled out one of the artist's renderings of the property. One glimpse of it made his heart thump, but he kept his enthusiasm tamped down and turned it to face Sokolov. "As you can see, the development will include approximately fifty homes. Some will be lakefront, and others will be on the golf course. They'll each be built on at least three-quarters of an acre."

Kade glanced at Sokolov to see him studying the rendering. Sokolov pointed to the largest structure. "What is this?"

"The clubhouse. It'll have a banquet room, a handful of smaller meeting rooms, a pool, tennis courts, and, of course, the pro shop for the golf course."

Sokolov met Kade's eyes. "So this isn't just a housing development. It's a country club."

Kade sat back and nodded. "I see it being a gathering place for the entire community, not just the residents of the neighborhood."

Sokolov looked down again. "And what of services? Will there be shops or restaurants?"

"Not in the development." Kade tapped the road drawn on the paper. "That leads straight north into Nutfield and straight south to the interstate."

"So this will be good for your town."

"Absolutely. The property taxes will be a boost, not to mention the increase to the number of tourists who'll visit annually."

"And what does the town think of that?"

"Depends who you ask, but local business owners are on board. I talked to one of the school board members, and she says they're all in favor. It won't add so many kids the schools will be overrun, but it'll increase their budget. It's a win-win."

"Why then is it not fully funded?"

"Because some people don't want to commit or even look too closely at it until they know it's going to be built, but the town manager won't bring it to the board until it's fully funded."

"What do you call that? There's an American expression…"

"A catch-22."

Sokolov smiled and nodded. "Yes. Catch-22. What does that come from?"

"A book, I think."

Sokolov sat back. "I am intrigued." He chuckled and added, "About this"—he tapped the artists' rendering on the table—"not the book."

"I have some floor plans drawn up, if you'd like to take a look."

Sokolov checked his watch, then pulled his jacket onto his lap. "I don't think I'll be buying one of the houses until we can walk through them, see what my wife thinks. But the investment opportunity sounds promising."

Kade forced himself to sit back, not to act too eager. "You're an investor?"

"I belong to an investment group in Boston. I wouldn't have considered this if I hadn't just spent the day looking at unsuitable properties. This is exactly what I'm looking for. And if I'm looking, then others must be, too." He pulled a business card from his breast pocket and handed it to Kade. "Please, email me all the information you have. My club meets Monday mornings, so I'll take it to them, and we'll get back to you by Monday afternoon."

"That sounds—"

"I'm so sorry to interrupt."

Kade turned to see Ginny approaching the table. Her cheeks were red, her eyes wide.

"Everything okay?" Kade slipped the business card into his pocket.

"I can't find my phone. I wondered if maybe it slipped out

when I was sitting here or"—she glanced at Sokolov, who'd crashed into her—"when I dropped my purse."

Sokolov stood. "My dear, I'm so sorry. I'll look."

"It's okay. I can—"

"Absolutely not. You sit. I'll search."

He set his jacket on the table, then crouched on the floor near where she'd fallen.

She slid in across from Kade and felt around the bench seat and in the crevice between the seat and the wall. "I never lose my phone. I can't believe it took me so long to realize it was gone. I got almost all the way home."

Kade peered beneath their table but saw nothing. Sokolov seemed to be conducting a thorough search of the rest of the restaurant.

When Ginny gave up looking, he said, "You're not having a very good day."

She pressed her lips closed and shook her head.

"I want to help."

"There's nothing you can—"

"Found it." Sokolov stood beside the table and presented the phone as if it were a priceless jewel. "Please accept my apologizes. It must have skidded out when I crashed into you."

Her shoulders relaxed the tiniest bit as she took the phone. "No harm done." She glanced at Kade. "Sorry again for interrupting. I'll just let you get back to it."

Sokolov shook his head. "We're finished, and I am leaving." He held out his hand to Kade, who stood and shook it. Sokolov's beefy grip was firm. "I look forward to hearing from you." Then, he turned to Ginny and held his palm out. She set her hand in it, and he covered her delicate hand with his other. "Once again, I apologize for causing you such trouble. I hope your day improves."

"I'm sure it will." Her words were kind, but she didn't smile. "Thank you."

# CHAPTER THREE

Ginny stifled a shudder as Sokolov walked out. "Who was that guy?"

Kade slid back onto the bench seat across from her. "Sokolov... uh"—he pulled a business card from his breast pocket and glanced at it—"Mike Sokolov. He's thinking of investing in my development."

"That's great." She'd heard all about the project and the roadblocks Kade had dealt with in the real estate club they belonged to. She tried to put some enthusiasm in her voice for his sake, but there'd been something creepy about that guy.

What a ridiculous thought. She'd never seen Mike Sokolov before. He was distinctive enough that she'd remember.

Ginny silently cursed her sister for her remarks that morning. Useless remarks with no details about who the people were who were supposed to be after her. Thanks to Kathryn, now Ginny was afraid of her own shadow.

She just needed this day to be over. She slid out of the booth. "I'll talk to you tomorrow."

But Kade slid out, too. "Why don't I drive you home? I can drop you back by your car tomorrow after lunch, that is if you don't need it in the morning."

Did she look so pathetic she couldn't get herself home? "I'm fine. Really."

"I know you are." He pulled his wallet from his back pocket and dropped a five-dollar bill on the table. "I'm sure Bonnie's ready to have the table back."

"It's really not necessary."

He slid the rendering back into his portfolio, then snatched his jacket from the seat. "I'll just walk you to your car then."

That wasn't going to work, either. "I didn't drive here. I walked."

He finished slipping on his jacket and faced her, eyebrows lifted. "Where do you live?"

"Just"—she waved toward the road—"back that a-way."

He grinned as if he'd just won a prize. "Excellent. Then I'll walk you home."

She wasn't sure if she wanted to cheer or groan. For months, she'd hoped Kade would ask her out, and now he was showing her all sorts of attention. But after the scene this morning... Did Kade feel sorry for her? Was that the motivation behind his sudden attention?

He tucked his portfolio under his arm and offered the other to her. "M'lady?"

She couldn't help a spurt of laughter. "Okay, then." She slipped her hand into his arm, and they headed for the door.

The wind had died down just a bit, but the air was chilly now that the sun had fallen behind the trees surrounding the town. Kade stopped on the sidewalk. "Which way?"

She nodded toward the far side of the street. Kade seemed to be in no hurry as they meandered past a few shops and her bank, then turned on a side street. Now that she was beside him, she wasn't sorry she'd let him accompany her. Her hand felt warm, tucked into his elbow. She'd made this walk a hundred times all by herself. There was something special about making it with another human being. And not just anyone.

"So," he said, "this place we're going... House or apartment?"

"House. A fixer-upper. I bought it when I moved here."

"Had you owned a home in California?"

Her soft *pfft* had Kade turning to face her. She offered a kind smile to offset the sound. "I lived in the Bay area. I couldn't afford to buy a parking spot. I was shocked at the real estate prices when I got here."

"Definitely better than California, but it's not as affordable as it was when I was a kid. With the economy growing and more folks escaping the high taxes and high prices in Massachusetts, New Hampshire is booming."

She looked around at the little town she was blessed to call home. "It's so beautiful. So... charming. I love everything about it."

"Even the weather?"

"Especially the weather. Of course, it helps that I can walk to town when it snows, so I don't have to navigate these hilly roads in my car if I don't want to."

He patted her hand, still tucked in the crook of his elbow. "I'm glad you like it. I love it, too. I've done a lot of traveling in my life, been all over the country and beyond, and there's no place I'd rather be than right here."

"Did you live other places, or just visit?"

"Vacations, mostly. And I used to travel with my dad on business trips sometimes."

"What does he do?"

"He's retired now." Kade steered them around a bush that had overtaken the sidewalk. "He and Mom live in Florida. But he owned a number of businesses. The most lucrative was a software company he bought in the eighties. He knew almost nothing about the industry, but he hired the right people. They developed software for specialized industries—independent insurance agencies and travel agencies, mostly. He sold that business for seven figures."

"Wow. I see where you get your entrepreneurial spirit."

He glanced at her, and his smile warmed her in the chilly breeze. "He's my hero." He chuckled, maybe a little embarrassed. "That probably sounds stupid coming from a guy in his thirties."

"Not at all. We all need people to admire."

"Okay, then. Who's your hero? Your parents?"

She focused straight ahead, stifling the scoff that tried to escape. "Not exactly. My father was always good to me. My mother... Well, let's just say I wouldn't pattern my life or my mothering skills after hers. But neither one was particularly heroic."

"That must have been hard," Kade said.

He had no idea. "When I was in high school, I had a friend whose parents were really kind to me. They worked together, made good money. But it wasn't the success that had me wanting to be like them. It was the fact that they were always so nice. I never heard them say a bad word *about* each other or an unkind word *to* each other. They treated their kids with respect and gentleness." She'd wanted their lives so badly, wanted to have parents who loved her and treated her with respect.

But her parents had never quite managed the love thing.

"I'm glad you found good role models," Kade said. "I'm sorry they weren't your own parents."

She shrugged. "I am who I am because of them." Though whether that was a good thing or not remained to be seen. How much value could a person have whose own family despised her?

Kade stopped and turned to face her. "Maybe you are who you are *despite* them."

"Oh." She searched for a better response, but he was so close that all intelligent thought flew from her head. Wow, he was attractive. Brown hair trimmed short, five o'clock shadow, strong jaw. His hazel eyes searched hers, and she couldn't think of a word to say.

They stood like that, face to face, until someone passed them on the sidewalk and jolted them from the trance.

He smiled and cleared his throat. "Anyway..." But he said nothing else as they resumed walking.

"It doesn't matter now. Mom's still in California." Or so Ginny assumed. "My father died last year."

"I'm sorry. Was he sick, or—?"

"Car accident."

"That must have been difficult."

"Yes." Her father had died, her mother had sent her away, and now her sister had abandoned her. Good thing Kade didn't know all of that.

"Why here?" Kade gestured at the little street and the old homes all around them. "There are so many newer places you could have bought."

She looked at the neighborhood she'd chosen. The houses had been built in the forties. They were mostly two-story, close together, but not like houses built in this century. They had big enough backyards for gardens and swimming pools. Each house was unique, interesting.

"I wanted a place that needed some cosmetic work. I thought maybe I'd update it and sell it. And I wanted to be within walking distance of town." Because most people were searching for peace and quiet, but Ginny needed people. She needed to hear voices and see faces and share smiles and laughter. Living alone, being alone... She could hardly stand it. That's why she loved Nutfield. It had taken some time, but she'd finally found friends here—true friends. People who invited her to parties, women who called her just to chat and check in. She'd made a home in Nutfield like she'd never had anywhere else.

"I lost you there," Kade said.

She smiled at him. "Nutfield is so charming, and the people are so warm."

"Once you get to know them."

"True. I've lived a lot of places. In the South, people are so nice when you first meet them. I had a hard time getting beyond the surface with anybody, though. And I think some of that was me and my family. We weren't exactly..." Where was she going with that? She certainly couldn't tell him what she'd been thinking. "Anyway, here, there's this... this shell around people, and they're not super welcoming at first, but I've learned that once they know you, know they can trust you, they pull you in."

He was nodding. "Exactly. It's sort of a cold-climate attitude. Underneath all the layers"—he plucked at his jacket—"we're not that bad."

Not that bad. Kade was about a hundred degrees beyond *not*

*that bad.* Handsome and kind and considerate. She could easily fall for this guy.

And wouldn't that be lovely, to fall in love? Despite her past, Ginny had always believed in love. She's always longed for her own happily-ever-after. Of course, if Kade knew all her secrets, he'd bolt like he was being chased by a moose.

But oh, to pretend something could come of it. To let her guard down...

They turned the corner onto her street, and she looked at her home, a white two-story with a detached garage that was currently housing a lot of her stuff. The gigantic sugar maple that shaded the front yard was just starting to bud. It had turned the loveliest shade of bright red in the fall. She couldn't help the swell of pride as she said, "This is it."

He gazed at the house, nodding. "I like it. Good bones."

"Thank you."

Across the street, a screen slammed, and an old man stepped outside. Ginny saw him nearly every day. He always wore a fishing cap and, on all but rainy days, sunglasses. He lifted his hand in a wave.

She waved back and smiled.

"Who's that?" Kade asked.

"We've only ever exchanged hellos," she said. "I looked at that house before I bought this one. It's bigger than I needed, though. He moved in a few weeks after I did. I went over there with cookies one day, but he didn't answer his door, even though I think he was home. Maybe he's an agoraphobic or something." She took her hand from Kade's elbow and stepped back. "Anyway, thank you for walking me home."

He took a tiny step toward her, and for a moment, she thought he might kiss her. She wanted him to kiss her. But they hadn't even had the first date yet. And hadn't she just told herself not to get her hopes up? Still, she couldn't help it when her glance flicked to his lips.

He smiled, and she popped her gaze back to his eyes, which

were crinkling at the corners. "It was a pleasure. I'll call you in the morning about lunch."

~

Ginny finished the second coat of paint in the room that would eventually be her office. It was technically a parlor, but she had no use for such a space. And with its position right inside the front door, this was a perfect place to work. She could look through the wide window at the street outside and watch the birds in the tree.

The walls were soft gray. As soon as the paint dried, she'd bring in the dark, weathered desk she'd found at an antique shop and hang the shelves she'd stained to match. Then, she'd decorate the space and make it hers. She couldn't wait.

And she wasn't going to think about anything else.

She'd done enough thinking the night before. She'd fallen asleep quickly, then awakened around three, Kathryn's words pinging in her brain, the image of her and her family leaving forever burned against her closed eyelids.

When she'd finally given up on sleep, she'd chosen one of her favorite playlists—a lot of Rush, U2, and Queen—and painted. She sang along at the top of her lungs to keep herself from thinking too much.

After she finished closing the paint cans, she silenced the song —Rush's "Limelight"—and glanced at the time.

Good grief, it was after eleven. Kade had called earlier and said he'd pick her up at noon. She'd been working so hard on not thinking, she'd lost track of time.

She rushed upstairs to the bathroom for a shower, reminding herself to scrub hard to remove the paint that had splattered on her hands and arms.

Forty-five minutes later, as she was slipping on her shoes, her doorbell rang, though *bell* was a strong term. It sounded like a combination of a needle being scraped across a vinyl record and the fuzz of a TV's bad reception. One more thing in her house that needed to be fixed.

She called, "Be right there," and hurried to put on her jewelry and add a bit of lipstick. After a quick appraisal in the mirror—she looked fine, thanks to the makeup that hid the dark circles—she ran down the hardwood staircase and swung the door open.

Kade stood on her doorstep looking better than he had the night before. How was that even possible?

"I'm sorry," she said. "I got distracted. Did you hear my shout?"

"I did. And that lovely doorbell."

"One more thing I need to replace. Let me just grab my purse."

"Mind if I come in? I'd love to see it."

"Sure." She stepped back, and he entered her home. As he did, the paint fumes reached her consciousness. Not exactly welcoming. But despite the smell, this place filled her with a sense of pride. That she could own a place like this at her age, especially considering where she'd come from, was nothing short of miraculous. But right now, she saw all the problems. The scuffed wood floors that would be refinished last. The missing balusters in the staircase, and the newel that needed to be repaired. The downstairs was nearly finished being repainted, but she'd only made it halfway up the staircase wall, and the line between fresh gray and old and dingy was obvious. "It needs a lot of work." She turned to see him looking into the office.

He stepped onto the plastic she'd laid to protect the floor. "Pretty." He sniffed. "Smells fresh."

"I hope the fumes don't bother you."

He smiled at her. "In our line of work, fresh paint smells like progress."

She liked his take on it. "This'll be my office as soon as the paint dries and I get the furniture in here."

"Excellent." He nodded, taking it all in. "These parlors aren't very useful anymore, so that's a great use of the space. You could even replace that window with a bay."

"I would love to do that. I don't know if it'll be in the budget, though."

"If you plan to sell it, you'd get it back."

"Yeah." But she didn't plan to sell it. She had when she'd

bought it, but now she couldn't imagine parting with it. "Come on. I'll show you the rest of the downstairs." She led him into the living room. This had been the first room she'd tackled, and it was her favorite in the house so far. The walls here were the same soft gray as those in the rest of the downstairs. She'd added a dark gray sofa with creamy white throw pillows that matched the two chairs that sat side-by-side opposite it. In the middle was a round coffee table. She'd already put pictures on the walls—artwork, not family photos. She didn't have many of those. And she'd added pretty lamps throughout the room.

"You're good at decorating."

Her cheeks warmed with pleasure. "Thanks."

"What else have you done?"

"Well, the kitchen's sort of a mess." She led him through the tiny dining room, which held her laptop and a pile of files, and into the old kitchen. "All I've done in here is paint and clean. I want to tear down that wall"—she pointed to the barrier between the kitchen and the dining room—"and open it up to make it one big room."

He surveyed the space, then glanced back into the dining room. He spoke from the doorway. "Good idea. You could even take down this wall." He knocked on the one that separated the dining room from the living room.

"I've thought of that. That would change the whole look of the room. But the cost..."

"Yeah, I know. All that work isn't cheap." He turned his attention to the kitchen. "So, what's the plan in here?"

She gave him a quick rundown of what she hoped to do—granite countertops, new tile on the floor, pretty backsplash. She yanked open the pantry door—it had a tendency to stick. The space was small and inefficient, the old shelves too narrow to hold much of anything. Right now, she had boxes piled on the floor.

"I plan to replace those old shelves and add new ones, maybe add a big spice rack, since it's so close to the oven."

"That'll add value." He looked around, then stepped back. "And upstairs?"

She closed the pantry door, then gave it another push with her hip to make sure it latched. One more thing on her to-do list. "Except paint the woodwork, which I've done throughout the house, and paint my bedroom, I've done very little up there."

"You'll get there. I have no doubt."

She was starting to doubt she would, not because she lacked the resolve or the resources, but because she didn't know if she should stay. Kathryn's words came back. Was Ginny a fool for not leaving like Kathryn had suggested?

"Are you ready?"

She shook off the worry and snatched her purse from the kitchen counter. "Ready."

It was lovely outside, sunny and in the fifties. She'd not moved to New Hampshire until early summer the previous year, so she hadn't experienced a spring yet. It was a magical time of year. After the long cold winter, the rebirth made her heart swell.

She climbed into Kade's Mercedes. On the outside, it looked brand new, but inside were signs of age. When he sat beside her, she said, "I like your wheels."

"It's a decade old now. My parents gave it to me when I graduated from college."

He'd gotten a Mercedes? Her parents hadn't even come to her college graduation. "It's nice."

"I like it. It's expensive to repair, though." He headed toward downtown. "Next time, I think I'll go with something a little more practical." They reached Crystal Avenue, and he turned to face her. "Do you mind a little drive, or are you in a hurry?"

"I have nothing scheduled today."

"Good." He turned toward the highway. "You like seafood?"

"Love it."

THE DRIVE TOOK LESS than twenty minutes. The coast was beautiful. She watched the surf splash against the rugged rocks, then turned her focus to the giant homes overlooking the sea on their left. They boasted old trees and gardens to match the majestic structures. Unlike most beach houses, which were usually packed so closely together a person could jump from one roof to the next, these homes were spaced a good fifty, sometimes a hundred, feet apart. "What are those places worth?"

Kade glanced at the one they were passing. "Depends. The ones in good shape? One to three million."

That was all? She couldn't imagine what they'd cost in California, or even south of here in Massachusetts or Connecticut. "Ever been in one?"

"There was one in Rye a while back that I walked through. Great house, and the views were amazing."

"You have any desire to live closer to the ocean?"

He shot a quick smile her way. "I love Nutfield. I'm happy to visit the coast, but I don't want to live here. In the summer, this traffic is bumper-to-bumper."

"I remember."

"Did you spend a lot of time here last summer?"

The road led them inland. She wasn't sorry to watch the ocean disappear from view. "A few times with my nephews and nieces when Kathryn and Matthew needed a babysitter." At least the kids loved her. But a decade from now when they hadn't seen her or, presumably, heard her name in years, would they even remember her?

She needed to keep her thoughts far from Kathryn and her family today. "So, where are we going?"

"We're almost there." A moment later, he pulled into the parking lot beside a two-story building about the size of a three-bedroom house with weathered gray clapboard siding. The sign read *Petey's*.

She studied the colorful... she wasn't sure what they were. They must have been related to fishing or boating. They hung from the siding and the railing of the porch and gave the building a festive, almost whimsical feeling. "What are those?"

"Lobster buoys. They mark the locations of the traps."

"They set the mood, then. Good food?"

"The best." He found a spot in the crowded lot and opened his door. She reached for her handle, but he stopped her with a gentle squeeze to her wrist. "I'll come around."

She'd never had a guy open her door before. She hadn't done much dating, but she didn't think most men still did that sort of thing.

Her door opened, and he held out a hand. She took it, surprised by the rush of warmth and pleasure, and stepped out of the car.

"Thank you."

"My pleasure." He let go of her hand when she was standing by his side, and she was sorry for the loss.

Inside, they were seated in a wooden booth with green leather-like seat covers and backs. The walls were plastered with plastic lobsters and wooden oars and photos of boats. Hanging from the ceiling were lobster traps and more buoys. There was a kayak leaning against the far wall. It wasn't a fancy place, but, based on the scents of fried food and fresh fish wafting from the kitchen and the fact that Ginny and Kade had been given the only open table in the room, she guessed the meals would be yummy.

They ordered their drinks—Coke for him, water for her. Amid the chatting and laughter of other customers, they studied the paper placemats that doubled as menus. The selections were just what she'd expect at a down-home seafood place.

"What's good here?" she asked.

"They make the best clam chowder in all the world, but everything's good. Should we do lobster?"

She considered that but got a glimpse of the table beside them, where a plate was piled inches high with fried goodness. "Don't judge me, but that looks delicious."

He followed her gaze and smiled. "A woman after my own heart."

After their drinks arrived and he placed their orders, he sat back and gazed at her. "Did you eat a lot of seafood in California?"

She shrugged. "Yeah, but it was salmon and mahi-mahi and ahi tuna. Good stuff, just different."

"We do seafood right." He sipped his Coke. "But that West Coast lifestyle must seem normal to you, being from that part of the country." Before she could answer, he said, "Wait, though. You said you'd lived a lot of places. Where else?"

"I was born in Louisiana. We lived there until Katrina."

"Were you in the path?"

"Unfortunately."

"Where did you evacuate to?"

"We didn't until after. My parents decided to wait it out."

His eyebrows rose, and he sat back. "Where were you?"

"New Orleans. It didn't work out, as you can imagine."

He was nodding slowly, no doubt remembering all the images he'd seen on TV. She remembered the images, too. And the smells, and the sounds, and the fear.

"How old were you?"

"Seven. I'll never forget it as long as I live. We lived in a little shack, and the downstairs completely filled with water." As she said it, the memories tried to force their way in, but she held them at bay. She'd lived through it once. She didn't need to relive it now. "My sister and I hid in the attic until our parents got us out of there."

"That must have been terrifying."

He had no idea. That was a story from her past she didn't tell. One of many.

"We left then. Since we'd lost everything, literally, we started over in Houston. After a few years there..." Would this be too much information? What would he think about her parents' lifestyle? And did it matter? It wasn't as if she'd chosen it. "My parents were sort of nomads for a few years. After Houston, we moved to Dallas, then Oklahoma City. After that, we lived in Colorado for a while, Kansas, back to Texas."

Kade sat back. His eyebrows lifted high on his forehead as if he'd never heard anything so strange.

"Then we moved to Indiana, but my parents hated the weather. We moved our way west again. Colorado Springs, Salt Lake City, a little town in Nevada not far from Reno. And then, at the end of my sophomore year of high school, we moved to San Francisco."

"That's... Wow. That must have been..." He seemed to grope for a word to describe it. Finally, he said, "But they settled in California."

"My sister was at Stanford, and I think they wanted to be near her. And now I'm here."

"All that moving must have been really hard."

The waitress delivered their meals—fried haddock, French fries, and coleslaw, plus a side of clam strips.

Ginny tried a bite of the haddock and groaned with pleasure. The crispy, salty breading was the perfect match to the flaky fish. "This is delicious."

Kade ate some of his meal, too, but his gaze hardly drifted from her. She could see the questions in his eyes.

She set her fork down. "I learned to make friends fast." If only she'd also learned not to get attached. But she'd never been able to keep her heart from latching onto anybody who was kind to her. In every new town, her parents had promised that this move would be permanent. And, fool that she'd been, she'd believed them, over and over. So every move brought with it heartache.

"Did you guys live in a motor home or something?"

Her laugh was short and humorless, but she forced a smile to cover. "That would have been nice. At least there'd have been some semblance of a home. We had a Chevy Astro, one of those full-size vans. Every move, if it didn't fit in the van, it didn't come with us."

Like the first bicycle she'd ever owned. Her parents had given it to her for Christmas. It was one of the Christmases they'd actually purchased real gifts. Other years, there'd been little under the tree—if there'd been a tree—and what was there was secondhand or came from the dollar store. Ginny had loved that bike—brand new, bright blue. She'd imagined herself riding it for the rest of her life, imagined all the amazing places she'd be able to see from the seat. They'd been living in Colorado, and the bike trails had been amazing.

The night they'd packed their belongings and left, her bike had been leaning against the little house they'd rented. It hadn't fit in the van.

Kade was watching her, lips closed. She didn't like the pity she read in his eyes.

"It wasn't that bad," she said. "I'm just feeling maudlin today because of Kathryn. It was normal for us. We always had each other."

"Your family must have been really close."

She tamped down a scornful laugh. She'd shared enough truth for one day, so she just shrugged and ate a fry.

"Were you homeschooled?" he asked. "With all that moving..."

"Nope. Every move, we started in a new school. Kathryn was great about making sure I did my schoolwork. Some of the schools were better than others, so if we went somewhere and I was behind, she'd tutor me. When we went to lesser schools, she tried to fill in the missing parts of my education. When she'd get too bossy and serious, I'd call her Professor McGonagall."

She'd expected a smile at that, but his frown only deepened. "You and your sister were close."

"When we were kids, yeah. After she started at Stanford, she got her own life, made her own friends. Even though, for a year, we lived close to her, we hardly ever saw her. She'd call and make sure I was doing well in school, but after a while, it felt like... I don't know, like she felt obligated to take care of me."

Kade's head titled slightly to the side, his eyes filled with compassion.

"Can you blame her, though? She has her own family to worry about now. She'd been taking care of me for years. When we were little, we were playmates, but after Katrina... Everything changed that night. I think she just wanted to leave all of us in the past. Leave all the memories." Ginny forced a smile and chose a French fry. "I don't really want to talk about Kathryn, if you don't mind."

"Of course. I'm sorry if I—"

"No, no. It's not your fault. How can you know my personal minefields?"

He took a bite of his haddock, and she did the same. Why had she told him all of that? She never talked about her past.

Kade set down his fork. "I wonder though... Weren't your parents involved?"

"My parents were busy." Doing what, she had no idea. Not working real jobs, but they almost always had food on the table. Ginny thought of the duffel bag her mother had given her the day she'd ordered her to leave, bringing back all the suspicions Ginny had carried since then.

What had her parents been doing for all those years? And how had they suddenly had the money to start businesses in California, in one of the most expensive markets in the country?

And what did all of that have to do with what Kathryn had said the day before? Was Ginny in danger? And how could she protect herself if she didn't know who she was supposed to be protecting herself from?

## CHAPTER FOUR

K ade tried not to stare at his lunch date.

With her long, nearly black hair, bright blue eyes, and high cheekbones, Ginny was stunning. But that was only one reason he had to fight to keep from staring.

The story she'd told about her past was so odd, so contrary to the life he'd always known. Who lived like a nomad? Who didn't collect more possessions than could be shoved in a full-sized van? What kind of strange people had raised this woman, and how had she grown to be so different from them?

She chose a fried clam, dipped it in tartar sauce, and popped it in her mouth. She didn't seem rocked by the information she'd just given him, but he was. She'd recounted the events of her past matter-of-factly, but he'd seen the pain in her eyes.

Ginny seemed almost... haunted.

Not that there was anything wrong with moving around a lot. A family was a family wherever they lived. But there was something about what Ginny had said, and how she'd said it, that told Kade hers hadn't been a real family. And, without at least the stability of a home, maybe extended family nearby, what must that have been like for her?

Ginny pointed a clam strip at him. "Tell me about your family."

He shrugged. "Not much to tell. We always lived in Nutfield. I'm the baby."

"So we have that in common. How many siblings?"

"Three. My sister, Andrea, is eight years older than I am. She lives in Salem, about forty-five minutes from here. She bought into a few businesses and a multi-level marketing business when she was in college. She's a stay-at-home mom who fits in work between taking care of her kids and her husband and her house. Andrea's the matriarch now that my folks are in Florida. She hosts all the family dinners and pretty much tells us boys what to do."

"Sounds a little like Kathryn. Large and in charge."

He chuckled "The next one, Rich, is six years older than I am. He's an attorney at a law firm in Boston. He and his family live in Londonderry, which is about a half hour from here."

"I've shown houses in Londonderry," Ginny said. "Nice town. The orchards are beautiful."

"And disappearing," he said. "Even as a real estate developer, I see the loss when a centuries-old orchard is razed in favor of another strip mall."

"I agree, but the town's charm remains." She nodded toward him. "And the next one?"

"Darren. I think you've met him. He's in the Chamber of Commerce, too."

"Right. I forgot he was your brother. He doesn't come very often."

"He's busy, married. They have a little girl, Kinsie."

"I think he's shown me pictures of her."

"Yeah, he's a proud papa. Annoyingly so," Kade added with a smile. "He owns a chain of gas stations between the coast and the mountains. He still lives in Nutfield, so I get to see him and his family."

"It must be wonderful having such a big family. Are you all close?"

"Definitely. We're busy with our own lives, of course. We always have a group chat going. Rarely a day goes by when we don't communicate. Even if it's just logistical stuff—who needs a babysitter when, who's got some event the rest of us are invited to—that kind of thing. Lately, we've been trying to figure out what to get our parents for their anniversary. Andrea thinks we should send them on an Alaskan cruise."

"Nice gift."

"Yeah. They're all really successful."

She wagged her French fry at him. "You're really successful, too. If you love your life, if you're going after your dreams, you're successful. Success isn't measured by income." Her cheeks turned a little pink. "I mean, I don't know your income, of course. I'm just saying..."

"It's fine." That blush was enough to nearly tongue-tie him. "I know what you mean."

"Good. It's just... My sister's four years older than I am, and I'm constantly comparing myself to her, as if I should be where she was at my age. Or worse, be where she is now." She gave a little shrug. "Thing is, I'm not on the path she was. She got married at twenty-four. I'm not even..." She laughed. "Well, obviously I'm not close to marriage, since I'm on a first date." Those cheeks went from pink to red, and her eyes widened. "I mean, if this is a date and not just two friends—"

"I hope it's a date." He couldn't help the smile tugging at his lips. "If not, I put on cologne for nothing."

She giggled and dipped her chin, then looked up from beneath her lashes.

Wow, she was adorable when she blushed.

They finished lunch while Kade entertained her with stories of the antics he and his brothers had gotten into when they were kids. The more she laughed, the crazier the stories he told. Anything to keep that smile on her face.

Back in the car, he pulled out of the parking lot toward the coast. "I wish we could spend the rest of the day together. Unfortunately, I have work to do this weekend, if I'm going to get on the agenda for the zoning board meeting next week."

"From what you've shared in the club, the development sounds like it'll be great for the town. Do you think the zoning board will go for it?"

"No reason for them not to. I own the land, and I have the right to develop it. It's zoned residential, so I need permission to add the golf course and the clubhouse, but there's no reason for them to deny me."

"But from what you've said, the town manager—"

"Bruce Collier."

"Right. Collier's against it. Do you think he can block it?"

"If Sokolov comes through with the funding and I get on the agenda, I'm pretty sure the council will approve it."

"Sokolov? That guy from last night."

He glanced long enough to see her eyes narrow.

"I didn't realize you knew him," she said.

"We met after he bumped into you. He'd overheard me talking..." Kade filled her in on what happened.

"Huh."

"You don't sound very hopeful," he said.

"It's not that. It's just... That guy gave me the creeps."

He chuckled. "Well, he practically tackled you. That doesn't surprise me."

"Yeah. Maybe." But she didn't seem convinced.

"Anyway," Kade said, "if Sokolov doesn't come through, then I'll ask my family to invest."

"I'm surprised you haven't done that already."

He glanced at her. "I'm trying to do it on my own. I mean, the land was a gift from my parents. My parents gave all of us an allotment of our inheritance when we graduated from college."

"Along with a Mercedes?"

"They're generous." He knew he sounded like a spoiled rich kid, but he wasn't. Not spoiled, anyway. None of his family were spoiled because their parents had raised them to work. "My siblings all achieved their goals without needing help. I want to do the same."

"Don't you consider it an investment? It's not exactly help."

He shrugged. "I'd rather do it myself."

"If it makes them money…"

"I know. You're right, of course." His siblings had all offered to invest, but Kade figured they'd offered not because they thought they'd make money but because they didn't think he could do it on his own. He desperately wanted to prove to them all he could.

He and his siblings were close, but they competed mercilessly. His dad had fostered that with games to see who was the fastest runner, who made the best grades, who could win at Monopoly. Even chores had had an element of competition. Who could stack the most wood? Who could shovel the most snow? Dad had taught them about the cutthroat world, and they'd learned well. As close as they were, there was always the undercurrent of competition.

And Kade always came up short.

"I hesitate to mention this," Ginny said, "since you're opposed to getting help, but I used to work for a real estate developer."

He'd take Ginny's help all day long if it gave him an excuse to spend time with her. "What did you do?"

"I interned there in college, then worked for them once I graduated. I started in the front office doing mostly clerical work, but by the time I moved here, I was managing projects."

"No kidding? So you probably know more about what I'm doing than I do."

"Not even close. Every project is unique. That being said, the guy who owned the business was a former airline pilot, and he drafted these meticulous checklists for every stage of the project. I guess pilots use a lot of checklists."

"Thank heavens. That's definitely not a profession where you want details to slip through the cracks."

"True. He didn't trust computers, so he had the checklists printed in binders."

"*Binders?* How long are these checklists?"

He chanced a glance, and she was smiling. "Long. Pages and pages long, but they include lots of descriptions and different variations in projects. I'm pretty sure there's one for the kind of thing you're developing. Anyway, I brought a few with me. I'd be happy to share one."

"That'd be wonderful. Thank you."

"Sure."

"Did you keep them because you think you want to develop real estate someday?"

"Who knows what the future holds?"

He thought of the woman beside him. Until this morning, his future had held the promise of a real estate development and little else. But today... Maybe God had more for him than he'd dared hope.

KADE PULLED into Ginny's driveway and parked.

"It might take me a few minutes to find that binder for you," Ginny said. "I can take it to the meeting with me next week, or, if you don't mind waiting..."

"I'd be happy to wait." Anything to extend his time with her, and he was eager to see the binder. He was organized, but this was his first major project, and details were bound to be overlooked.

He opened her car door and held out his hand, slightly less surprised by the zing of desire when she slipped hers into it. The first time he'd touched her, he'd been nearly rendered speechless.

She stood and led the way inside and to the kitchen. She froze at the door.

"Everything okay?" But when he looked past her, he saw what had surprised her.

The pantry door was open.

He remembered her shutting it. It had stuck, and she'd pushed her weight into it.

The door had been closed when they'd left. He was certain.

Adrenaline flooded his veins.

Ginny turned to him, her face pale. Her eyes were wide, her mouth open. "I swear I closed that."

"You did." He took her hand and tugged. "Come on."

"Where?"

"I want you to go—"

"No. We must be remembering wrong." But the look in her eyes told him she didn't believe that any more than he did.

He wasn't going to stand there and argue. He wrapped his arm around her and all but dragged her toward the front door.

Though she plodded along beside him, she said, "Kade, this is my house. I'm not going to—"

"Yes, you are." He led her outside and unlocked his car. "Get inside, lock the doors, and call 911."

She didn't move. "I'm not leaving my house."

"Don't make me carry you, Ginny Lamont."

"You wouldn't dare."

He placed his hands on either side of her face and looked into her eyes. "I just want to make sure it's safe. Is that so bad, for someone to protect you?"

"I don't..." She blinked, swallowed. Her gaze flicked to the house, then back to his. "It's probably nothing."

"Humor me. If you don't want to call 911, then don't. But get in the car and lock the doors. Right now." He added, "Okay?" as if it were a request, but he would protect her if he had to toss her over his shoulder and carry her down the street.

The sun shone, the birds twittered overhead. But suddenly, the world felt very dark and uncertain.

"If you insist." Though she tried to sound flippant, he could see the terror on her features. He hoped his face didn't look like that. He wanted to at least appear fearless, even if he didn't feel it.

He opened the car door and, when she was settled in the driver's seat, handed her the keys. "Be prepared to drive away if you need to. Don't worry about me—I'll be fine." He added that last part with as much confidence as he could. She was probably right, and the house was probably safe. But there were no guarantees, and though he didn't have the finely tuned instincts of a soldier or a spy, something had felt very wrong.

After meeting her eyes one last time, he ran back inside.

Silently, he searched the downstairs, one room at a time. The office was empty, as was the living room. He even checked behind the sofa, just in case. He walked through the dining area into the kitchen. Of course, it and the pantry were empty. He opened the door off the hallway that led to the basement but decided to check it last. After a quick look in the downstairs bath and the coat closet, he climbed to the second floor.

If he weren't conducting a search for an intruder, he'd feel like *he* was the intruder. In the first room on the right, he found a couple of boxes, probably filled with things she hadn't unpacked, since her house was in a state of reconstruction. The closet was empty. The next bedroom had a long table covered with knick-knacks and photos and other decorative stuff. There were a few packages of things she'd bought but hadn't opened yet. Again, the closet was empty.

The bathroom had her things scattered all over it. Makeup, hair dryer, a straightener like he'd seen his sister use, a hairbrush. A towel had been haphazardly bunched onto the rack. She'd probably be mortified he'd seen the mess. Under different circumstances, he'd find it amusing. He approached the shower and yanked back the curtain. The tub was empty.

One more room. He opened the last door upstairs and stepped into Ginny's bedroom. She'd told him she'd painted this room, but she'd done much more than that. The walls were a light blue, which coordinated perfectly with the comforter, pillows, and curtains. Every surface was decorated artfully. The room smelled sweet—vanilla, he thought, though he had no idea where the scent originated. He walked to the far side of the queen-sized bed and then checked underneath it. No bogeyman jumped out. He opened the closet and found it filled with Ginny's clothes hanging from the rack and piled on the floor.

Now that he was sure the house was empty, his heart rate slowed.

Ginny was a bit of a slob, but otherwise, everything seemed in order.

He heard a bang, then the pounding of feet.

His heart nearly came to his throat, and he bolted toward the hallway. "Ginny!" Had she come in? What was happening?

He rushed down the stairs, hanging onto the railing and barely keeping his feet. He looked out the front door to his car, only to see her in the driver's seat. She waved and opened her door.

He pushed the screen and shouted, "Stay in the car. Lock the doors. And call the police!" He ran through the house to the back door, which was wide open.

It had definitely been closed before.

Her backyard was wide, the grass bright green after the long, cold winter. On the far side, a black wrought iron fence separated her property from the neighbor's.

He walked outside slowly, looking around, prepared for a fight. The doors of the detached garage were closed. Whoever had been in her house would surely have run, not hidden. Though the intruder had stayed longer than Kade would have guessed. Why hadn't he left when Kade and Ginny were outside?

Kade studied the grass, and sure enough, it was pressed down in places.

The intruder had escaped.

If Kade had called the police, they might have caught him.

If Kade had searched the basement first, he'd have caught him. And then what would he have done? He was no weakling, but working out in the gym wasn't exactly hand-to-hand combat training.

And then the worst scenario had his stomach dropping. What if he'd let Ginny come in the house by herself? What if she'd been alone?

He looked all around the outside of the garage, then went in its side door and found it filled with furniture but no bad guys. Back outside, he approached the bulkhead that led to the basement.

It was padlocked, which explained why the intruder had been forced to return to the first floor to get out of the house.

He went inside and down to the basement. With every step, his heart rate kicked up a notch. It was dark and dreary and inhospitable. The floor was concrete and swept, but the space was dirty and dank and smelled of years of moisture.

Wisely, Ginny hadn't stored anything down here. It was empty except for the washer and dryer.

Convinced the house was safe, Kade climbed to the first floor and went outside. He approached the driver's side of his car while Ginny stepped out.

"All clear?" The words were bright and cheerful, but he saw the fear behind them.

"Did you call the police?"

She shook her head, her gaze not quite meeting his.

"Why not?"

She shrugged.

What did that mean? "Let's go inside and talk."

He held out his hand, and she took it. But holding her hand wouldn't be enough, not right now. He pulled her into an embrace.

She hugged him back, then stepped away, a question in her eyes.

"I'm so thankful you're safe." He took her hand again. "Come on."

Inside, she led him to the living room and sat on the sofa. He sat beside her, keeping her hand in his.

"There was somebody in the basement."

She gasped and covered her mouth with her fingertips. "Are you kidding? I'm sorry. I should've... You could have been hurt."

"*You* could have been hurt."

"Oh." As if it had just occurred to her, which only irritated him.

He forced himself to take a deep breath, trying to calm his pounding heart. He had to think clearly now.

"Did you see him?" she asked. "What did he look like?"

He recounted the events while she listened silently.

"Maybe it was just a burglar," he said. "Except... it didn't look like anything had been disturbed. Maybe he'd just gotten here."

"That would make sense." The fear in her eyes told him she didn't believe it.

But... "No, it wouldn't, unless he broke in because he was hungry. A burglar would start with the expensive things, not the pantry."

She glanced at the flat-screen TV hanging on the wall, then stood and walked into the dining room. "My laptop is here."

He followed and stood beside her. "Probably not a burglar, then."

"Maybe it was somebody who was hungry," she said. "A homeless person."

"This isn't San Francisco. How many homeless people have you seen in Nutfield?"

She said nothing as she walked into the kitchen. When she reached for the pantry door, he said, "Don't touch. There might be fingerprints."

She crossed her arms and wandered from room to room, eventually leading him upstairs. He probably should have waited in the living room, but even now, even knowing the house was safe, he couldn't leave her side.

She glanced in each bedroom. When she got to the bathroom, she looked at him with a sheepish grin. "Now you know my secret."

"You're a slob."

She smiled, though it was slight. "Not a slob. Just not... compulsively neat. And I was late, so I didn't have time to clean."

"Otherwise you would have?"

Her smile got a little wider. "Probably." She shrugged. "Maybe."

He chuckled as he followed her to her bedroom. At her bureau, she reached for a jewelry box.

He clasped her hand in his before she touched it. "Fingerprints, remember?"

She glanced around the space, then at him. "I'm not going to call the police."

"What? You have to."

She pulled her hand from his and rifled through the jewelry box. "Everything is here."

"You have to call the police."

She ignored him and wandered to the closet, where she studied the contents, focusing on the shelf above her clothes.

"He was in here."

He followed her gaze. There were plastic containers of various colors on the shelf. "How can you tell?"

She pointed. "He put them back in the wrong order. The purple one goes on the end. The red one is next then the orange and yellow."

"You have an order for that, but..." He indicated the clothes on the floor and lifted his eyebrows.

"I'm just saying, he was here. Will you grab them so I can see if anything's missing?"

When he hesitated, she stretched on her toes and reached for the purple one. She was just tall enough to reach the bottom and inch it out. When it cleared the shelf, it would probably land on her head.

Stubborn woman. He took down the boxes and set them on her bed. They were lightweight, about the size of shoeboxes.

She opened the first, dug around a bit, then did the same with the rest. Though he didn't look too closely, he saw photographs, some costume jewelry, a few trinkets.

"Nothing's missing. They're a little... wrong. I think he looked through them, but as far as I can tell, he didn't take anything."

"What was he looking for?"

She touched the pendant that hung from her neck and turned toward her bureau. Over her shoulder, she said, "Could you just...?" She gestured toward the door. "I want to see if he went through my personal things."

Kade stepped into the hallway and hoped she wouldn't discover even her intimates had been disturbed.

She stepped out a moment later and started down the stairs.

He followed. "Well?"

"No stone unturned."

His stomach tightened. "I'm sorry. It's such a violation."

She sat on the sofa and pulled her knees to her chest, wrapping her arms around them.

Her eyes were still wide, avoiding eye contact, and her lips were turned down at the corners and closed tightly, as if she were trying to hold something inside.

"What are you thinking?"

She shook her head and swallowed. "It's probably not related."

"At this point, I think we need to assume everything's related."

She took a deep breath and met his gaze. "Kathryn warned me that someone followed me here, that someone's after me. She told me to run."

Kade waited for Ginny to explain, but she said nothing else.

He finally said, "Who? Who is after you?"

She shrugged.

"What do they want?"

When she said nothing, he stood and paced. "You don't know who's after you or what they want? Come on, Ginny. You have to have some idea of what's—"

"I don't, okay?" She stood and crossed her arms. "I have no idea what's going on. I never knew... anything about anything. Kathryn thinks I'm a liar or an idiot. Since I truly don't know, I must be an idiot." She ran both hands through her long hair, then blew out a long breath. "It's not your problem."

"No you don't." His voice was louder than he'd intended. He lowered it but kept the vehemence there. "You don't get to just... just blow me off when you're obviously in danger. Somebody was in your house. Do you get that? If I hadn't been here—"

"I get it, okay? I'm not *really* an idiot." She threw her hands in the air as if she'd never been more frustrated. "Scratch that. Kathryn thought I was. You obviously think so."

"Don't put words in my mouth." He returned to his place on the sofa and sat.

She glared down at him, and he held out his hand. "Please, sit with me."

She ignored the hand and sat, arms crossed once again. She

gazed past him, staring at nothing. Her eyes were narrowed, her lips pinched tight. Everything about her had shuttered in the last two minutes because he couldn't control his temper.

"I'm sorry, Ginny. I'm not angry with you. It's just very hard to believe."

"I know." Her gaze flicked to him. "I don't really know anything."

She didn't *really* know anything. Which meant she knew something.

"Tell me what Kathryn said."

Ginny looked toward the ceiling. "She said she was running, and that I should run too. Change my name, get a new ID, not tell anyone where I was going. She said I wasn't safe here, that my being here has brought them."

"Who's them?"

"Kathryn said she saw someone at Dad's funeral. But I don't understand... Mom and Dad were business owners in San Francisco. Their work was legitimate... I mean, I had thought it was, but then..."

Her arms were still crossed as if she were holding herself together. Kade touched her shoulder. "Then what?"

"It's all so convoluted. I don't understand it, and telling you what I know isn't going to help anything."

He snatched his hand back. "I see." She clearly had no faith that he could help. Fine, then. He'd leave her alone—if he thought she was safe. But he didn't think she was safe, so she was stuck with him.

Her eyes filled. "I'm sorry. I didn't mean it like that. I just meant that... I don't need to drag you into my nightmare. It's my problem. You don't need to make it yours."

"I'm in it now, Ginny."

Her heavy sigh told him what she thought of that. "You don't have to be. I appreciate you going through the house, but whoever it was is gone for now."

"Fine. I'll leave, but not until we call the police."

"We can't. I can't do that."

"You have to. Someone was—"

"I know. But the police are…" She slapped her hand over her mouth as if she'd been about to say a bad word.

"The police are what?"

"I can't believe I almost said that. The past is creeping in on me." She lowered her head into her hands. "I'm so stupid." The words were muffled against her fingers.

"What are you talking about?"

Her shoulders shook, and she kept her head tucked where he couldn't see her tears. But he knew they were there. He was a jerk. She'd just had someone rifling through her things, and Kade was only making it worse.

"Hey, it's okay." He scooted closer and wrapped his arm around her shoulders. "I just want you to be safe."

She leaned against his chest, her face hidden behind her hands. She felt so small and soft and vulnerable, tucked there against him. He had the urge to lift her and set her across his lap the way his father used to hold Andrea when she cried. Fortunately, Kade knew better than to give in to that particular urge.

Finally, her tears subsided. She stood and crossed to the bathroom, then walked back, dabbing her tears with a tissue. "I'm sorry. It's just… I thought my sister was lying or exaggerating or… I don't know. I didn't realize…" She gestured to the room vaguely. The tears and tissue had removed most of her makeup, and despite the blotchy skin and red-rimmed eyes, she was still beautiful.

Beautiful and exceedingly frustrating.

"Here's the deal," he said. "You need to either tell me what's going on, or I'm calling the police to report what happened here."

She met his gaze briefly before focusing back on her lap. "Okay. That's fair." She swallowed, seemed to be working to meet his eyes. "I honestly don't know anything about this. Just what Kathryn told me and what happened today. My parents were drifters. Every place we lived before Reno, we skipped out in the middle of the night. That's why there was no moving truck or taking anything beyond what we could fit in the van. I knew we lived differently than other people, but I never understood what it meant. As I got older, I assumed they were skipping out on rent, but I think it was worse than that. In Reno, things started to change. They made more money and were settled for a while. I mean, a long time for us—nearly an entire school year. We left there on good terms—we even had a U-Haul trailer with some of our things in it. We moved to San Francisco, and my parents bought a condo. They *bought* it—in San Francisco. When we'd been living in dumpy rent houses since we'd left New Orleans. Suddenly, my parents had the money to start a business. They opened a restaurant, then another one. Things were better. I didn't know why and I didn't care. I was happy to have settled down. I made friends. I went out for the soccer team."

He smiled at that. "Were you good?"

"I was terrible, but they let me on the team anyway. Said I had a lot of team spirit."

"I can see that."

Her smile was short-lived. "I wasn't paying attention to what they were doing. Does that make sense? They were my parents, and I was just so happy that things were... Well, things were never normal at my house, but I liked my school, I liked my new friends. I liked our home. A real home, not the kind that sits on concrete blocks. Can you understand that?"

"You were a kid."

"So maybe I stuck my head in the sand. So what? I had enough to worry about with school and friends and... and all the stuff that goes along with being a teenager without worrying about where my parents were getting the money." She squared her shoulders as if she expected him to argue with her. "I trusted them. They were my parents. Even with all their faults, I trusted them."

"Of course you did. Why wouldn't you have?"

Her shoulders drooped, and the challenge emptied a balloon . "Because I should have known. I should have known Mom and Dad would never live life on the up-and-up."

"What were they doing?"

She shrugged. "No idea. Something much bigger than the nickel-and-dime stuff they'd done before San Francisco. Not that I know much about that, either, but, in retrospect, I think they were con artists."

"You think they moved on to bigger and better things?"

"Bigger, anyway, yeah."

"You don't know what?"

Her head shook slowly. "I have no idea. I never paid attention. Maybe I never wanted to know."

"Why would people be after you?"

Her eye contact slipped, and she shifted slightly away from him. "I don't know."

Except something in her body language told him that wasn't entirely true.

"No guesses?"

She stood and walked toward the kitchen. "Maybe if I knew what my parents had been doing..."

"Your mom is still in California?"

She shrugged as if she weren't sure. What would that be like, to not know where your own mother was? "I haven't heard from her." And obviously Ginny hadn't called her—or if she had, she hadn't reached her. "I don't want to get her into trouble. I don't want to be the reason anybody looks into her."

"Is that why you're reluctant to call the police? What were you about to say earlier...?"

"'The police are dangerous. Never tell them anything.' It's a mantra our parents repeated many times."

Wow. What kind of parents...? Ginny was in serious danger, and she was afraid to go to the authorities because of her parents' twisted desire to protect themselves and their illegal activities.

"I understand you're worried about your mother, but right now, your first concern is yourself. You need to call the police."

"And tell them what?"

"Everything you just told me."

She was shaking her head. "I can't do that. If my mother goes to prison... I mean, it could happen. But I can't be the cause of it. Even Kathryn never did that, and she's hardly seen or spoken to Mom in years."

He looked down at his own hands, clasped in his lap. The frustration showed in the way his skin pulled taut over his knuckles. He focused on relaxing before he faced her again. "Then at least report the break-in. You don't have to tell them the rest."

She held his gaze while she considered it. Finally, she nodded. "Fine. I'll call them."

# CHAPTER FIVE

Ginny waited in the living room while two police officers wandered through her house. Because having an intruder violating her space hadn't been degrading enough, she needed to add two more strangers to the list. Kade's seeing everything only bothered her because now he knew her secret tendency toward messiness. That was nothing compared to everything else he'd learned about her today.

So much for the first date that had gone so well. She wouldn't blame him if he steered clear of her after this.

But maybe not. He was still there, a steady presence by her side. He hadn't said much after he'd told the police what happened, just sat beside her, held her hand.

She could get used to that, get used to him. She knew she shouldn't. Friday morning, she'd thought her life was simple, all figured out.

Today, it seemed complex and dangerous. Too dangerous to pull another person into. Still, she couldn't bring herself to ask him to leave.

Kade had told the police all he knew, and she gave them all the information she was willing to share. They searched the house, dusted for fingerprints, and even talked to some of the neighbors—nobody had seen anything unusual. When they were finished, they told her what she already knew—there was nothing they could do. It looked like the intruder had come in through a back window, but there were no fingerprints on the frame. Though they found lots of others in the house, the cops weren't optimistic. No prints on the frame meant the guy wore gloves.

Probably not a teenager pulling a prank.

Since the intruder didn't appear to have taken anything, there were no stolen goods to track. And nobody'd seen him—or her, Ginny supposed—so they had no description to go on.

When they were finished telling her what they'd found—essentially nothing—she walked them to the door, Kade by her side.

The older of the two police officers, a tall gray-haired man, faced her after his partner stepped out. "Ma'am, if you were my daughter, here's what I'd tell you to do. First, replace all the locks and add deadbolts. These locks"—he jiggled the knob on her front door—"aren't going to stop anyone. And those old window locks are too fragile. You don't have to replace them. All you need is a board wedged between the bottom sash and the frame to keep it from rising. You know what I mean?"

A good solution. New windows were far out of her budget. She nodded, and he continued.

"Install an alarm system. You'd be amazed at how fast a loud siren will run off an intruder. Finally"—he leveled her with his gaze—"buy a gun and learn how to use it."

She stepped back. The cop was suggesting she buy a gun? She definitely wasn't in California anymore.

"Whoever broke into your house," he said, "wasn't looking to steal. I don't know anything about you or your life, so I'm just throwing this out there, but could it have been an old boyfriend?"

She glanced at Kade, whose gaze had shifted from the officer to her.

She focused on the cop. "I've never had a serious boyfriend."

"You're kidding." The police officer shook his head. "Men these days... They have all the brains of boiled shellfish." He looked at Kade with a slight smile, then returned his focus to her.

"If not an old boyfriend, then maybe somebody who has a bone to pick with you. An enemy, a business rival?"

"I'm afraid I'm not that interesting."

"Hmm." The officer's radio squeaked, and he silenced it. "I can tell you, we haven't had any other reports like this in Nutfield. I'll check to see if any of the neighboring towns have, but I'd be surprised. This"—he spun his finger in a circle indicating her house and the events of the day—"this is very unusual. So keep your eyes open, let us know if you think you're being followed or if anyone shows you extra attention. Not that there's much we can do, but if anything unusual happens, let us know. We'll try to keep an eye out for you. Okay?"

They wanted to watch out for her? The thought felt so foreign that any authorities would care. That *anyone* would care. "I can do that."

"And I'm not kidding about the gun. You don't need a permit in New Hampshire. You can buy one today and bring it home."

"Just like that?"

"You have the right to protect yourself. And the responsibility. To yourself, your parents, your loved ones. Buy a gun, learn to use it, and then be prepared to shoot if you have to. Understand?"

"Yes, sir."

After the door closed behind him, Kade turned . "I can help you with the locks and with the gun."

She headed toward the kitchen for a drink. "The locks I'm fine with. I'm going to need to think about the gun."

He followed and stopped in the doorway. "Get your things."

She turned. "Right now?"

His eyebrows rose as if she'd asked a stupid question.

She needed to think, to process. She pulled two glasses from the cabinet and filled them with water. Obviously, Kade was in a hurry to be finished with her and get on with his day. He'd told her he had other things to do, and she'd kept him hours longer than he'd planned to stay. "Look, I can manage." She held a glass out to him, thinking he must be as thirsty as she was. "I know you're busy."

He closed his eyes, drew in a deep breath through his nose, then blew it out. His features relaxed, and he opened his eyes. "Your life is in danger. There's nothing more important than making sure you're safe."

She set the glass he hadn't taken on the counter. "For me, maybe, but for you, there's nothing more important than—"

"Would you stop? Get your things and get in the car."

"You're not the boss of me." She put as much teenage attitude as she could in the words and added a grin so he'd know she was kidding.

He smiled back. Finally. She hadn't seen his face free of worry in hours. It warmed her almost as much as his touch had. She set down her own drink and rested her hand on his arm. "I'm not trying to be obstinate. I'm just saying, I can manage shopping by myself, and you have other things to do. Why don't you go home and work on your presentation to the zoning board." Their conversation from earlier popped into her head. "Let me get that binder for you. It'll be a great place to start."

His back stiffened. "I'm not thinking about that right now. I'm worried—"

"I know, okay? Worrying about my safety isn't going to get your development built. And I really am capable of managing the hardware store by myself."

He leaned against the doorjamb. "Will you at least let me install the new locks?"

"That would be great. I mean, I could figure it out, but if you know how..."

"I've done it plenty of times on properties I've flipped. If you have a tape measure, I'll see what size boards you need to get for the windows."

She opened her junk drawer—one of many in her house—and dug around until she found the tape measure. She handed it to him, then grabbed a notepad and a pen. "I'll take notes."

He took those, too. "You find that binder for me, okay? This'll only take a few minutes."

He headed for her back windows while she went upstairs and

into the first bedroom on her right. She was pretty sure her old work things were in a box in there.

And she was right. It was lucky she hadn't brought much with her from California. Most of the things in her house she'd purchased since she'd moved here. She met Kade back downstairs with the binder in her hand. He was bent over the notepad, scribbling.

"Got it," she said.

He finished what he was doing and handed the pad to her. "I got all the windows measured and wrote a list for you." He stood beside her so he could read what she was looking at. He'd labeled each window—front right, front left, etc.—and added measurements to the sixteenth of an inch. Meticulous.

"You see at the bottom"—he pointed to the last notation—"I recommend that brand of lock. They're easy to install and well made. Any chance you have a drill?"

"I do. It's in the shed."

"Good. You'll need to see what size hole cutter and buy that while you're there. I don't know what to recommend in terms of a security system. Maybe ask them at the hardware store. I can do some research if—"

"I probably won't do that today. Surely whoever broke in this afternoon won't come back tonight. That'll give me some time to figure it out."

He stepped back so he could face her. "You're going to stay in this house tonight, all alone, without a security system? Do you really think you'll sleep?"

She considered the question, didn't like the answer. "I know what you're saying, but—"

"We can call one of those security companies and have them do the install. Maybe you could stay with a friend until they get out here."

"I'm not leaving my home." She took a deep breath. "Look, I've lived here for almost a year, and nothing like this has ever happened. It's weird it happened today, I'll admit, but I don't fear for my life. Whoever that guy was, he came when I wasn't home on purpose. He was looking for something. Even if he didn't finish the job, he'll wait until I'm not home to come back. Don't you think?"

"That's not a risk we should take. We're talking about your life."

"No. We're talking about my stuff."

His brows lowered, and he closed his mouth tight. "Just look at security systems when you're there. If you see one, buy it, and I'll install it."

"You have to—"

"I can work tomorrow."

He was stubborn and obstinate and determined to protect her. There was something intensely comforting—and attractive—in that, so much so that she couldn't even pretend to be annoyed. "How about this—I'll let you help me stay safe if you'll let me help you with your development."

His eyebrows rose. "Really? You want to help?"

It was the least she could do, but she realized as she'd asked the question that she did want to help, and not because she owed him. "I would be honored. You work on getting acquainted with the binder while I'm gone."

A smile, a real, full smile, crossed his lips. He held out his hand to shake, and she placed hers in it. He closed his other around hers. "Deal."

As GINNY DROVE to the hardware store, the events of the day—and the day before—pressed down on her.

She'd always prided herself on being able to focus on what she wanted, keep her thoughts free of fear and worry. It was how she'd managed to graduate from high school with honors, go to college, and then rise so quickly in her first job—all despite the uncertainty and unsteadiness at home. It was how she'd managed to keep going after her father died and her mother sent her away in such a strange and sudden way. It was how she'd managed to start over in a new town in a new state with a new career and be successful so quickly. Positive thinking had fueled her life.

*As a man thinketh in his heart, so is he.*

Even though Ginny loved that proverb from the Bible, she wasn't sure what to think about God. Most of her new friends in Nutfield were Christians, and they had convinced her to go to church a few times with them. Samantha Kopp hosted a Bible study in her home one night a week, which Ginny attended sporadically. She'd been raised with no religion at all, but she'd always believed in a higher power. Nobody could look at the beauty and complexity of creation and think it had all happened by accident. The God of the Christian church, though? What she'd learned about God so far had resonated. Like that proverb, for instance. But she wasn't convinced. She believed what she chose to focus on directed her life.

After the intruder, Ginny needed to focus on Kathryn's warnings and make a plan.

She navigated into Manchester. At least she could get to the hardware store on autopilot. Her mind was a million miles away.

In Nutfield, Ginny had friends. She had a business and a life. She desperately needed roots, a home, a family. In Nutfield, she'd begun to cultivate those things. Sure, the friends she'd met weren't technically family, but they were the closest thing she had.

And there was Kade. She had no idea what would become of that, but she wanted to explore it.

At what cost, though?

She needed more information about what she was dealing with.

She parked in the hardware store's lot, took a deep breath, then pressed her sister's number on her car's Bluetooth screen. Maybe, now that Kathryn was safely away, she'd feel comfortable sharing more information.

But Ginny got a recorded message saying the number had been disconnected.

Wow. That was fast. She swallowed the disappointment, the sadness. The next number on her screen was her dad's. If he were alive, he'd answer her call. He was the only one who'd still cared for her.

Except, though Daddy had been kind to her, even tender with her sometimes, though he'd encouraged her and even told her he was proud of her when she made good grades, Dad had never been honest with her.

He wouldn't be now, even if he were alive.

She missed him anyway.

And then there was Mom's number. Ginny hadn't spoken to Mom since Dad's memorial service. Not that she hadn't missed her mother and longed to hear her voice. Mom had never loved Ginny, not like a real mom should, but she was the only mother Ginny had.

Before she thought too much, she pressed the button. It rang twice, and her mother answered.

"Why are you calling me?" Her voice was rough, a leftover effect of years of cigarette smoking.

Ginny's heart pounded. "Kathryn left."

"She had to." A long exhale. Ginny could picture her stubbing out the latest butt in the old gold ashtray they'd had forever. "That was your fault. I told you to run. I didn't tell you to run to her."

"She called you?"

"That's the deal. You move, you call. So there's nothing you need to tell me that I don't already know."

"My house was broken into today. Someone searched it."

Silence. Then, "Did they take anything?"

"I don't think so. The duffel bag's in a safe place. Is that what they were looking for?"

"How in the world should I know?"

"You do know, Mom. Just tell me—"

"Do what your sister did and run. Take the money and your valuables. When you get where you're staying, get a burner and—"

"I remember the instructions."

"Obviously not. I told you to lay low, and I told you only to call from a burner. So this time, do a better job of hiding."

"But I don't want to run. This is my home."

"You were always such a"—expletive—"whiner. Get those stars out of your eyes."

"I have a life here, Mom."

"Run. And don't look back."

"But if you'd just tell me—"

"And don't call me until you're settled. With a burner, for"—expletive—"sake."

No point in answering, not because Ginny didn't have plenty to say, but because the three short beeps in her ear told her Mom had already disconnected.

Ginny stared at the car's dashboard as if it could bring her mother back and fingered the necklace she'd worn ever since Dad's death. It was a rose gold circle pendant with what looked like an onyx in the center. It was probably just a piece of black glass, but it was special to her because he'd given it to her just a week before he died. It hadn't been her birthday, nor a holiday. Just a gift because he'd been thinking of her.

A cheap trinket was all she had left of her family.

Whatever. She had shopping to do.

The store was packed. A sunny April day, and everybody in Southern New Hampshire was celebrating the warmth. She passed people with carts loaded with plants and flowers and fertilizer and tools. People were smiling and cheerful. Some even wore shorts, T-shirts, and flip-flops as if the temperature were in the nineties, not barely seventy.

Ginny glanced at the displays of flowers in the lawn-and-garden department. She'd planned to add colorful annuals to the small flowerbeds in her front yard, but now she wasn't so sure.

Her mother's words resonated in her mind. *Run and don't look back.*

She smiled at a toddler riding in her mother's shopping cart. The girl waved at her, and Ginny waved back until the girl and her mom disappeared around the corner.

There was such joy in this place today. Ginny needed to fixate on it and not on the many questions plaguing her.

No. She needed to fixate on the problem, not put it out of her mind. She needed to focus. Positive thinking wasn't going to keep that intruder from coming back.

She found the aisle with locks, located the brand and size Kade had recommended. After a few moments of deliberation, she chose a set for the front door—a lovely wrought iron that would go well with the dark red she intended to paint the door one of these days. She picked a similar handle-and-lock combo for the back door, simpler but with elegant lines.

After waiting patiently for someone to help her, she instructed one of the employees to cut the lengths of wood she'd need to secure her windows.

Wood stacked in the cart and locks chosen, she headed to the aisle with security systems.

So many to choose from, and they weren't cheap. Some were less than a hundred dollars, but this wasn't the kind of thing one should skimp on. The better ones were pricey. Kade had done a little research and texted his suggestions. She located the ones he liked. Expensive.

Was she really going to plop down three hundred dollars to secure a home she didn't intend to stay in?

And that was the real question, wasn't it?

She couldn't avoid the decision anymore. It was time for her to choose. Should she do as her mother and sister demanded and leave Nutfield for good?

Or should she take the risk and stay?

To leave meant starting over in everything. In business, with friends. But it also meant she'd be safe from... from whoever was after her.

To stay meant fighting for the life she'd built in Nutfield. It meant she'd keep the business, the house, the friends. But only if she stayed alive.

Maybe a smart person wouldn't risk her life for little things like a house and a job. But it wasn't those that had her vacillating.

It was the people she'd have to leave.

Jack and Harper, Sam and Garrison, Rae and Brady and the rest of that crew, clients, people Ginny worked with, people she'd become friends with at the real estate club, in the Chamber of Commerce, at the food bank.

And she'd have to leave Kade.

The concern he'd shown her, the care and tenderness... She'd felt valued in a way she never had before. Sure, her friends would've helped her if they'd known what had happened. But Kade... He barely knew her, and he'd been there for her.

She closed her eyes, shutting out all the different boxes and displays in front of her, and remembered the moment Kade had run outside, had pulled her from the car and wrapped her in his arms.

She'd felt safe there. She'd felt... at home.

And now she was considering leaving? Starting over in a new town in a new state with nothing? She couldn't have cared less about the money she might lose, the business, the clients.

She cared about the people. She cared about Kade.

All she'd ever wanted was a family. In Nutfield, she'd found one.

And she wasn't sacrificing it. Not for a nameless, faceless threat.

She opened her eyes, found the most expensive of the security systems Kade had suggested, and put it in her cart. She could handle the price tag.

She'd need the best if she was going to protect herself from the enemy.

In the car on the way back to Nutfield, her phone rang. She looked at the caller ID—it was Rae, one of her new friends. And... she just remembered. Brady, Rae's husband, was the chief of police.

When she answered, Rae said, "We heard about the break-in. Anything we can do?"

That Rae, a woman she hardly knew, would call... Emotion clogged her throat, and she swallowed it down. "I need to buy a handgun. Do you have any suggestions?"

# CHAPTER SIX

A car door slammed outside, and Kade stood from his seat at the dining room table and looked out the front window. Sure enough, Ginny was opening her trunk.

He jogged into the evening light. "Can I help?"

She turned to him, a plastic sack dangling from her arm. "That'd be great."

Wow, that smile...

Inside the trunk were cut boards and a laminated box that held the security system. "You went ahead and bought one."

"Got the one you suggested."

The rush of pleasure had him scolding himself. He needed to get a grip. "I'll get it installed tonight."

She looked at the sky, the few stars already twinkling overhead. "Maybe we should wait."

"Unless you've reconsidered staying with a friend, I'm not leaving until it's installed."

He expected her to balk or argue, but she didn't. Instead, she rested her hand on his forearm. "That's very kind of you. Thank you."

The rush of pleasure turned into a full-blown tidal wave. He had the urge to pull her into his arms and promise to protect her forever.

Forcing himself to deal with the matter at hand, he lifted the box from the trunk and followed her inside.

After they unloaded the wood, he replaced her locks with the new knob-and-deadbolt combos she'd picked out while she settled the boards in place on each of the windows.

When the new locks were installed and tested, he found her at the coffee table. She'd removed all the pieces from the security system box and spread them out, and now she was studying the instruction booklet.

"I see you've got a jump on me."

She glanced at the pieces of plastic and metal and electronics on the table. "It's like tackling Everest."

"Call me Sherpa Kade."

She lowered the instructions and eyed him from head to foot and back. "You're a bit tall for a Sherpa."

He hoped his cheeks weren't turning red. Her attention did weird things to him. He lifted the keys for the new locks. "Where do you want these?"

"Just toss them on the counter in the kitchen."

He did, then joined her. "What do you think?"

She set the instructional booklet on the table. "I think I should have gone to engineering school."

He chuckled and grabbed it. "How hard can it be?" After he'd flipped through the first couple of pages of instructions, he groaned, which made her smile.

"Told you."

"We can do this," he said. "We're educated adults. We went to college."

"That's right. I am woman. Hear me roar."

"I am man. Hear me... whine."

She laughed out loud. "I've heard you say a lot of things, but I've never heard you whine."

"You've never seen me install a security system." But he was kidding. The instructions were clear if complex, and within an hour, they'd made headway. He'd finished installing the sensors on the doors and was about to work on the camera when her stomach growled.

She giggled. "Excuse me."

"Phew. I didn't want to say anything after our huge lunch, but I'm starving."

"Come on, then." She led the way into the kitchen, and he stood at the counter while she searched her refrigerator. "Let's see. I have leftovers from McNeal's last night." She opened the container, then shoved it back in the fridge. "Not enough for two." She opened the crisper, then the meat drawer. "Got it." She snatched a bunch of packages and set them on the counter beside him. "Chef salad?"

"Sounds delicious." He'd prefer a steak, but he'd take anything as long as he could eat it across the table from her.

She beamed and snatched the leftover container out of the refrigerator again. "Chicken fingers will be a good addition."

"What can I do?"

She scanned him from head to foot. "What *can* you do? You know your way around a kitchen?"

"Um, I can cut stuff."

She grabbed two cutting boards, two knives, and a peeler and set them on the counter. "I'll wash and tear the lettuce. You peel the cucumber and slice those cherry tomatoes."

They got to work, shoulder to shoulder. He did what she asked, but he had to work to focus on his task. Watching her was mesmerizing. Her hands were deft. Her smile, constant. Her laugh, quick. Her wit, as sharp as the knife she used to chop the fried chicken strips.

She gasped. "Boiled eggs!"

He chuckled. "I've never seen someone so excited about eggs before."

"They'll be good. And I need to get the cheese."

When he'd finished his tasks, he watched as she chopped ham and cubes of cheese, added some chunks of avocado—another "staple" nobody would find in his fridge—sliced the boiled eggs she just happened to have on hand. "They're chock full of protein, you know," she explained. And then she mixed salad dressing from scratch.

She was pulling two huge bowls from the cabinet when she said, "Why don't you set the table. The silverware is"—she pointed with her elbow—"in there. And the napkins are in the pantry."

He did as she asked, setting both of their computers in the living room to get them out of harm's way. A moment later, she carried the salad and half a loaf of French bread she'd warmed in the oven to the table, and they sat for their second meal of the day together.

She reached for her fork to eat, but he stopped her with a hand on her wrist. "I didn't do this at lunch, but after everything... Do you mind if I pray?"

"Oh." Her smile faded, but only a little. "I guess not."

His hand was already there with hers, so it only made sense to hold it. As it slipped into his, the events of the day came back to him. "Father, thank You for protecting Ginny today. Thank You for protecting her house and her things. As we do everything we can on our end to keep her safe, please fill in our gaps. Protect her tonight in this house. Protect her from whoever broke in today and whatever is going on. Give her..." He paused, swallowed, and added in his thoughts, *give us...* "understanding about what's going on and wisdom to know what to do about it. Bless our food tonight. In Jesus's name, amen."

He squeezed her hand. When she looked at him, her eyes were wide, and a tear was making its way down her cheek.

"Hey." He wiped it with his fingertip. The gesture was intimate and felt perfectly right. "I didn't mean to make you cry."

She sniffed, and that perpetual smile returned. "Nobody's ever prayed for me before like that. Or like..." She shook her head, swallowed again. "Or like anything, I guess. That was very sweet."

Nobody had ever prayed for her?

She brushed her hair over one shoulder. "I mean, I go to Bible study at a friend's house every once in a while, and they pray, but for everybody. You know?"

He held her gaze. "It was my pleasure. And I'll keep praying for you until this is all straightened out." And maybe longer than that.

She didn't look away, just tilted her head to one side. "Thank you, Kade. For everything you did today. And for... for your kindness, your understanding. It means more than you can imagine."

He'd do that and a million more things if that would keep her from leaving. Kathryn had told her to run, and now an intruder had broken into her house. Maybe, if he really cared about her, he'd suggest she take her sister's advice. The problem was, if she left, then he'd never see her again. And even though he'd only spent one day with Ginny, he didn't think he could accept that.

So the only option was to keep her safe and pray she'd stick around.

THEY CHATTED OVER THE MEAL, and he worked to keep from staring at her.

Funny thing was, every time he looked at her, he found her looking at him.

Something was happening between them, and fast. Something he'd never experienced. He felt connected to her—and he liked it.

He tried to focus on his meal. The salad was cool and fresh, the fried chicken crispy, and the cheese creamy. Spicy dressing added the perfect kick to pull it all together. "It's good."

"It's probably not as substantial as you're used to. I eat a lot of salads." She nodded toward the living room. "I saw your computer. Did you go to your house to get it?"

"I told you I wasn't leaving." He sipped his drink. "I keep my laptop with me most of the time."

"Yeah?"

He shrugged, sliced an oversize piece of chicken. "I got into the habit in college. I always worked, so I had limited opportunities to study. If I had five or ten minutes between classes or had some extra time, I'd take advantage. I kept the habit after I graduated. There never seems to be enough time."

"That's smart. I've gotten accustomed to doing a lot on my phone."

"I don't like working on my phone if I can help it." He lifted his hands. "Fat fingers. And home is too quiet."

She set down her water glass and beamed at him. "I'm the same way. I need people around."

"The noise of a crowd."

"Yes." Her eyes were bright. "The energy... There's something about it that gets my creative juices going."

He chuckled. "We have that in common, then."

She stirred her salad. "I thought I was weird, you know? Because my sister was always searching for peace and quiet. And my college roommate needed silence to do anything productive. I'd sit there and chatter, and she'd shush me."

"I get it. Maybe it's because we're the babies in the house. We're used to things going on over our heads."

Her smiled faded a little. "Everything was over my head."

"I didn't mean like we were too dumb to get it. Just too young."

"I know." She returned to her dinner, and he did the same. Then, she said, "Did you get some work done?"

"A lot. That binder is going to be priceless. I can't thank you enough for sharing it."

"I'm just happy to be able to do something for you after all you've done—"

The doorbell screeched like the nails of an angry cat running across a chalkboard. He winced at the sound. "Tell me you bought a new doorbell at the store today."

She pushed back in her chair. "I should have added it to the list."

"Are you expecting someone?"

"Oh. I should have told you. Do you know Rae and Brady Thomas?"

"The police chief? I've seen him, but I don't know that we've ever met." Kade followed Ginny to the door. "Did I miss something? Why are they here?"

"Rae called..." At the door, she reached for the handle.

He stopped her with a hand on her arm. "Let me, just in case."

She stepped out of the way. "Thank you, brave knight."

He chuckled, unlocked the deadbolt, and yanked the new handle. It felt sure and solid in his hand.

On the front porch stood a tall man and a pretty woman. Kade stepped aside.

Ginny said, "Come in. Thank you guys for coming over. You really didn't have to do this."

The couple stopped in the foyer. "Kade, these are my friends, Rae and Brady Thomas."

Rae had shoulder-length strawberry blond hair and green eyes. An oversize bag swung from her forearm. She stepped forward with a friendly smile and shook his hand. "Hi, Kade."

Brady was taller than Kade, maybe six-four? And he looked enough like the quarterback whose name he sort of shared that Kade figured he'd heard enough jokes about it for a lifetime. Brady held out his hand. "Kade...?"

Kade shook it. "Kade Powers. Nice to meet you."

Brady's eyebrows lifted, but he didn't smile. "Any relation to Darren?"

Everybody knew Darren. "He's my brother."

"His gas stations are always clean and well maintained."

Rae bumped her husband with her hip. "He's a gas station connoisseur."

Brady smirked at her. "It's always good to know where there's a clean bathroom when you spend as much time as I do in the car."

Kade updated Brady on what his older siblings were doing while Ginny led the way to the living room.

Rae peeked into the dining room before she sat on the sofa. "We interrupted your dinner."

"Not your fault," Ginny said. "We got started late, and we're about done, anyway. Have a seat, Brady."

He sat beside his wife, and Kade and Ginny took the two club chairs.

Kade still didn't know why Brady and Rae were there. When

he caught Ginny's eye, she answered his unspoken question. "I asked what kind of a handgun I should buy."

"You decided to do it?" Kade asked. "Good for you."

Ginny shrugged. "If I'm going to stay in my house, then I need to protect it."

"Wherever you go," Kade said, "you need to protect yourself."

"That, too." She turned to Brady. "You guys didn't have to come over, though. I really did plan to buy one."

"I read the police report." Brady had a no-nonsense air about him that Kade appreciated. "And you're wise to get a firearm. What happened here today is not normal. People don't break into houses and search them for fun. And from what the report said, it seemed the intruder worked hard to replace everything so you wouldn't know he'd been here."

That was true. Kade hadn't articulated that, but now that Brady had, he realized it was one of the things that had struck him as odd. As sinister.

"Are you sure you have no idea what he was looking for?" Brady asked.

She shook her head, but her eye contact slipped, and her gaze bounced around the room before it found the chief again. "Nope."

He narrowed his gaze and said nothing. The man was perceptive.

Rae looked like she was about to speak, but without taking his eyes from Ginny, Brady quieted her with a hand on her leg. "The thing is, Ginny, I don't think I believe you."

"Brady!" Rae's voice was indignant. She turned to Ginny. "I'm sorry. My husband can be—"

"Honest," Brady said. "I'm being honest because you're a friend, and I want to help you, but I can't help you if I don't know what's going on." He sat back in the sofa. He was trim and fit and seemed to envelop the space. "I don't suspect you of anything, Ginny, except maybe withholding information we need to keep you safe."

She swallowed, and her gaze flicked from Brady to Rae to Kade and back. "I really don't know anything."

"That you're willing to share with us right now." Brady let the words hang in the air. He didn't speak, and when Rae looked like she might, he tapped her leg. Secret married-couple sign language.

Kade wasn't going to break the silence, either. Ginny was holding out on them. He suspected Brady was right. They needed to know everything if they were going to keep her safe.

Though tension rolled off Ginny in waves, she said nothing.

Impressive in her determination to keep whatever she was hiding to herself. Impressive and irritating all at once.

Finally, Brady leaned forward. "If anything changes and if you feel like you need help or more protection, or if you decide to tell us more, please don't hesitate. If you've done something illegal—"

"She hasn't." Kade hadn't meant to speak, but the words were out there now.

Brady turned to him. "You know what's going on?"

"Not really, but I'm just saying..."

Brady's eyebrows lifted. "You're saying you trust her? Or you're saying you know enough to know she hasn't done anything illegal."

"Both." Kade made the word sure and strong. "I trust her, and she hasn't done anything illegal."

After a moment, Brady nodded. "Fair enough." He turned to Ginny again. "I'm here if you want to talk. Or you can talk to any of my men. We might be a small town, but we have our share of crime and"—he cut his gaze to his wife's—"strange situations. Let's just say we've had a lot of experience."

Rae's head bobbed. "That's true. And you can trust Brady and the police. They're going to do everything in their power to make sure you're safe. But they can't help you if you don't tell them the truth."

Ginny swallowed, and a beat passed before she said, "If I think of anything..."

After a long moment of watching her, waiting, Kade assumed, for her to share something else, Brady turned to Rae. "Go ahead."

She reached in her huge bag and pulled out a pistol. She

checked to make sure it wasn't loaded, then pointed it toward the floor and handed it to Ginny.

Ginny accepted the weapon silently. "Is it loaded?"

"No magazine," Rae said, "no bullet in the chamber." She reached back into her purse and pulled out the magazine and a box of ammunition and set them on the coffee table.

Ginny smiled. "I only know what you mean because I watch TV."

Brady was eyeing her through narrowed eyes. "You know how to shoot it?"

"Haven't the slightest idea." She held the handle between her thumb and forefinger. It dangled toward the floor. "I've never even held a gun before."

"That's obvious." Kade stood and pulled her to her feet. He shifted her so that the barrel was pointed toward the wall and positioned her right hand as it should be.

Her grip was tight as a stretched rubber band. "Relax. It's not going to explode."

She giggled and tried to comply, but he could feel her stress.

"You want your hand as high on the handle as you can get it. Scoot it close to the tang."

She moved her hand up the gun. "Tang is delicious. We drank it all the time as kids."

He stifled a chuckle. "I'm glad to see you're taking this seriously."

"You're the one making up words."

When he had her right hand positioned properly, her pointer finger straight on the side, he positioned her left hand across the other side. It was awkward, though, so he wrapped his arm around her back and worked with her left hand in his. "You want as much skin on the gun as you can get. That keeps it secure. Here, wrap these fingers over those..." When she got her hands right, he said, "There you go. That's it."

He caught Brady's half-smile across the room and realized how close he and Ginny were. Her back was pressed against his front. Her hair, carrying the faint scent of apples, tickled his lips. Funny how well she fit. Heat radiated through him, a heightened aware-ness of the woman in his arms—and the two people watching. He stepped back and swallowed. "Anyway, we can practice another time."

She pointed the gun at the floor and looked at him, her cheeks pink. "I guess."

She sat, and he did, too, considerably warmer than he'd been a moment before.

"I was going to offer to teach you to shoot it," Brady said, "but Kade seems like an able instructor."

"We all learned to shoot when I was a kid." He looked at Ginny. "I'll be happy to teach you."

"Okay." She set the gun on the coffee table. "I really appreciate this. I'll get it back to you when..." But she faltered and shrugged. "Eventually. Or maybe I'll just buy myself one."

"We have plenty." Rae cut her gaze to her husband, an affec-tionate smile on her face. "Before we were married, Brady gathered quite a collection. And now that we have kids, they're all locked away in a safe." She focused on Brady. "Speaking of the kids..."

"Right." He stood. "We left them with my folks for date night. We'd better get home before my dad breaks out the candy and gets them on a sugar high."

After they traded thanks-for-comings and nice-to-meet-yous at the door and Rae and Brady left, Kade and Ginny returned to their meals.

She was about to dig into her salad once again when he said, "So, I take it from the locks and the security system and the gun that you decided not to take your sister's advice."

She set her fork down and glanced at the pistol, which she'd rested on the table beside her. "This is my home, my life. I'm going to fight for it."

# CHAPTER SEVEN

Ginny wasn't looking forward to this.

She climbed into Kade's warm pickup—apparently the man had two vehicles—Sunday afternoon. While he'd finished installing the alarm Saturday night, he'd somehow gotten her to promise to join him for church on Sunday.

He didn't attend the same church as Sam and Rae and the rest of their crew. Ginny had liked theirs, the pretty old building in the center of town. Kade's church was very different. Newer building, younger people, louder music. At first, she'd found it strange, a little uncomfortable the way people lifted their hands during the songs, all the talk of the Holy Spirit. The sermon was interesting, though. The pastor, a trim forty-something man wearing jeans and an untucked shirt, had talked about the difference between the plans people make for themselves and God's plans for them.

That God would have a plan for her life was such a strange idea. Did He really care how she spent her time or money? Had He really designed work for her to do, as the pastor had said, even before her birth? She couldn't imagine. God always seemed so far away, like a white-haired grandfather who found his grandkids amusing when they were visiting but forgot about them when they were out of sight.

Maybe her perception of God had been way off. Or maybe the people at Kade's church—and Sam and Rae's for that matter—were crazy.

She wasn't prepared to rule out either scenario.

After church, Kade brought her back home to change into something she wouldn't mind getting dirty. He'd waited in his pickup, which she hadn't even known he'd owned until this morning when he'd driven her to church in it. It was an older model two-seater with a long truck bed. Clean on the inside, beat-up on the outside.

She settled on the bench seat. "I'm not ready for this."

"Ready or not, you need to do it."

Fifteen minutes later, Kade turned his pickup down a dirt track that was so narrow and rarely traveled, she wouldn't call it a road. He drove about a hundred yards between trees that were so close together, she closed her eyes more than once, certain the truck was going to smack their branches. The road angled upward, and the trees tapered off and deposited them in an open space maybe twenty-five yards across. He stopped at the crest of the hill.

She could feel him looking at her, but she couldn't force her gaze away from the view.

Trees towered around them. On the right was a huge grass-covered mound. In front of her, the landscape dotted with leafless trees angled down in a rocky slope to the glimmering surface of Clearwater Lake.

Houses surrounded the lake at almost every spot except right below them.

"This is yours?" She glanced long enough to see the pride in his features.

"You see that dock with the little boat?" He pointed to the left, the north edge of the lake, and she followed his finger to the dock where a quaint blue fishing boat floated on the calm water. "From about twenty feet on this side of that to"—he pointed toward the right end of the lake, the southern edge—"to that little inlet right there."

"How long is it?"

"About a mile and a half on the water."

She whistled. "I knew you owned lakefront property, but I had no idea."

"The only undeveloped land on Clearwater Lake is mine."

"Wow."

He shrugged. "It's not like I earned it. My parents gave it to me."

"It's beautiful."

His features lit as if a light shone on them. "I've been incredibly blessed."

"I'm glad you realize it. For a rich kid, you don't seem too spoiled."

His jaw dropped in mock offense. "Are you saying I'm *a little* spoiled?"

"Maybe more than a little"—she cut her gaze around the land that had been a gift—"but I like you anyway."

His gaze met hers and held a long moment. "It's mutual."

*Oh.* When he looked at her like that, she could hardly think. She should look away, think of something to say.

He cleared his throat. "Anyway, we're here to shoot."

That broke the connection. She groaned. "I'm not sure I should be around a loaded gun. I'm a bit flighty. Once a boyfriend took me to drive golf balls."

Kade's eyes narrowed on the word *boyfriend.*

Ginny continued. "He was explaining what to do and had just said something along the lines of, 'Always check behind you...' But it was too late. The words didn't register in time. I caught him on the shoulder with my backswing."

"Was he terribly injured?" Kade's eyes lit up as if he found the injury amusing.

Ginny playfully punched him in the shoulder. "It definitely left a mark." And then she remembered why she'd told the story. "Seriously, what if I accidentally—?"

"You're not going to shoot me or yourself. I promise."

She wasn't so sure about that. Her brain didn't always connect with her actions.

Five minutes later, Kade had set a board across two sawhorses in front of the grass-covered mound. He fetched a grocery bag full of empty cans from the truck. "Good thing the recycling truck hadn't come yet. I have plenty of targets." He set nine cans on the board. "Why don't you grab the gun and ammo from the truck?"

She'd left them in a canvas bag, and she was happy for them to stay there. "I'd really rather not."

He shrugged. "I'll get them, then."

"I mean, I'm not sure I want to do this."

Over his shoulder, he called, "I knew what you meant."

A moment later, he set the canvas bag on the tailgate and motioned her over.

"This is pretty simple." He held the magazine in one hand and a bunch of bullets in the other. "You just slide them in like so." He pressed the bullets into the magazine. "You want to try?"

She shook her head, and he sighed.

"Fine. You can load the next round." He took her elbow—maybe he hadn't trusted she'd go with him—and stopped about four yards from the cans. He handed her ear plugs, which she put in her ears while he did the same.

She worried she wouldn't be able to hear him, but when he spoke, his voice was audible, if muffled.

"Remember how I told you to hold it?" he asked.

She tried to put her hands the way he'd shown her the day before. When she didn't quite get it right, he helped, though this time, he didn't wrap his arms around her from behind. She wished he would. Then maybe she could have distracted him enough to make him forget the whole teach-Ginny-to-shoot craziness.

As if she'd be bold enough to initiate a first kiss. No chance. And he seemed like a man with a mission today.

When he was happy with the placement of her hands, he demonstrated how she should stand. Left foot slightly forward, both knees bent a little. "A natural athletic stance," he said.

"'Natural' and 'athletic' are two words nobody's ever applied to me."

He chuckled while she stood the way he'd told her to.

"Good." He gave her an approving nod. "I don't want you to move your trigger finger. Keep it against the shaft of the gun and away from the trigger."

She was happy to comply.

"Now, you're going to lift the gun to eye level and aim at the can."

"Which one?"

"Whichever one you want. You'll use these sights. You put that one"—he pointed to the one on the far end of the gun—"in the center of these two." He pointed to the ones nearer her eyes. "Focus on the far sight. The closer ones and the target will be blurry, but that's okay. Just keep your eye on that far sight and aim at a can."

She did what he asked. She got the can in her sights and kept in there. "Now what?"

"Move your finger to the trigger."

Okay. So far, so good.

"As slowly as you possibly can, like super-slo-mo, press that trigger."

"Just like that."

"So slowly you think it'll never fire."

She kept the can in her sights and did what Kade asked, slowly, slowly pressing the trigger. Her heart rate increased. Was this going to hurt? How loud would it be? Did it always take this long? It never took this long in movies. Maybe she was doing it—

The boom had her gasping.

Four yards away, the can flew off into the grass.

She'd expected a painful kick, but it hadn't hurt. She stared at the can on the ground, shocked. She'd done it? On her first try? A wide smile crossed her lips, and she tried—unsuccessfully, she was sure—to temper it. She turned to Kade. "Did I hit it?"

"It saw you aiming and jumped to protect itself." Kade's eyes glimmered with amusement. "It's all in the excellent instruction."

She giggled. "Probably."

"I'm kidding. That was amazing."

"I'm twelve feet from it. I bet anybody can do that."

He shook his head. "Do it again."

She turned to the targets, chose a Dr. Pepper can, and aimed. Again, so slowly she thought it would never happen, she squeezed the trigger. And again, the boom surprised her. This time, she didn't gasp.

The can flew off the board.

The shell hit her hand and fell to the ground.

"I did it."

"Again."

She hit the third, then the fourth. At his prompting, she hit all nine.

He took the gun from her hands and set it on the canvas bag on the ground. "You're a natural."

"You were right earlier. Good instruction."

"It's all about using the sights."

"I felt like my hands were shaking and moving constantly."

"Sure. Your body is constantly moving, pumping blood, breathing. You can't be perfectly steady. But you don't have to be. This time, I don't want you to aim at the can. I want you to aim at a certain spot on the can."

"This time?" She rubbed the skin between her thumb and forefinger.

"Does it hurt?"

"A little."

He looked at where she was hurting. "That's normal. You'll get used to it."

As much fun as it had been, she wasn't sure she wanted to do it so much she got used to it.

Kade nodded toward the pistol. "Leave that there while I arrange more targets."

"We've had enough for today."

He ignored her and set nine cans—all Coke—on the board.

This time, he ensured the words were facing her. "I want you to aim at the C."

"There's no way."

"It doesn't matter if you hit it exactly. It's just what I want you to aim at. Grab the gun and ammo and let's go back to the truck."

Wow, he had a pushy side. "I really would rather—"

"Just do it, please."

She huffed, grabbed the gun and the canvas bag, and walked to the pickup. She set them beside the box of ammo. "I think that's enough for today."

"Load the magazine like I showed you."

"You're not the boss of me."

His lips twitched, but he didn't allow the smile to come through. Instead, he turned to her and took her hands. "There was a man in your house yesterday, Ginny. A man. In your house. If I hadn't been there, he'd have been in your house alone with you."

"I know, but..."

He squeezed her hands. "But what?"

"Shooting cans is one thing. I don't think I could shoot a person."

"If he was coming after you? If you thought he might hurt you?"

She swallowed hard. "I don't think so."

His lips closed in a tight line. "I'm going to assume that your self-protection instinct will kick in." He let go of her hands. "Go ahead and load the magazine."

She did what he asked, then fired off more rounds from a little farther away.

She hit the target every time.

When the last can fell, she aimed at the ground and turned to Kade.

Kade's eyebrows rose. "You're a closet secret agent, aren't you?"

"You figured me out."

"You want to go again?"

By now, her hand was really hurting. "Let's call it good for now."

"Fair enough. We'll come back and try again soon."

He left the board and sawhorses and walked her to the passenger seat. After she'd slipped in, he set the canvas bag with the gun and ammo on the floor at her feet. Then he met her gaze. "I appreciate that, even though you didn't want to practice today, you did your best and tried to learn. I'm impressed."

She shrugged. "As long as I have to do it, I may as well do it well."

He stayed there another moment, and his gaze flicked to her lips.

Her whole body paused as she waited for him to close the distance between them. But he didn't.

He stepped back and closed the door. As chilly as the April air had been outside, she felt colder now than she had all day.

THE WEEKEND SUNSHINE had given way to rain by Monday. Ginny hated rain. It always conjured images best forgotten, images that had been burned into her brain by Katrina when she was only a child.

But today, she wouldn't let the rain get her down. Because, though in many ways her weekend had been hard, in other ways, it had been amazing.

Kade had been amazing.

His kindness made it impossible for her to feel depressed, despite the rainfall outside.

After target practice, they'd gone to lunch, then spent the rest of the afternoon at her house working on his presentation to the zoning board. The money hadn't come in yet, but he was hopeful Sokolov would come through. Kade was far more organized than most people she'd worked with at this stage, with his budget planned to the penny, the contractors lined up, the schedule—including accounting for rainy days like this one—in place.

They'd expanded the list of ways the housing development and country club would benefit the community. Ginny had put together a PowerPoint presentation, and Kade had sent the proposal to the printer. He was all set for the meeting the next day.

Today wasn't about Kade's project, though. Today was about Ginny's.

She had to figure out who had broken into her house and maybe even find a way to get in touch with them, whoever they were. Because her mother had given her that duffel bag full of cash. She hadn't told Ginny what she was supposed to do with it, and she assumed she wasn't supposed to give it to strangers who came calling. But Ginny didn't owe her mother anything, not after the way she'd treated her, not after their conversation Saturday.

Ginny would hand that duffel bag over to whoever wanted it if doing so would mean she could keep her life in Nutfield.

It had crossed her mind to give it to Kade. It could solve his problems entirely, and, if the project was as successful he thought it would be, she'd make the investment back. But if people were after her, the money was her only leverage. And anyway, Kade wouldn't want it, not if he knew its origin. She had no idea what the money represented. She did know that the people after her were criminals.

Would they use the money for harm? Was it wrong for her to give it to them? Did it belong to them, and had Ginny's mother stolen it?

She had no idea.

Maybe the bag held a clue. She was at the bank when they unlocked the doors that morning. Five minutes later, the bank manager left her in the room with her safe deposit box on the table and the door closed.

Ginny opened the bag. Even though she'd known what it contained, the sight of all those bundles of bills shook her. Where had it come from?

Whom did it belong to?

She took each bundle out. There were some bundles of hundreds, but most were twenties. She'd never counted it before, though it wasn't hard to figure it out. Each bundle should hold a hundred bills. There were eight bundles of hundreds, so eighty thousand dollars in hundreds. There were twenty-four bundles of twenties—forty-eight thousand dollars. She flipped through each one looking for... something. A name, a phone number, an email address. Nothing.

She studied the bands surrounding the bills, again looking for a clue as to who the money belonged to. But the bands had nothing written on them.

Ginny glanced at the door, praying it would stay closed. It would, she knew. She had privacy here, but she couldn't help the apprehension.

She searched the bag itself. There were no pockets, no secret compartments. She didn't know exactly what she'd hoped to find. Maybe a note that read *If found, please call...*

No luck.

She placed all the money back in the duffel, shoved it into the box, and returned the box to its proper space.

That had been no help at all.

Ginny usually walked to the real estate office to work, but when she left the bank, she went back home to work. With appointments settled and paperwork managed, she turned her attention to her parents' businesses.

Ginny dialed the number for Tammy Jean's Cajun Cafe in Oakland. Her parents had opened Tammy Jean's—named for Ginny's paternal grandmother, her favorite granny, who'd been killed in Hurricane Katrina—shortly after they'd settled in California. At first, Dad had done most of the cooking, and Mom had managed the staff. The restaurant had been a success, and they opened another one, then bought a couple of other fledgling restaurants and made successes of them. Neither of Ginny's parents had worked in the restaurants in years. They'd spent their time managing them and, in Dad's case, serving on some committees for non-profits, doing some overseas traveling for business—what business, she had no idea—and playing golf.

It had never occurred to Ginny before her dad's death, but it did seem odd that a handful of restaurants could make enough money to afford her family the lifestyle they'd lived.

She checked her watch. Two o'clock on the East Coast meant eleven a.m. in California. The phone rang three times before a breathless woman answered. "Tammy Jean's."

"Britt, is that you?"

A pause, then, "Ginny? Oh, my gosh. I can't believe it." Ginny could picture the head hostess. She was maybe twenty-five, blond, pretty, and great with customers. "How are you?"

Such a loaded question, but Britt didn't need to know all the details of her life. "I'm fine. Is Wang Lei around?"

A little gasp. "Your mom didn't tell you?"

Ginny didn't have time for Britt's dramatic streak right now. "Tell me what?"

Britt lowered her voice to nearly a whisper. "He was murdered."

Ginny's stomach looped. "Oh no. When?"

"It's been a while. Last fall, maybe September? It was right before your mom sold the place."

"She sold it?"

There was a beat of silence. "You didn't know?"

"We don't... I moved away. I don't talk to her much."

"Still, though, that's totally weird that she wouldn't tell you."

Britt didn't know the half of it.

"Can I speak to the new manager?"

"The owner's here. Hold on a sec. And hey, when you're in town, stop by. I'd love to see you again."

Not that Ginny would ever go back to the San Francisco area, but she said, "That'd be great."

While she waited, Ginny opened a new document on her laptop and typed *Wang Lei, murdered, September. Business sold right after.*

Finally, a man came on the line. "This is Ted."

"Hi Ted. This is Ginny Lamont, Darlene's daughter. I was wondering—"

"Look, Ginny, is it?"

"I—"

"I bought this business with cash." His voice was loud enough that Ginny pulled the phone away from her ear. "Sunk everything I own into it, and I'm not going to let your people wrench it away from me."

"Wait, I'm just trying—"

"We're legitimate now, got it? Don't call here again. And don't come in. I'll have the cops on you so fast your head'll spin."

The phone slammed in its cradle, and Ginny winced at the sound.

What in the world?

She typed the gist of the conversation into a document, her hands shaking. It wasn't often she got yelled at by perfect strangers. And had them threaten to call the cops on her, as if she were a criminal.

When she'd noted what he said, she pushed back from the kitchen table and got a glass of water.

It was okay. She could do this.

There were plenty of other businesses to call, other people to ask. Somebody would give her the information she needed. Somebody had to know what kinds of people her parents had been involved with.

She returned to the computer and her phone and dialed her parents' second largest restaurant, another Cajun place, this one in Richmond.

But the manager had quit, and nobody knew where he'd gone.

The restaurant had been sold, and the new owner refused to speak to her.

When she called the third restaurant on the list, there was no answer. A quick Google search told her the place had closed its doors.

More calls, no answers. All the restaurants her parents had owned had been sold or closed, the managers gone.

Ginny finished typing a final note, then pushed back from the table. She moved into the living room and paced. Those restaurants had been her mother's largest source of income. Why would she sell them?

Why would somebody want Wang Lei dead?

She knew her parents were into something illegal. The restaurants must have been involved. She'd only hoped to ask the managers if they knew anything. Having worked so closely with her parents all those years, she thought maybe they'd picked up on something or knew if her parents had had enemies. But now... The managers had been in on it, whatever it was. Or at least somebody thought they had.

But what?

She felt like the answer was so obvious, it was staring her in the face.

"Think, Ginny." But she didn't have enough information.

Back at the table, she took a deep, calming breath, and dialed the club.

Most of the time, she didn't allow herself to dwell on the fact that her parents owned a place like *Pretty Little Things*.

She'd heard her parents discussing "pretty things," but hadn't known what they were talking about, and when she asked, they just waved it and her away. *Just one of our businesses. Not your concern.*

And of course, she hadn't investigated, too wrapped up in her own life to care.

But then she'd seen the name on her dad's desk, and she'd looked up the address.

Not exactly the classiest area of town. The next time she'd gone downtown, she'd driven by it, thinking she'd go in, maybe introduce herself to the manager, see what kind of place it was. *Pretty Little Things*—she'd imagined a gift store.

It was the curvy, cartoon women on the sign that gave it away.

And the blacked-out windows.

Her parents owned a strip club.

Fine. Whatever. She'd never known anything about it, and she didn't want to know now. But she needed information. She found the number and dialed.

The man who answered the phone sounded bored. "Pretty Little Things. We open at four. We take cash and credit cards. No checks. We serve a full menu. Need anything else?"

"Uh... Yeah. Hi. I'm looking for the manager."

"You got him. I'm always looking for new girls, so just come in—"

"No, no." Her cheeks burned at the thought. "I'm not looking for a job. I'm calling because... How long have you worked there?"

"You a reporter or something?"

"No. Um..." She vacillated about telling him who she was.

"A cop?"

"No, no. Nothing like that."

"Look, I know what you're asking. It's a bad idea for you to come. Maybe you think it'll be fun, a lark, but trust me, you don't want to be here. Anything else?"

She took a deep breath. "I'm so sorry. I'm a little discombobulated. See, I think my parents used to own that club, and I'm trying to... to learn about their business."

"If they don't own it anymore, then it isn't their business."

An excellent point. "My name is Ginny Lamont. My parents used to own your... club. I wondered if they still do."

When the man spoke again, his voice had lowered to nearly a growl. "I bought the place last fall. Your parents' associates have been sniffing around, trying to get in with me, but I got no desire to go to prison for a bunch of crooks. I make all the money I need. So if that's what you're—"

"What kind of... of work did they do? I mean..." She was struggling to articulate. "My parents were into something illegal. What do you know about that?"

There was a long pause before the man's voice softened. "Listen. If you don't know, then you're lucky. Don't dig in someone else's graveyard. Let it go."

"I can't. Somebody's after me."

The man uttered a curse word under his breath. "Then you're as good as dead."

~

AS GOOD AS DEAD.

Ginny pushed away from the table and stood. She wasn't going to write that in her notes. That would make it too real.

She looked around her kitchen, her dining room. Everything was the same, but dread and fear crawled at her back. She shuddered and wrapped her arms around her middle.

*As good as dead.*

She walked into the living room, pulled in a couple of breaths, and blew them out. She was safe here. She checked the new lock on the back door, then crossed to the front. Both doors were bolted shut. The windows were barricaded.

Her gun had been lots of different places since she'd gotten it Saturday. In her night stand, in her purse, in the little drawer in her coffee table. Every spot she'd found for it either seemed too exposed or too far away to do her any good.

Right now, it was in a drawer in the kitchen. She pulled it out, set it on the counter.

She was safe.

For now.

But what would happen when the intruder came back? Would she be safe then?

*As good as dead.*

She didn't want to think about her parents anymore. She needed to get out of the house.

A walk would make her feel better, but it wasn't just raining. It was pouring, and the wind was whipping. No umbrella in the world could protect her from that.

Fine. She'd drive. She just couldn't be alone right now. She needed people. She needed...

She grabbed her phone and dialed.

Kade answered on the second ring. "Hey."

His voice relaxed her a little. "Working hard?"

She heard a few taps on a keyboard, then, "I think I'm ready for tomorrow."

"Did you hear from the guy from Friday?"

"I'm still waiting. It's killing me."

She'd never asked a man out, but she needed a distraction

badly. "I've been stuck in the house all day. I thought maybe, if you had time, we could, I don't know..." Ugh, she should have thought this through. It was too late for lunch, too early for dinner, and pouring rain.

"Let's take a drive," he said. "It'll kill time while I wait to hear from Sokolov."

"Are you sure you don't mind? I know you're busy."

She could hear the smile in his voice when he said, "I'll be there in twenty minutes."

By the time she'd thrown on makeup, put on her shoes, and grabbed her things, he was pulling into her driveway. She slipped on her hooded raincoat, activated her alarm, and ran out to meet him.

She slid into his passenger seat feeling both excited and embarrassed that she'd called. "Hi." She took off the black hood that made her look like the grim reaper.

"Hi yourself." He faced her, and a grin spread across his face. "You look beautiful."

"Thank you." He looked beautiful too. Strong and kind and protective.

"Where shall we go?" he asked.

"I don't care. Anywhere but my house right now."

His grin faded. "Did something happen? Something I should—"

"No more intruders, and the alarm works great. I feel very safe there." Mostly. Except when people three thousand miles away told her she was as good as dead. "It's just claustrophobic on a day like today. And I've had a rough couple of hours."

He backed out of her driveway and headed away from town. "Doing what?"

"I called the businesses my parents used to own."

"Used to? What happened?"

"Looks like Mom sold them." She gave him the rundown on her phone calls. She didn't mention that one of the businesses was a strip club. And she held back the last man's final remark. She wanted to tell him, but... It all sounded so crazy. She didn't want

Kade to think she was being dramatic. And she knew what he'd say —that she should tell Brady what was going on. She wasn't sure if that was a good idea or not.

It would be one thing to give the duffel bag to whoever had broken into her house. It would be entirely different to start something that might land her mother in prison.

When she was done, he said, "What do you think about what you've learned so far?"

"My parents were criminals. That much is clear. And they were into something dangerous."

He was nodding. "You don't have any guesses?"

"How could I? I was just a kid, and then I went to college. I should have paid better attention. I should—"

"Don't do that." He glanced at her, then took her hand. The connection with him, after everything she'd learned, stirred something in her heart. His hand was warm. His eyes were kind when he looked at her. He knew all these ugly things about her, but he wasn't backing off.

He braked at a stop sign and faced her. "You can't go back in time, and it's not as if your knowing would have changed anything. I'm glad your parents protected you at least a little." He focused forward again, but not before she saw the way his lips tightened, pulled down at the corners.

"What? What did that look mean?"

"Just that..." He signaled, then turned onto a street she'd never traveled before. The homes were far apart, probably each on its own acre, and set far off the main road, hardly visible through the rain. Lights shone here and there, but mostly it was a dark road on a dreary, oppressive day.

She started to prompt him to finish his statement, but he squeezed her hand and continued. "I'm just trying to imagine what it would be like to have parents who hadn't protected me. Not that we were in a lot of dangerous situations, but I always knew I could count on their support. I still can." He glanced at her. "I'm sorry you don't know what that's like."

A wave of... What was it? Affection, tenderness? It overwhelmed her, made her want to scoot closer and cuddle against his side. To feel the protection he was taking about.

Thank heavens for the center console that kept her firmly in her seat.

They'd spent the entire weekend together. He'd said their lunch Saturday was a date, yet he'd not kissed her that day or since. The few guys she'd dated in the past had been pretty eager to get to the kissing part of the relationship—and beyond. Which was why she'd never had a boyfriend for very long. She'd never trusted any of them enough to go *beyond*.

Now here she was with a guy she did trust, possibly too much, and he hadn't even tried to kiss her.

Maybe he was over the idea of dating her. Maybe all her troubles made him want to run.

Of course. She had a target on her back. Why would anybody who knew the truth about her want to be near her?

And yet, here he was. Holding her hand, spending time with her.

She didn't know what to think. She did know she liked him. A lot. Maybe too much. Maybe she was already falling in love. And falls weren't exactly stoppable. A person didn't get halfway into a fall and then change her mind.

Ginny felt like she'd taken a leap off a high cliff, and there was no escaping what would come next.

And she didn't want to. Because she believed in love. Even though she'd rarely witnessed it, even though she'd never seen it demonstrated in her own family, she believed in true, abiding love. She believed in soul mates and happily-ever-afters. She believed in strong families and good parents and children who felt secure. She'd never had it, but she believed in it, and she wanted it.

And right now, regardless of how Kade felt about her, she believed in him.

"I'm sorry," Kade said. "I shouldn't judge your family."

Based on the tone of his voice, he'd misread her silence for offense. "With everything I've told you, you have every right to judge. And you're right. They didn't protect me. They didn't even particularly like me. My mom didn't, anyway. Kathryn did when we were girls, but that changed when she went to college. Dad loved me in his own way."

Kade said nothing, but she could tell by the way his lips were pressed together what he thought of her father's love.

She touched the necklace her father had given her. Dad had loved her.

But Kade was right too. A good father would never have done what hers had. She knew that. She knew what she'd received from her father was a pale imitation of true fatherly love. But it was all she knew.

"Did your mother sell the condo?"

"Oh. I don't know. I just assumed she still lived there."

"You really think she sent you running to safety and didn't protect herself?"

Reluctantly, Ginny pulled her hand from Kade's and slid her phone from her purse. She checked the real estate listing website. Her mother's house hadn't been listed for sale, but that didn't mean it hadn't sold. Kathryn's house hadn't been listed, either.

She went to the San Francisco County's real estate assessor's website and typed in the address of the condo she'd called home for much of her life.

The details of the property loaded.

"She sold it in September."

He nodded slowly, his eyes narrowing. "So she sold everything."

"Yup."

"Maybe you should call her, see if she'll tell you what's going on."

Ginny set her phone in the center console and crossed her arms against the chill.

Kade adjusted the heat. "Bad idea?"

She sighed. "It's such a good idea, I did it on Saturday."

He looked at her, then back at the road. "You didn't tell me."

"It's... embarrassing."

He laid his hand on her knee, palm up. An invitation she happily took as she slipped hers into it.

"Your mother's behavior is not a reflection of you. What happened?"

"I told her about Kathryn, but she already knew."

"I thought you said they hadn't spoken in years."

"We have a... a thing we're supposed to do when we relocate. Mom told me when she sent me away. We're supposed to call her and tell her where we are and give her the new address in case she needs it." Ginny left out the part about always calling from a burner. That was too weird.

And she hadn't done it. She'd called from her own phone. She hoped that wouldn't come back to bite her.

"She insists on knowing where you're living," Kade said. "But she didn't reciprocate and tell you where she moved to?"

"That sums it up."

"What did she tell you?"

Ginny stared at the drops of water sliding down the side window. Not straight down but diagonally because of the air hitting the moving car. That's what her life felt like, headed in the wrong direction because of unforeseen forces beyond her control. "To do what Kathryn did."

He turned into a neighborhood and pulled over. After putting the car into park, he faced her. "She told you to run away."

Ginny nodded.

He pressed his lips together. "But you're still here."

"This is my home. This is more my home than San Francisco ever was. I have a life here."

He squeezed her hand, then kissed her forehead. "I'm glad you're staying."

"You don't think I'm stupid?"

"You can't run for the rest of your life."

"But what if...?" She swallowed. "I don't even know who I'm supposed to be afraid of."

"Let's see if we can narrow it down. Based on what you told me, it sounds like the restaurants were involved in whatever your parents were doing. I have a theory, but... Why don't you Google it, see what you can find?"

She grabbed her phone and opened the internet browser. "What do I type?"

He shrugged. "I don't know. Try *crime in restaurants.*"

She did and scrolled through the results. "These are all about shootings and burglaries and..."

"Maybe *criminal activity in restaurants.*"

She typed that and scrolled again.

More about shootings and burglaries. But then there was a post that had her stopping, clicking.

*How to Use a Restaurant to Launder Money.*

"Oh."

She turned the screen so he could see it, and he nodded. "That was my guess."

"How did you know?"

"You've obviously never watched *Ozark.*"

"That's a TV show, right?"

He smiled. "I heard it was good, so I tried it. But I don't like shows where I'm supposed to root for bad guys."

A good moral position. What if the bad guys were your parents, though?

She tapped on the article. It was a tongue-in-cheek how-to on money laundering through restaurants.

"What does it say?"

She perused the article quickly. "Looks like any cash business can work. They take the dirty money—"

"Like, money from drug sales or whatever, I guess."

"Yeah, I guess," she said. "Money a criminal can't just put in his bank account without raising flags."

"Okay, go on."

"They take dirty money and filter it through the restaurant. They add it to the cash received every day, a little at a time so as not to raise alarms. They put it in the bank, then give the 'clients'" —she put air quotes around that word—"access to it. Once it's clean, the clients can do whatever they want to with it."

"The criminals."

"Right. Mobster stuff, I guess. Racketeering, extortion, protection scams."

Kade added, "Drug dealing, arms dealing—"

"Human smuggling—getting illegals across the border." And that prompted another thought. A thought that made her ill. But she had to face it, face who her parents really were. "Human trafficking."

They fell silent.

"Bad stuff," he said.

"Bad people." She closed her eyes, tried to imagine her parents doing business with people like that.

Despite her mother's cigarette-damaged voice and trashy language, she cleaned up well. She was a strikingly beautiful woman with dark hair and pretty light brown eyes, tall and slender. She knew how to apply makeup to make herself look classy. She was pleasant and likable—to people besides her own family members.

Ginny's dad had grown more distinguished with age. He'd looked sharp in the suits he wore nearly every day and had more than his share of Southern charm.

Both of them had lost the drawl in their accents and developed lovely high-society Southern speech patterns that endeared them to others.

They'd been so good at wearing their masks, even Ginny had believed them.

She wished she couldn't picture her parents with criminals and crime bosses, but she could. She could see it, and she didn't doubt what she'd discovered for a moment.

"My parents helped the worst kinds of people get away with their crimes. They profited from it." The thought made her sick. "I profited from it. It sent me to college. It paid for my housing, my food." She swallowed, swallowed again. Nausea churned in her belly. She covered her face with her hands, too ashamed to look at Kade. "I didn't know. I swear—"

"I know."

Tears filled her eyes, slipped through her fingers as she hid her face. She didn't wipe them, couldn't bring herself to even search for a tissue. She wanted to curl into a ball and hide.

What kind of people had her parents been?

What kind of person was she?

"Hey, hey." His voice was tender, gentle. He rested his hand on her head, stroked her hair. "It's okay. We'll figure this out."

How could he even look at her? She was so embarrassed, so ashamed of her family, her roots. Her own stupidity for turning a blind eye all those years.

Kathryn had known. Why hadn't she told her? And how had Ginny missed it?

"This is not your fault, Ginny. Your parents did this. Your parents were criminals, and the money they made was dirty. But that's not your fault. You didn't know. You weren't complicit. You were a child."

She had been. But now she was an adult. An adult who'd always been so cheerful, so trusting. So stupid.

"This does not define you," Kade said. "Your parents don't define you. Your sister doesn't define you. Only God gets to define you. And He says you're precious and priceless and worthy."

How could that be?

"Look at me." His voice was still tender, but she could hear the imperative in it.

She didn't want to. But she couldn't hide forever. She wouldn't. Because Kade was right. She was not her parents.

She pulled in a deep breath, blew it out. She pulled a tissue from her purse and wiped her tears. Then, finally, she looked at Kade.

His gaze was warm and tender. "That's better."

"I'm sorry. It's just..."

"It's a lot of information to take in after a weekend of taking in troubling information. At least now we know what we're dealing with."

"Not really." She wiped the last—*please let them be the last*—of her tears. "We know we're dealing with criminals, but nothing else. I want to know who they are."

"I want to know what they want," Kade said.

The problem was, she knew what they wanted. She'd told Kade everything else. She should tell him this, too. There was no reason for her to keep secrets from Kade. He was trustworthy.

She took a deep breath, opened her mouth to speak.

The phone rang through the car's speakers. Kade glanced at his phone, which he'd left in the center console, then straightened. "It's Sokolov."

# CHAPTER EIGHT

It seemed like Kade's whole life was riding on this phone call.

The phone rang again.

Now was a terrible time to talk business, but Ginny's eyes were wide, eager. "Answer it, for heaven's sake."

"I feel like—"

"Answer before he disconnects."

"We'll continue this—"

The phone rang again. Man, that was loud.

She waved her hands toward the screen on his dash that read *incoming call.*

She was serious.

He pressed the button. "Kade Powers"

"I'm glad I caught you," Sokolov said. "I have good news."

His heart thumped in his chest. "Okay."

"I met with my friends this morning. They liked your proposal, and they want to invest."

He worked to keep his voice steady. "That's great. Do you know how much—?"

"We are willing to complete the funding. I will fax the Letter of Intent to you right away. Tell me your fax number."

He gave the fax number of the office store he used in town, and Sokolov said, "Excellent. I'll send it."

Just like that.

Kade glanced at Ginny, who wore a wide smile. She clapped her hands together silently and mouthed, *Yay!*

He couldn't believe it. All that worrying, and God had come through.

"The only thing is," Sokolov said, "one of the investors owns a construction company. He'd like the project."

Ginny's smile faded.

Kade focused on the screen. Ginny was too distracting, and he needed to concentrate. "I have a company I've worked with for years," Kade said. "They're hard-working and trustworthy. And local."

"His business does work in New Hampshire, and he'll hire some locals for the job. Perhaps you've heard of them. They are New England Builds, but most people just know them as NEB."

"I've heard of them," Kade said.

"So you know they're reputable."

"I don't know that. I don't know much about them at all. Look, I appreciate the thought, but I'd feel more comfortable with my own guys."

"Do you have an agreement with them? A contract?"

"No. Not yet, but—"

"NEB can start breaking ground as soon as you're ready. They're fast, efficient..." His voice shifted from businesslike to friendly. "Really, Kade, there's nothing to worry about. They know what they're doing. My friend isn't insisting because he needs the work. He likes to know who he's working with. All of us prefer contracting with NEB. We trust them. If you have other investors you'll lose if you change construction companies—"

"No, I don't. It's just... they're friends."

"This is business. You must learn to separate business from friendship or you will never succeed."

Kade wasn't sure about that. What was wrong with working with friends? "And if I decide I'd rather work with my guys?"

After a long pause, Sokolov said, "Then we'll have to pass, I'm afraid."

Kade blew out a breath. "Can I think about it and get back to you later today?"

"Today, tomorrow, next week. There's no hurry at all."

No hurry for them. "Thanks. I'll call you back." He ended the call and looked at Ginny.

"What do you think?" she asked.

"It's a fair request. They're going to give me, a total stranger, money to build something. They want someone they trust overseeing the project. I get it."

"But?"

"But I like the company I use. They've always played fair with me. These guys... I know nothing about them."

She glanced at the clock. "How much do you think we can learn by the end of the day?"

He loved her attitude. He shifted into drive and made a U-turn. "Let's find out."

She nodded, but her focus was on her phone.

Of course it was. His problems weren't hers. She had enough problems of her own. "So, your parents—"

"Uh-uh. We're done talking about them." She didn't glance away from her phone. "Okay, I found NEB's website. I'm searching for..."

The whoosh-whoosh of the windshield wipers kept him company until Ginny decided to finish her sentence.

"I'm searching for contact information for developers who've used or are currently using NEB."

"That's a good—"

"Shh. I'm focusing."

Alrighty then. He'd just drive.

She pulled a notepad from her purse. "Sometimes it's easier to just write things down."

She went back and forth between her phone and her notepad. Finally, she looked at him. "It's a good start. I've found about twenty people we can call. We'll probably only reach half of them, but ten endorsements—"

"I'd take that."

"We should cut the list in half and each make some calls."

"You don't have to do that." Kade couldn't imagine a worse way to entertain a woman. "Seriously, I can manage."

"Are you kidding? Something to think about besides my problems? I'm all in." She peeked at the backseat where he'd rested his laptop case. "You don't happen to have the binder in there, do you?"

"It goes with me wherever I go. If it were a blanket, I'd be Linus."

She grinned. "Good. There are some questions in there to ask contractors. We can use them as a starting point, a conversation starter with these developers."

He glanced and caught her pleased smile. "Wow. You think of everything. That's a great idea."

How did somebody go from crying about her parents' misdeeds to business mode in the space of fifteen minutes?

The tears hadn't been false, and neither was the smile she wore right now. It was as if she couldn't help it. Her cheerful disposition wouldn't be contained.

Considering everything she'd gone through, her optimistic spirit was a gift from God. He didn't think she realized that, but he sure hoped she would someday.

They were reaching the outskirts of town. "Where shall we go?"

"Dunkin' Donuts?"

"Great idea." He turned toward it, and five minutes later, they pulled in.

After they'd ordered coffee and found a booth in the corner, she handed him a sheet of paper with business names, contact names, and phone numbers.

He pulled out the binder, found the questions she was talking about, and read through them. They covered everything from a company's hiring standards to how they handled cleanup after a project. "This was a great idea."

She beamed. "What's most important to you?"

"I'm all about integrity. The bottom line matters, but I care most about making sure we're following the law and providing a safe work environment."

"Excellent." She circled three questions. "So we focus on these."

He was beaming right back at her. Weren't they a pair? He grabbed his list and stood. "I'm going to go over there so we don't bother each other." And so he wouldn't be distracted by her beautiful face when he needed to concentrate. Fortunately, the restaurant was nearly empty.

As she started dialing, he walked away and did the same.

Not quite an hour later, he shoved his phone in his pocket and slid into the booth across from Ginny. She was on the phone, but she smiled at him quickly before she made a few notes.

"Thank you for being so candid," she said. "So, in all, you'd say—"

There was a pause, and then, "Excellent. We really appreciate your help." She laughed, said, "Ain't that the truth. Okay, you have a good day."

Finally, she set the phone on the table. "Phew."

"I reached everyone I could," Kade said, "so if you still have names—"

"Nope. I'm done. Just..." She made another notation on her notepad. "What'd you learn?"

"Nothing bad," Kade said. "No red flags. All the developers seemed very happy with NEB's work, said they were professional and trustworthy."

"I got the same impression." She turned her notepad so he could see it.

Her handwriting was horrendous. He inched closer to the page and squinted. "Does that say...?" He worked to decipher the last line. "Anthill... under the bed?"

She giggled, snatched the notepad back, and read the line. "It very clearly says 'on time, under budget.'"

He turned the paper back to face him and tapped his finger on the words. "But what's that between *under* and *budget*? And are you sure that's an O? It looks like an A to me. And what happened to the...?" There were multiple missing letters. "Sheesh, can you read this?"

"When I make paper notes, I have to type them while they're still fresh."

"So... no?"

She glared. "Listen, buster."

His chuckle bubbled over. "I haven't been listen-bustered in a long time."

She lifted her cup and regarded him over the lid. "Then you were past due."

He couldn't think of a good comeback because her eyes, her smile, stymied him. "I can't tell you how much I appreciate all you did this afternoon."

She lifted her shoulders in a no-big-deal shrug. "I told you last week I wanted to help. I'm just glad you let me."

"Let you?" He scoffed. "I couldn't have done it without you. So..." He glanced at her notepad and his. "What do you think?"

"I'm not about to give you advice. This is a huge project, and you have to decide what's best. I can tell you that I didn't hear anything that gave me pause."

He sipped from his coffee, half listening, half just enjoying watching her talk as she shared what she'd discovered. Seemed similar to what he'd learned. The company did the jobs professionally, kept their promises, and treated their employees well.

"I'll be happy to type what I found out so you can see it. Or I can just read it to you, since you clearly have a reading disorder."

He nearly spit out his coffee. "I can read letters. I never mastered chicken scratch."

Her blush did things to his body he wouldn't discuss in polite company.

She flipped through her notebook. "Yeah. I don't see anything worrisome. One guy said they had a conflict but it was resolved easily. Misunderstanding." When she reached the last page of her notes, she set the notebook down. "How about you?"

"Everyone seems happy with them."

Kade was accustomed to the construction company he'd been

working with. He hadn't built many things, just a few office build-ings, a restaurant, and a strip mall between town and the highway. The company he'd used had managed each project well, and Kade had made friends with the owner. But Sokolov was right. This was business, not friendship. There was no reason not to use NEB.

Ginny was watching him while she sipped her coffee, both hands on the mug. Her blue eyes regarded him, eyebrows raised.

"I'm going to do it," he said. "I can't see any reason not to."

She smiled, though it was not as wide and cheerful as usual. "You're sure?"

"Are you not?"

She shrugged. "I don't know. You did your due diligence. They know your budget. The company is obviously legitimate."

"But?"

She looked out the window at the dreary day and took her bottom lip between her teeth.

Which sent his mind reeling far, far from real estate devel-opments.

She spoke, and he forced himself to focus on her words, not her lips. "I'm feeling very cautious because of"—she waved toward nothing in particular—"you know. Everything. I suspect my reser-vations have nothing to do with truth and everything to do with my own issues."

That made sense, but… "Are you sure there's nothing else?"

"That guy Sokolov rubbed me the wrong way the other night. But considering the day I'd had and the fact that he bumped into me—"

"He wasn't exactly graceful."

"But he was gentlemanly about it," she said. "And he could have stolen my phone if he'd wanted to. I wasn't even paying atten-tion when he found it."

"Me, either. So there's that." But she didn't look convinced, and her smile was far from the cheerful, honest one she'd given him earlier. This felt polite, maybe forced. "It's just me, Kade. Don't let my unfounded worries stop you."

He considered all she'd said. Her worries did seem unfounded.

The truth was, without the money Sokolov offered, Kade's project was dead for another year.

"Honestly," he said, "meeting Sokolov felt like a gift from God. I think I'd be a fool not to accept his offer."

Her smile widened to the one he was coming to love. "Then what are you waiting for? Call him."

~

AFTER HE CALLED SOKOLOV, they tossed the remains of their coffee and headed to the office store in town. Kade left Ginny in the car and ran in to collect the fax and the things he'd sent for printing earlier that day. He made one last vital phone call while he waited in line.

When he climbed back in the car, he settled the poster-sized artists' rendering and the bag filled with proposals in the backseat and faced her. "Just got off the phone with Collier's secretary. I'm on the agenda for tomorrow's meeting."

She beamed at him. "It's all coming together for you."

"This calls for a celebration."

"What did you have in mind?"

"Dinner?"

Her smile faded. "You must be busy. Don't feel like you owe me anything for my help. You can just take me home."

Was that what she wanted? To go home? Based on her initial reaction, he didn't think so. "Wow, woman. You sure know how to make a guy feel wanted."

"I don't mean it like that. Just... you've wasted enough time with me for one day."

He leaned away and faced her. "Wasted time? Is that what this was?"

"Oh." All joy leached from her face. "I just mean, not for me. This was great. But you must have better—"

"Why do you do that? Why do you always assume you're in the way? Unwanted?"

She turned toward the window.

Because she'd been treated that way by the people who were supposed to love her most in the world. He brushed her hair back so he could see her profile. "Just so there's no misunderstanding," he said, "I came for you today because I'd thought about calling you all morning, but I didn't want to seem too eager."

She turned her head just enough that he could see her eyes, but she didn't look at him.

"I spent the afternoon with you because I like you. I like spending time with you."

"But all my baggage—"

"Doesn't change that."

She nodded almost imperceptibly.

"And I invited you to dinner because I can't bear to part with you yet. I want to celebrate my victory, and there's no one I'd rather celebrate with than you." She was still looking beyond him, so he shifted to catch her eyes. "Your family were idiots if they didn't realize how special you are."

If he wasn't mistaken, he thought he saw the beginnings of tears before she blinked them back.

"I, however, am highly intelligent, despite my reading disorder."

She smiled at that.

"And I know quality when I see her. Okay?"

"Okay."

"Good. I know the perfect place to escape this dreary day."

Twenty minutes later, he dropped Ginny beneath the portico of a restaurant and parked. Then, he snatched his laptop case and the bag he'd gotten from the copy store and jogged through the rain to the door. This was his favorite steakhouse in the world. The food was delicious, the service excellent, but it was the ambience that made it perfect.

The hostess said, "Two for dinner?"

Kade rested his hand on Ginny's back. "Near the fireplace, please."

Ginny's eyes lit. He'd thought she'd like it here.

They were seated at a table for two about ten feet from the

flickering flames. The floor-to-cathedral-ceiling stacked stone fire-place was the centerpiece of the dining room. The scent of the wood fire filled the space. Exposed beams overhead and knotty pine siding gave the room the feeling of a rustic lodge. It wasn't crowded tonight, probably owing to the pouring rain and it being Monday. All the better for him, because it meant they had good seats, and he wouldn't have to share Ginny with anybody.

She looked around. "How have I never been here?"

"You like it?"

"It's absolutely wonderful. I love it."

"Me, too." He tried to hide the swell of pride. "I helped build it."

Her attention snapped to him. "You did this?"

"The owner's a friend."

"Wow." She took in the space, her gaze resting on the fireplace. "That's magnificent."

"Thanks. My friend's idea. I just made it happen."

She turned to him again. "I'm impressed."

He shrugged that off. "Anyway, order anything you like. Dinner's on me."

After they ordered their drinks—iced tea for her, Coke for him—he reached for his laptop bag. "I hope you don't mind, but I wanted you to see the proposals."

She leaned forward. "I'd love to."

He dug in the sack and handed her one of the full-color bound packets he'd had printed, then watched as she looked.

The cover had a scaled-down version of the artist's rendering of his development. She murmured, "It's beautiful. Now that I've seen the property, I can really picture it."

She opened to the first page, then flipped through the proposal one page at a time, uttering little "mms" and "oohs" as she went. Finally, she flipped the cover closed. "This is perfect."

He blew out a long breath. "Thank you for saying that."

"I can't think of a thing I would have added." She glanced at the cover, ran her fingers over the picture. "I can't wait to see it in real life."

"You and me both." He took the proposal and slid it back in the bag and into his laptop case. "Enough about my stuff. Tell me about your real estate business. How is that going?"

She filled him in on her business, making him laugh with her stories about strange things clients had done. The food was delicious, the fireplace warm and cozy, and the company perfect. They talked about her business, his business, and he couldn't remember what else. But they never ran out of things to say. And he never tired of looking at her.

When dinner was over and they were the last customers in the restaurant, he knew it was time to go, little though he wanted to.

He stood and held out his hand. Her fingertips were cold, so he led her to stand in front of the fireplace. She warmed them while they gazed at the flames. "Why don't you wait here, and I'll get the car and crank the heat?"

"Don't be silly. The rain won't hurt me."

He was about to argue, but when she looked at him, her blue eyes wide, her pink lips so close...

He'd been thinking of kissing her all day. But the car, with the console—so awkward.

And in Dunkin' Donuts after talking to contractors all afternoon? That seemed about as romantic as a bologna sandwich.

But here... The place was empty. It was just Kade and Ginny and a crackling fire, and he couldn't wait another moment.

He slid his hands on either side of her face, his fingertips just reaching the soft strands of her hair. He bent down slowly, waiting for a sign she wanted him to stop.

She didn't flinch or move or maybe breathe. He didn't either as he closed the distance and touched his lips to hers.

They were soft and tender. She tasted of the chocolate dessert they'd shared. Delicious and perfect.

Her hands rested on his hips, then slid around his back, and he deepened the kiss while his body reacted, ached for more.

When he nearly exploded with desire, he forced himself to stop. Mustering his self-control, he leaned away.

She rested her face against his chest, and he pulled her into an embrace and kissed the top of her head.

He hoped she was feeling some semblance of what he was, because that was mind-blowing.

And he was falling for this happy, free-spirited woman.

This woman whose life was in danger.

# CHAPTER NINE

Though Ginny told Kade she could handle a little rain, he insisted he get the car and meet her outside. When he parked beneath the portico, she rushed outside.

By the time she reached the car, Kade was holding her door open for her. She started to thank him, but on the way to his eyes, she got sidetracked by his lips.

She'd never experienced a kiss like that. Soft and tender, warm and insistent. She'd never responded to a kiss like that, either. She'd read about those kind of kisses in romance novels, kisses that made your toes curl. Kisses that make all rational thought flee. She'd always thought those kisses the stuff of fairytales.

She'd been wrong.

Kade's lips had been perfect.

Right now, they smiled, and her eyes lifted to see the heat in his eyes.

She had to breathe. To think.

To get in the car. Right. She slid into the seat.

A moment later, he joined her and drove away. By the time they were on the highway, he'd pulled her hand into his.

The ride was quiet but not uncomfortable. She couldn't stop thinking about that kiss, and about the things he'd said earlier tonight. That he wanted to be with her. That he hadn't been able to stop thinking about her.

Thank heavens it was dark and he couldn't see her silly smile.

Did he have a similar one on his face? When she glanced at him, his eyebrows were lowered, his mouth closed tight.

"Hey, what's wrong?"

He squeezed her hand. "Nothing."

Well, that wasn't true. She shifted so she could see him better. "Please tell me the truth. I don't appreciate being brushed off."

He glanced her way. "I was thinking about our earlier conversation."

"Which one? We've had a lot today."

"About your parents."

Her too-full stomach twisted. "Let's not talk about that tonight."

"Okay."

But she could tell he was thinking about it. "Let's focus on your meeting tomorrow. Assuming the project gets approved, what's the next step?"

"We'll break ground as soon as possible."

"Within a week? A month?"

"I've got everything in place. We just need the town on board and the funding to come in, and we can begin as soon as NEB is available."

"That's so exciting."

"Yup."

He didn't seem excited at all. Or particularly happy. Did he regret kissing her? It hadn't seemed exactly spur-of-the-moment. In fact, he'd taken his time with it. Given her time to stop him. As if that would ever happen. She'd looked forward to that kiss for days. And it had well exceeded her expectations. Why would he regret something he'd done so thoughtfully? Something that had been so good?

Maybe it was the project. "Are you nervous?"

He blew out a long breath. "I'm not nervous about my project. It's going to be fine. The events of the weekend, your sister, the intruder, what you learned today... That's what I'm thinking about."

"Why? It's fine. I'm fine. Why ruin a perfectly wonderful evening with that?"

He pulled onto her street and parked in her driveway. Then, he turned to face her. "How do you do that? How do you just push it out of your head?"

Her house was dark. She hadn't left a light on or closed the blinds, and the windows were gaping and black. Her heart thumped with fear, and she turned back to Kade. What had he asked her?

Right. How did she push away unpleasant things? "If I don't want to think about something, I just don't. I focus my mind elsewhere. If there's something out of my control, I ignore it."

"Seriously? Just like that? What a gift."

"Sometimes. The problem is, some things aren't out of my control. When I was a kid, I could have made more of an effort to know what my parents were doing. Not that I could have fixed it, but I could have been informed, prepared. But it was unpleasant, so I ignored it. I pretended everything was fine and lived in my own little fantasyland."

He took her hand again. "It's like a defense mechanism."

"Maybe. And when I have a problem"—the dark house loomed over them—"and I don't know how to fix it, I put it out of my head."

"How does that help?"

"It doesn't. Which is how I land in situations like this. By pretending they aren't real." Like the duffel bag her mother had given her. She'd put it out of her mind, figuring she'd give it back to her mother when she saw her again. But now... Could she do that, knowing what she'd learned?

Should she turn the money over to the police?

She had no idea.

"What are you thinking about?"

Ginny shook her head. "Nothing. Did you ask me a question?"

"How do you do that, pretend things aren't happening?"

She put the duffel bag out of her head.

It was just that simple.

"I trust the world will make everything right because... I don't know. I guess because I'm a decent person, so things should work out decently for me."

Kade's eyes narrowed. "Do you think that's how it works?"

"I don't know how it works, whatever *it* is. I know what you believe. I'm not against what you believe. It's just..." She glanced at the clock. How was it nearly eleven? And how did they get into this conversation? "You have a meeting tomorrow. I should go."

For the first time since they'd left the restaurant, he smiled. "You do that to me, make me forget everything else." He opened his door.

"You don't have to come in with me." She swallowed and kept her gaze away from the dark house. "I can manage."

As if she hadn't spoken, he walked around to open her door. The rain had stopped, though moisture lay heavy in the air. At the house, he took her keys and turned the lock, then stepped inside. The alarm beeped the warning that it was about to go off, but Kade was in no rush. After a moment, he moved out of the way so she could follow him in and make the beeping stop. She flipped on the foyer light and turned to him. "Thank you for..."

He closed the front door. "I'm going to take a quick look around, if that's okay."

"Why?" Fear bubbled in her middle as she remembered the last time she and Kade had come in together. "Did you see something?"

"Nope. But unlike you, I can't just put unpleasant things out of my mind. So if I want to sleep tonight, I need to know you're safe. Stay put."

Before she could raise a protest, he moved away from her. He searched the downstairs, flipping on lights as he went. He opened all the doors and looked behind the sofa. A moment later, he bounded up the stairs. She heard doors opening and closing, and then he came back down.

"I really appreciate you doing that."

He smiled and walked past her to the door that led to the basement, opened it, and went down.

A moment later, he returned with a smile. "Nothing but dust bunnies."

"You didn't check the attic."

His eyebrows lowered in that concerned look she'd come to know. "I didn't think of that. Where's the access?"

"I was kidding." She put as much amusement as she could into her voice. "The access is in the second-floor hallway, but there's no way to climb them and pull the steps up behind you. It's designed that way to keep people from getting trapped."

His eyebrows hadn't budged.

"Seriously, I was kidding."

"If you're sure."

Man, he was cute when he was worried. And when he wasn't. "I'm sure. And I appreciate you doing that. As confident as I tried to sound, I was scared to come into the dark house by myself."

"Good."

She stepped back. "Wow, thanks."

"You should be scared, Ginny. After everything you told me today—"

"Let's not. We both need to sleep."

"I'm just saying, you need to stay on your toes." He stepped closer and took her hands. "I need you to protect yourself."

"I will. I promise."

"Have you been keeping your gun nearby, practicing holding it?"

She didn't want to lie, but she didn't think he'd appreciate the truth. She shook her head.

"Tomorrow, hold it over and over until it feels natural. When the weather clears, we can go shooting again."

"You don't have to—" His eyebrows lifted, and she cut herself off. "Okay."

"Thank you." He stepped closer, and for a moment she thought—hoped—he'd kiss her again. But he just gave her a quick peck on her forehead. "Get a good night's sleep."

~

Ginny was dropping her whole wheat toast into the toaster the next morning when her phone dinged with a text.

It was from Kade. *Are you awake?*

She typed, *Fixing my avocado toast.*

She was watching for the blinking dots to tell her he was responding when her phone rang in her hands.

She answered, not caring if he thought she was overeager. "Good morning."

"Did you sleep?" His voice was deep and soothing. It somehow calmed her and energized her at the same time.

She flipped her frying egg. "I had good dreams."

He chuckled. "I had some memorable dreams myself."

She felt that silly smile again and thanked the heavens he couldn't see her warming cheeks.

"What in the world is avocado toast?" he asked.

She explained her favorite breakfast concoction.

"No offense," he said, "but that sounds really gross."

"I'll make it for you sometime. It's delicious." She mashed half an avocado. "Are you ready for the meeting?"

"About that," he said. "I wanted to ask a favor. After our talk yesterday and all your help, I feel like you know as much about the project as I do."

"Not even close."

"Enough to be helpful, though."

Her toast popped, and she spread the mashed avocado on top of it, then slid the egg over it. "I'm happy to help. What do you need?"

"I was thinking, since you know the project, and since you have so much experience with real estate developments, maybe..." He paused, cleared his throat. "Will you come to the meeting with me? You can act as, I don't know—"

"An assistant?" She carried her plate to the table.

"I don't know if that's the right word, but—"

"You're asking me to assist you, so assistant feels appropriate."

"But not like you work for me or anything. I don't want you to think I see you like that."

"I'm not offended, Kade." She sprinkled her breakfast with salt and pepper. "I'm flattered you think I can add anything. What time is the meeting?"

He blew out a long exhale as if he'd been nervous to ask. "Two."

"Hold on a sec. Let me check my schedule." She put him on speaker, then navigated to the calendar app. "I have a closing at ten but nothing this afternoon. Assuming the closing doesn't get moved, I can be there. Is there anything you want me to do beforehand?"

"Could you meet me at one-thirty just to talk it through with me? I want to make sure I'm not missing anything."

"I'll be happy to meet you. The proposal was perfect, though. I'm sure you have it well in hand."

"Still..."

She found the concern in his voice honest and endearing. "You have a lot riding on this."

"I have to get it right."

She tapped the calendar to add an appointment. "Where shall we meet?"

"McNeal's?"

"Perfect. See you there."

A phone call that afternoon from a client kept her at the office longer than she'd planned. When she finally got off the phone, she walked in the waning mist to McNeal's. She was five minutes late, and Kade was already seated in a far booth focused on the paperwork spread in front of him. He stood when she approached and kissed her cheek. "Thank you for doing this."

She sat and looked at what he was studying. It was the binder she'd given him. Yellow sticky notes were poking out all along the sides.

"I'm worried I don't have enough information," he said. "What if they ask me about this stuff?" He pointed to a blank spreadsheet with columns labeled for every tiny detail of a project.

"Maybe giving you that binder was a mistake."

He ran his fingers through his hair. "I don't have all this information yet. I don't know how I could."

"You'll fill this out as the project goes along. It'll help you track costs. More than that, it'll help you with your next project to know exactly where your money went." Gently, she closed the binder. "You've got this, Kade. I have no doubt."

The little wrinkle between his eyebrows showed he was unconvinced. He sipped his drink. A glass of iced tea sat in front of her. "I hope you're right."

"You've done this before, right?" She slid the tea closer and added sweetener. "You've gone before the planning committee?"

"A few times. And they always approved me until January when I went with this project. It was one thing to get turned down mid-winter. It wasn't as if I would have broken ground then. But if they don't approve it today, it'll be late summer before I can try again, which means we either build in the winter or wait until next year."

She sipped the tea. "You don't want to build in the winter?"

"There are so many days when the guys can't work because everything's buried under snow or ice. It takes longer and costs more."

A good point. But something she'd heard in church—his church—on Sunday prickled in her memory. "Isn't this exactly what the pastor was talking about? You make your plans and do your part, and you trust Him with the results? Because God's got a plan, right? I'm sure I'm butchering it, but wasn't that the point?"

His eyebrows lifted, erasing the concern on his face. "You were listening."

"Of course."

He nodded. "You're right. I've prayed about it for months. I've done everything I can to prepare, and I even asked for help along the way—something I'm not very good at, to tell you the truth. I've done my part. The rest is up to God."

She nodded, though she wasn't so sure about the God part. Did

He really care that much about a little real estate project in New Hampshire? Didn't God have better things to worry about?

Kade took her hands. "Thank you. We haven't even gone to the meeting yet, and you've already helped me."

She looked down to hide the smile she knew was beaming on her face.

He squeezed her hands and let go. "If you can just take this"—he opened the binder to one of the sticky-noted pages and turned it toward her—"and keep this section open. Most of the details I think they'll ask about are here. If I can't pull an answer from my head or find a number quickly, can you supply it?"

"Absolutely."

"And if I look lost or if I need help—"

"I'll jump in. But I don't think that's going to happen."

He stood and dropped a five dollar bill on the table. "We'll see."

# CHAPTER TEN

I t was ridiculous how nervous Kade was.

Ginny was right. He'd done this before multiple times. The last time, they'd told him to come back when the project was fully funded, and now it was. He shouldn't have anything to be nervous about.

But as he stepped into the meeting room in the musty old town office building, sweat broke out on the back of his neck.

He and Ginny scooted into chairs near the front of the room. He sat on the end of the row, the poster-sized picture of the development propped against the side of his chair.

The council members were seated at long tables facing the audience. Bruce sat in the center. If Kade wasn't mistaken, his chair was higher than the others. He wouldn't put it past the man to find a way to make himself look bigger than he was.

His term didn't end for another year, and it couldn't come soon enough. He'd been town manager for a long time, and throughout the years, his plan had been to keep Nutfield from entering the twenty-first century. Even this meeting attested to that. In most growing communities, the planning committee met twice a month. But Bruce refused to budge on the once-per-quarter schedule that had been enacted by their forefathers, probably right after they'd signed the Declaration of Independence. Never mind that the meetings had gotten so long that they'd had to move them back from seven p.m. to two in the afternoon in order to cover all the business.

As expected, every seat was filled, and people stood in the back and out the door.

Ginny looked around at the crowd. "Wow. I didn't know these were such events."

"Nobody wants to be here." He cut his gaze to Bruce, puffed up like a sovereign over his kingdom. "Except him. He loves this."

She looked. "That's Bruce Collier?"

"One and the same. Enemy of progress."

"Maybe he just fears change."

"If that's the case, then he has no business being the town manager."

She perused the crowd. "So, are all these people going to bring new business?"

"I should have warned you. It'll be a very long meeting. I hope you can get some work done."

She pulled her phone from her purse and waggled it in front of him. "Don't you worry about me. I'll keep busy."

He sat back and settled in for a long wait.

More than three hours later, most of the folks who'd brought business to the meeting had spoken, had their projects voted on, and left. The room was nearly empty by the time Kade's name was called.

He and Ginny stood and stepped up to a small table in front of the council members. There were two chairs there. He pulled out one for Ginny, and she sat and opened the binder.

He lifted his notes and the proposals from the bag and set them on the small table. Then he positioned the poster board on the easel.

He handed the proposals out, greeting every member by name. That wasn't hard. He knew them all, and he liked most of them.

When he reached Bruce, he said, "Afternoon, sir."

Bruce scowled at him.

Kade moved on, finally reaching the person seated in the last chair. "Afternoon, Mrs. Boucher."

The older gray-haired woman smiled at him. "Oh, for heaven's sake, Kade, you're a grown man. Call me Constance."

He winked. "Yes, ma'am." He and Mrs. Boucher's son had been friends in school. No matter how many times she told him to call her by her first name, he just couldn't do it.

Finally, he stood by the table, snatched his notes, and addressed the council.

"First, let me introduce you to Ginny Lamont. Ginny is a real estate agent here in town. She has experience with large-scale real estate developments, and she offered to assist me on this project."

Most of the council members nodded at her. Bruce, of course, scowled. Ginny was a newcomer, and thus, not to be trusted.

Ginny seemed confident and cheerful, as always. She nodded to him, and he turned to the council and continued.

"I came before this body in January with the same proposal I bring to you today." He walked to the easel to stand beside the picture. "As you know, I own the parcel of land on the south side of the lake. If you'll open to page two, you'll see the boundaries of my land."

Except for Bruce, all the members flipped to the proper page.

Bruce said, "A gift from your father, if I'm not mistaken."

Kade nodded twice. "A very generous gift, yes."

"And what does he think about your little"—he waved toward the easel—"hobby."

Kade hoped the anger that boiled in his middle wasn't showing on his face. "My father fully supports my career."

"I guess he doesn't care, now that he lives in Florida."

"Bruce." Mrs. Boucher turned to face the town manager. "Let the man talk."

Bruce harrumphed.

Kade continued. "I intend to develop the property into a country club complete with a golf course, swimming pools, tennis courts, and an upscale meeting room. Though it will be a private club, the membership dues will be reasonable, affording Nutfield residents and those in the surrounding towns the ability to join if they choose to. Everyone will be welcome on the golf course. There will be homes on the property, some abutting the lake, others overlooking the fairways and greens. If you'll take a look at page three, you'll see the number and variety of houses—"

"Expensive houses," Bruce said. "They'll just draw a bunch more people from Massachusetts with more dollars than sense. Why would we want those kinds of people here?"

Kade smiled. "I'm glad you asked. If you'll turn to page four..." He flipped through his notes. Where was that list?

Ginny cleared her throat. When he looked, she was holding out what he needed. She winked as he took it.

He went through the benefits to the town he and Ginny had compiled. Most of the council members were nodding, some even smiling, as he spoke.

"Go ahead and turn to page seven, and let's talk details." He took them through his plans, the costs he anticipated, the phases he planned, and the timeline for each.

Bruce's scowl turned smug as he closed his proposal. "Mr. Powers, this is all interesting, but, if I remember correctly, we told you not to come back until you were fully funded. Are you?"

"I am."

Bruce's eyes narrowed. "So your father decided to 'invest.'"

Again, Kade's anger simmered at the way he'd said the last word, as if this were anything but an investment.

"As a matter of fact, no. If you'll turn to page fourteen..." He waited as they did so, then took them through the list of investors.

Bruce studied the page as if there'd be an exam. His finger jabbed at it. "Who is this Sokolov Investment Group?"

"They're a group of financiers from Boston."

"We don't know these people." He focused his attention on his fellow council members. "Do we really want to let total strangers come into our town and buy property?"

"To be clear," Kade said, "the property belongs to me. They're buying shares, but I will own the majority share and will be making all the decisions."

Bruce harrumphed again. "I don't think we should trust people we've never met."

A niggle of anxiety rose in Kade's stomach. That's exactly what he was doing, trusting a whole group of people, only one of whom he'd met, and only for an hour.

A man whom Ginny had told him made her nervous.

But Sokolov and his friends wouldn't have any say in his project. Kade would have all the control.

He opened his mouth to argue, but Mrs. Boucher jumped in. "We're not being asked to trust strangers, Bruce." She focused on the other men and women on the board. "We're being asked to trust Kade Powers. His family has roots in this town that go back as far as any of ours. Every project he's ever brought to us has succeeded." She faced Kade again. "I don't see any problem with it."

Kade endured a long question-and-answer session and managed to answer every question without needing Ginny's assistance once—though her presence alone helped him keep his cool as Bruce's questions kept coming and coming. Finally, the council brought it to a vote.

The project passed by a vote of eight to one.

Kade gathered his things, eager to get out of the building so he could show his excitement. Before they could leave, though, Bruce called, "Kade, if you'd just wait. I need to speak to you."

He nodded to the man, feeling like he'd just been called out for being naughty in class. Everything in him wanted to tell Bruce what he really thought of that idea. But he'd been raised to respect his elders whether they deserved it or not. "We'll be out here, then."

Kade and Ginny stopped in the musty hallway.

Her smile was bright as the sunshine trying to peek through the clouds outside. "You did it."

"We did it."

"I did nothing but hand you a piece of paper."

He stepped closer, too elated to stop himself, and settled his hands on her hips. He looked down into her beautiful eyes. "That was a pivotal piece of paper."

Her gaze flicked to his lips, and he couldn't help himself. He leaned down to claim a kiss.

He loved how warm and willing she was. The confidence she'd shown in him after he'd been so vulnerable, so worried about this meeting, was a strong aphrodisiac.

Noises and murmuring in the room just beyond the door had him remembering where he was. He stepped back. "Sorry. I don't know what came over me."

Her eyebrows lifted, and he laughed.

"Well, maybe I have a suspicion." He forced down the lingering desire. "You don't have to wait. I'm sure you have stuff to do."

She checked her watch. "Actually, I'm showing a house later, so I should go get ready for that."

As people filed out of the room, he gave her a quick kiss on the top of her head. "I'll call you later."

She took his hand and lowered her voice. "You're right, that Bruce is a piece of work, but you kept your cool. I'm proud of you."

It was an effort to keep his chest from expanding.

"Congratulations." She squeezed his hand and joined the crowd leaving the meeting.

After everyone else had gone, Bruce stepped out of the room, set his feet, and crossed his arms. "Tell me more about this investment group."

"You looking to develop some property?"

Bruce smiled just enough to show his yellowing teeth. "I don't trust people I don't know."

"Which is why you shouldn't be the town manager. Look, just because you don't know somebody doesn't mean they're bad. These guys have invested in properties all over Massachusetts. Great, successful properties."

"And why did they decide to invest in you?"

In him. Not in the project, but in him.

That was an excellent question, actually. Kade had no idea.

Because even if the project plans were excellent, that didn't mean Kade was capable of pulling it off. Sokolov and his people must have done their homework on him or they wouldn't have bothered.

Kade told Bruce what he knew about Sokolov and how they'd met.

"Seems pretty fishy to me," Bruce said.

"Fortunately, the council didn't see it that way." Kade snatched his things from the floor. "If there's nothing else—"

"Who was that woman?"

"Ginny? She's a real estate agent. I told you that."

"Where's she from."

"San Francisco."

Bruce's eyebrows rose on his age-spotted forehead. "California?"

"Is there another one?"

"What do you know about her?"

This was getting ridiculous. "I know she's lovely and kind and knows a lot about real estate. And I know it's none of your business. If there's nothing else—"

"You think I'm a washed-up old fart who hates change."

Bruce nailed it, but Kade said nothing.

"But I care about this community," Bruce said.

"So do I." Kade set his things back on the floor. "This is my home. Pretending the rest of the world isn't out there isn't going to protect it. The school needs more money, the roads need to be repaved, the police force needs new cars, and there's not enough money for any of that. What I'm proposing will increase the tax base and, thus, revenue. It'll also bring new customers to the businesses in town. It'll be good for everyone."

"Maybe. If you do what you're promising to do."

"When have I ever not finished a project?"

Bruce's eyes narrowed, and he stepped back. "Look, Kade, you're a decent kid, but this is a big project. And now you've gotten in with outsiders. Strangers even you admit you know nothing about—this Ginny person and those new investors. My job is to protect this community, and that means I need to know who's investing in it. So if you won't do your homework, then I will."

Kade lifted his things once again and turned toward the hallway that would lead him out. "Do whatever you need to do."

Kade seethed all the way outside. Sokolov's money would spend just like everyone else's. He and his friends would have zero control over the project.

Except that Sokolov could pull his funding. Which, Kade admitted, gave him plenty of leverage.

But why would Sokolov care? For him and his friends, this was a business investment.

Kade wished he were more like Ginny and could push away that niggling worry. As he reached his car, what Bruce said came back to him. Not just about Sokolov but about Ginny.

Had Kade made a mistake by bringing her with him today?

What kind of information might Bruce discover? If he found out the truth about her parentage, would it hurt Kade's project?

More importantly, would it hurt her?

KADE DROVE to Ginny's house the next morning as nervous as he'd been before the council meeting.

The more Kade thought about Bruce's words, the more like a threat they sounded. If the guy decided to look into Ginny, what would he find? And what would he do with that information?

The rain and clouds that had moved in over the weekend had blown out to sea, leaving the air crisp and cool. In the giant sugar maple in Ginny's front yard, birds twittered and squirrels jiggled the bare branches. It wouldn't be long before buds appeared around town and flowers bloomed on the apple trees in the orchards.

And he broke ground on his real estate project.

Developing the lakeside property had been his dream since he'd graduated from college, since his parents had given it to him. In one way or another, everything he'd done since then had been leading to this moment in his life. All the prior development projects had been practice for this. The money he'd made had gone into the bank to fund this. Other people went to movies and watched sports and dated. Not Kade. He'd spent his free time reading books, meeting people, and studying other developments. Because this was the project that would launch his business.

This was the project that would set him apart from his brothers and sister.

This was the project that would prove he was competent and successful. Prove he'd been worthy of the gift.

But as he parked in Ginny's driveway and walked to the door, he asked himself—at what cost?

The door swung open, and Ginny greeted him with a smile that had his heart thumping. As usual, she looked gorgeous. She wore black slacks with a blue sweater that made her eyes sparkle. "Sorry to keep you waiting. I'm almost ready." She held the door open, and he stepped inside while she headed for the kitchen. Over her shoulder, she said, "I was looking at listings for a new client, and I lost track of time."

"I'm in no hurry."

She was often just a little late. A minute, maybe two. In anybody else, that would annoy him, but with Ginny, he found it endearing.

He found everything about her endearing.

She returned with her purse and jacket.

He took the jacket and helped her into it, then pulled her hair out. The feel of the long silky strands in his hands did something wonky to his brain.

She turned to face him, so close he could feel her breath. Her cheeks were flushed as if something wonky had just happened in her brain, too.

They were supposed to go to breakfast, but he'd be happy to stay here and kiss her all morning.

Her eyebrows lifted as if she knew what he was thinking.

"Food." He practically grunted the word, not because he

wanted to eat but because they needed to talk, and he needed to talk to her before he kissed her again.

"If you say so." She engaged her alarm and then preceded him out the door to the car.

Though McNeal's served the best breakfasts in Nutfield, he drove to a little diner in the next town over that had been there as long as Kade could remember.

As they walked inside, he said, "Ever been here before?"

She gazed at the sign above the door that read *North Star Diner*. "Never even heard of it."

He pulled open the door, and they stepped into the tiny dining room and waited at the hostess stand.

The place hadn't changed in years. Laminated table tops, peel-and-stick tile on the floor, acoustic ceiling tiles. The scents of bacon and sausage and real New Hampshire maple syrup made his stomach growl. Clanking utensils and pots and pans served as the musical backdrop.

Most of the tables were filled.

A white-haired woman wearing an apron called from the door that led to the kitchen, "Sit wherever you like. I'll be right with you."

"Shall we?" With a hand on the small of her back, Kade led her to a table in the far corner and pulled out her chair. "It's not exactly fine dining."

She shrugged off her jacket and studied her menu-slash-place-mat. "I bet the food's good."

"You ever had biscuits and gravy?"

"Honey, my kin are from Louisiana." Her deadpan expression and exaggerated Southern accent made him smile. "What do you think?"

The white-haired waitress stopped at their table. "Coffee?"

They flipped over their cups, and she filled them. "You kids know what you want?"

That was the second time in two days he'd been called a kid. He was tempted to order chocolate milk and animal crackers but feared the waitress would take him seriously.

After they ordered, Kade sipped his coffee and set it down carefully.

"What is it?" Ginny said.

"What?"

But her smirk told him she wasn't buying his false nonchalance.

He folded his hands on the table. "I have to tell you something."

She folded her hands and set them on the table, too. He wasn't sure if she was teasing him or trying to take him seriously. "Clearly."

"After you left the meeting yesterday, I had a conversation with Bruce."

"Uh-huh."

"I'm sure you gathered the fact that he doesn't like strangers."

"I actually cracked that code."

"Well, he sees you as a stranger. Which I knew he would, but I wasn't worried about it. I guess I didn't understand what..."

Her eyes narrowed. "Just say it."

"He gave me the impression he intended to look into Sokolov and the other investors."

"That's not surprising. Are you worried about what he'll learn?"

Kade shook his head, swallowed. "He also said he intends to look into you."

She tilted her head to the side. "And you're worried about what he'll find?"

"Aren't you?"

She paused, bit her lip, looked past him for a minute. When she met his eyes again, she shrugged. "It's not as if my parents' being criminals is public knowledge. They've never been arrested, at least not as far as I know. They were upstanding members of the community. Dad sat on a number of boards at non-profits."

He nodded, and a weight lifted off him. "Right. If he looks for information, he'll find out they owned restaurants. Nothing wrong with that."

Now, she sat back a bit, looked away.

The coffee churned in his empty stomach as he watched emotions play across her face. "What?"

She unrolled her napkin, set the utensils carefully on the paper placemat.

Clearly, there was something she hadn't told him.

He sipped his coffee and waited.

She sipped hers, too, then set it down and met his gaze. "One of the places my parents owned was a..." She swallowed, looked away. Seemed to meet his eyes again with effort. "They owned a strip club."

He sat back. "Ah."

"So Bruce might find that." She shook her head. "I'm sorry. If I'd had any idea my parents' business could come back to hurt you—"

"I'm not concerned about me. I'm concerned about you."

Her burst of laughter was short and humorless. "Bruce Collier is the least of my worries."

"He could hurt your business. He could—"

"I have no control over what my parents did or what they owned. Were my parents criminals? Apparently. But me? I've never even gotten a traffic ticket. I have nothing to fear from that man." She leaned toward Kade again, her blue eyes gazing deep into his. "If you think this can hurt you, then maybe we need to stop..." But her words trailed off, and her cheeks turned the faintest shade of pink.

"Stop seeing each other?" he finished for her.

She sat back and swallowed. "Yeah. That."

"No." He held his hand out, palm up, on the table, and she took it. Funny how perfectly her hand fit in his.

Her life fit in his.

Okay, it was way too soon to be thinking that way. He knew that. He also knew he'd dated a lot of women, but none of them had affected him like Ginny did. None of them intruded on his thoughts all day and then had starring roles in his dreams at night. None of them understood him the way she did. She believed in him and encouraged him in his hopes for the future. She didn't think what he wanted was too much, too fast, as others had told him. She didn't begrudge him the time he spent on his project.

This thing with Ginny was brand new and fresh. But they'd already survived their share of troubles. He'd seen her cry, he'd seen her terrified, he'd seen her strong. In the short time he'd known her, he'd seen a lot of facets of her, and he'd yet to see one he didn't like. No, not just like. Respect. Admire.

This thing with Ginny was new, yes. But all lasting relationships started somewhere. New didn't have to mean temporary.

She was looking at their joined hands, watching as his thumb rubbed across her knuckles.

He gave it a little squeeze. "I'm not going to throw you over because that crusty old curmudgeon doesn't like new people. If you're not worried, then I'm not worried."

Her smile was natural and sweet. "Good. Then let's not worry together."

He could do that. He wanted nothing more than to do that.

But there was still plenty for them to worry about. Because he may have just decided to pursue this... whatever it was with Ginny. But that didn't change the situation. There were people threatening her, and somehow, Kade and Ginny had to figure out who they were and how to stop them.

# CHAPTER ELEVEN

Ginny couldn't believe all that had happened.

Six weeks had passed since the town planning meeting. Six weeks since Kathryn left. Six weeks since an intruder had broken into Ginny's house.

And nothing had happened. Nothing bad, anyway.

Ginny's home had remained secure. Kade's investors had sent the money they'd promised and then stayed out of his way. Bruce hadn't spread any rumors or confronted either of them.

She stood on the hilltop overlooking Kade's land at Clearwater Lake. The air was cool this early summer morning. The sun shone overhead, turning the surface of the lake a dark blue. A few fishing boats cut through the still waters, far enough away that she could barely hear their motors from here. The only other sounds were the rustle of the breeze in the trees, the chirping birds, and the low murmur of voices behind her.

In a moment, she would return to the gathering crowd. Right now, she was content to breathe in the beautiful day and wonder at her good fortune.

She'd given up trying to find out who the money in that duffel bag belonged to and put the whole ugly business out of her mind. She'd worked on her real estate business and helped Kade get his development going.

The best thing about the previous six weeks, the thing that had made them the most wonderful six weeks of her life, was the time she'd spent with Kade.

They'd shared at least one meal a day. They'd bounced ideas off each other for their respective businesses. They'd gone target shooting a few times a week, which she'd learned to love. They'd joked, laughed, watched movies, and eaten popcorn.

They'd kissed.

They'd done a lot of kissing.

And the shocking thing was, Kade had yet to push for more. It wasn't because he didn't want more. She could see the desire in his eyes every time he left her for the night.

Six weeks before, she'd worried she might be falling for him. Well, she was still on the descent and loving every minute of it.

She'd even taken to going to church with him. Between church and Bible study and all that Samantha and her friends had taught Ginny, she felt like she was finally beginning to grasp this whole God thing.

Maybe He wasn't just some force that had set the world in motion then stepped away. For the longest time, she'd believed God had left His power on the planet for people to learn to wield. Not for bad, of course, but she'd had these ideas about the power of thoughts, the power of belief.

Those things were true. But they were true because God was real and working and powerful.

Not only that, but she was coming to understand that no force on the planet, weak or strong, was without allegiance. The spiritual realm wasn't comprised of neutral beings willing to do the bidding of humans who called upon them.

No, the spiritual world was comprised of benevolent forces versus sinister forces, good versus evil.

At least that's what the Bible said. And Ginny was starting to believe it, not just because of the words but because of the people who'd shared it with her. People who'd seen miracles. People who'd had everything stacked against them and had no reason to hope but had chosen hope anyway.

If the Christian God was real, then Ginny wanted to know Him. Because... wow. To have a Father who would send His own Son to die for her? She couldn't imagine. To have a Father who cared about her, who knew her every move, who knew all her thoughts and loved her anyway...

Her mother had barely tolerated her. Her father had been selfish and distant.

Ginny couldn't imagine a God of love.

She stared at the sparkling waters of Clearwater Lake and spoke to the God she was trying to believe in. *I want to know You. If You're there, if You're real, show Yourself to me. Help me see You.*

A hand settled gently on Ginny's back, slid against her T-shirt and around her waist. She didn't have to look to know Kade had joined her.

"Enjoying the view?" he asked.

"It's wonderful, this vista."

He smiled and kissed her forehead. "It's really going to happen."

One day, after she and Kade had done some target practicing, Kade had given her a tour of the property on a four-wheeler. He'd shown her where he intended to put the clubhouse about halfway down the hill and about where the roads would go and the different plots of land. They'd continued down to the lake, where he'd pointed out his plans for a dock and boat slips. On the rocky shore, they'd built a campfire and roasted hot dogs and marshmallows and watched the sun set.

Now, she was seeing the vision he'd laid out for her that day. It was coming together just like Kade had planned. The roads had been cleared and paved, the plots marked, and a few houses were already being built. Construction had begun on the clubhouse a few weeks before, and today they would break ground on the golf course. "It's beautiful."

He glanced over the land. "It will be soon enough. We've come so far."

She loved that word, *we*. As if she were part of his plans, his future.

*Lord, is there any way...?*

But she was afraid to finish that prayer, afraid somehow she'd jinx it. She knew that was ridiculous, but still...

"Do you need my help with anything?"

He squeezed her waist. "You've done everything I asked and more. Thank you. I don't think I could have done this without you."

"I just made a few calls."

He took her hands. "Ginny, having you with me has made an enormous difference in my life. Maybe I could have done it alone, but I guess what I'm saying is, I'm really glad I didn't have to. I always thought this development was my dream, but now that I know you..." He smiled, shook his head. "I'm dreaming bigger now. I'm dreaming of having a family. Of you."

"Oh."

"I just wanted you to know that. Because all of this"—his gaze roamed the land before it rested on her again—"wouldn't mean nearly as much to me without you by my side."

She swallowed, unsure how to respond. Before she could think of something suitable, he continued. "Would you pray with me?"

"Of course." She was still reeling from his words, wishing she'd responded with something more appropriate than *Oh*. And the whole *Let's pray aloud together* thing felt awkward, especially with other people around. Kade's family had already shown up, as had a few friends from town. She wished they were alone, wished she could kiss him and tell him how she felt about him. Instead, she bowed her head and let him do the talking.

She didn't have anything to add, so she listened to his sweet words asking for favor on the day and the project. In her head, all she could add was *Yes, Lord, do that. Do that.*

It wasn't much, but maybe it wasn't nothing, either.

When he finished, he squeezed her hands and turned toward the crowd. More people were making their way on foot between the parked cars up the narrow lane. "I'd like you to stand with me until I get started, if you don't mind."

Joy bubbled up as they walked down the short incline to the level area. They'd set up tables earlier that morning, where Ginny had arranged carafes of coffee and bottles of water. Beside those were muffins and Danishes and bagels she'd bought from a bakery in town.

Thanks to the blue skies, the tent Kade had reserved hadn't been necessary. The trees surrounding them offered ample shade. An event company had brought in chairs, and people were already starting to fill them.

Kade's siblings were there, as were most of their friends from the real estate club, from church, and from the food bank where they both volunteered.

Ridiculous how much it meant to her that Kade wanted her by his side. He introduced her to people and included her in conversations and praised her for her help. Ginny brushed off his praise and tossed it right back to him.

While Kade chatted with a banker, something caught Ginny's eye.

On the far side of the clearing stood a man with a full head of blond hair. He wore jeans and work boots. She'd barely glanced at his face before he'd turned away, but there was something familiar about him.

She could swear she'd seen him before.

The man climbed in his car and drove away. Why come all the way out here if he hadn't planned to stay?

Once everyone arrived, Kade called the ceremony to order, and people filled the chairs. He squeezed Ginny's hand and let it go, and she walked to a seat in the front row.

They'd had a groundbreaking for the clubhouse a month or so before. They'd decided to do this one for the golf course to bring out more of the community, to help them see what had already been done and get them excited about it. Based on the crowd that had gathered, their plan had worked perfectly.

"Thank you all for coming." Kade's gaze skimmed the people. "I can't tell you what your support means to me. Some of you invested. Others helped me with planning. Others offered counsel or prayed. Some of you"—he glanced in the direction of Bruce Collier—"ensured I knew what I was getting myself into. Whatever role you played, I want you to know I appreciate it. This project would never have gotten this far without your help. So thank you."

Ginny glanced behind her, saw most people smiling back at Kade. Bruce, of course, scowled. Her gaze met Sokolov's.

He was watching her.

Fear skittered down her back. She shuddered and turned toward the front again.

"I wanted you all to see the progress we've made already," Kade said. "I know some of you thought it was a shame to develop this property." Again, his gaze flicked to Bruce. "And I understand that thinking. There's a temptation to leave the land rustic and untouched."

"Hear, hear," Bruce said.

Kade had the grace to smile at him. "It was a temptation, but we've done the right thing by resisting it. This property is too beautiful for me to keep to myself. Too beautiful to remain hidden from the world."

Kade introduced the designer he'd brought from Florida, a man who'd designed multiple top-tier golf courses on the East Coast. He explained his vision as the crowd followed his outstretched arm to the land, perhaps imagining what the course would eventually look like.

When the man was finished, Kade thanked by name everyone who'd been involved, including the investors, bankers, and more. One by one, he invited them to the front, and each one dug a shovelful of dirt and tossed it onto a growing pile. The ceremonial groundbreaking progressed quickly, and when Kade was finished, the crowd broke into applause.

People stood and chatted. Some approached Kade to congratulate him. Some wandered toward the refreshment tables, while others headed for their cars.

Ginny told Kade's siblings good-bye. After they'd walked away, she was ready to join Kade. Before she moved, a hand brushed her arm. She turned to see Mike Sokolov. "Ginny, right?"

Her stomach filled with acid for no good reason. She held out her hand. "Hi, Mr. Sokolov."

"Call me Mike." His hand was hot and sweaty when he shook hers. He wore khaki slacks, a green collared shirt, and a gray herringbone flat cap. He was bigger than she'd remembered, with wide shoulders and thick arms. His accent was strong, but his words were clear. "It is good to see you again."

She couldn't say the same. Why this man so rubbed her the wrong way, she had no idea. "I'm glad you made it. Are there others from your investment group here?"

"Just me," he said. "I'm mostly retired, so I had time."

She turned to take in the property. "What do you think?"

"I think our Kade Powers is going to be a very wealthy man."

"He has a great vision for this land."

"And for women, I'd add."

She stepped back, not sure how to respond to that. "Well, I guess—"

"It was lovely to see you again, Miss Lamont." He turned and walked away.

How very odd.

She was walking toward Kade when Bruce caught her eye. She'd never spoken to the man in person, and she didn't want to now. But when he headed her way, she stopped and forced a smile.

He held out his hand as he approached. "Bruce Collier."

"I remember." She shook his hand. "Ginny Lamont."

"You're hard to forget." He stood back and crossed his arms. "I've done a little research on you, Ginny. You're quite the *pretty little thing*."

The name of her parents' strip club hung in the air between them. She glanced at Kade—had he heard? But he and the course designer were answering questions in the middle of a small crowd.

She focused again on Bruce. "What are you getting at?"

"We don't need your kind in Nutfield."

"You mean real estate agents?"

"I mean smut brokers."

She rocked back on her heels. "I am not my parents."

"I'm not sure what you two are planning, but I won't allow any of that sick business or the people associated with it to come into my town."

"We're not planning—"

"Smut's like a disease, and you're a carrier."

"How dare you?" Her voice had risen. Across the space, Kade glanced her direction.

Bruce showed his yellowing teeth. "Your boyfriend's going to lose everything when the truth comes out." He pivoted and started toward the parked cars.

She stared after him, dumbfounded.

"What did he say?"

She turned at Kade's words and forced a smile. She wanted to tell him. And she wanted him to never know. Either way, she wasn't about to do anything that would ruin this moment. "Just Bruce being Bruce."

Kade studied her with narrowed eyes. He opened his mouth to say something, but someone called his name.

"Go. I'm fine." She forced herself to smile, opening her eyes wide in an effort to look happy despite her pounding heart and shaking hands. "If you don't need me for anything—"

"Just wait and I'll walk you to the trailer."

Beyond Kade, men stared at his back, waiting for him to return.

She stood on her tiptoes and kissed his cheek. "It was a great success. Congratulations."

Before he could stop her, she rushed toward her car. She was careful not to get close enough to anybody to be pulled into conversation.

Her mind was too full of threats and innuendos to focus on anything else.

~

GINNY SEARCHED real estate listings the next morning, looking for houses to show a new client. The trailer on Kade's land was empty, as usual. She'd hired another agent, who would be there most of the day in case anybody wanted a tour of one of the two show houses that had already been built and decorated. The young man would arrive soon enough, and she could head out to meet her client.

She hadn't intended to get such an early start, but she'd needed to do something to get her mind off Bruce Collier and his threats.

She'd bugged out of the dinner Andrea had hosted for Kade and the rest of their siblings and their families the night before, blaming a headache for her need to stay home. At least the headache hadn't been a lie. It had pounded ever since she'd left the groundbreaking ceremony. But she'd have cancelled, anyway. She'd gone home early—before Kade could come by and question her about what Bruce had said—turned off her phone, and tried to rest.

This morning when she'd turned on her phone, she'd had a strange message left the night before from an editor at the *Nutfield Gazette* asking her to call him as soon as possible, but when she did, the call went straight to voice mail. She left a message, of course. She hated to think what that was about. Maybe Bruce was already at work trying to discredit her in a demented effort to stop Kade's project. Which would make no sense. The project was well underway. There was no stopping it now.

The last thing she wanted was to hurt Kade's development. But it wasn't as if Bruce were universally loved in Nutfield, and Ginny had made a lot of friends in town. Maybe they would stand by her. Maybe her clients would be the voice of reason, defend her, tell others how she'd helped them find homes, how she'd never been anything but honest.

Maybe the people of Nutfield would believe the best of Ginny, not the half-truths Bruce might spread.

The problem was, maybe they wouldn't.

Her cell rang. She glanced at the screen. It wasn't Kade. Not that she was ready to tell him about Bruce's threats yet, but it would have been nice to hear his voice. He'd seemed both concerned and irritated the night before when she'd told him she couldn't go with him—and then asked him not to come by.

She'd hurt his feelings. But maybe it would be best for everyone if he kept his distance from her until Bruce played his hand.

The phone rang again, and she pushed away thoughts of Kade and swiped the call to connect. "Ginny Lamont."

"Hey, it's Bonnie Smith."

Ginny's newest client. "Glad you called." She searched through the listing paperwork she'd printed. "I've already pulled the listings on a bunch of houses. There's one in particular—"

"About that."

Ginny set the papers down. "Do you need to reschedule? I try to take Sundays off, but Monday—"

"No. It's just... We found another Realtor we think will suit our needs better."

"Oh." Ginny pulled in a deep breath. "I hope I haven't done anything to offend you." Though how she could have since their last meeting, she had no idea.

"It's just... We found someone else. That's all. Thanks anyway."

"Well, if you change your mind, please call me. I'd love to—"

The phone beeped, indicating the woman had disconnected.

How strange.

Ginny snatched the listing sheets she'd already printed and thought of the hours she'd spent working for Bonnie, both during their meeting and that morning. Now, she'd have nothing to show for all that time.

She stuffed the papers in the recycling bin. It was fine. She'd lost clients before. Granted, never before the first showing, at least not without a decent reason. But this wouldn't kill her. She had plenty to keep her busy, between the work she'd already arranged and the properties she was selling here at Clearwater Heights.

A car parked outside, and she peeked out the trailer's window. Her associate was there, which meant Ginny could leave.

Her stomach growled. She hadn't eaten anything the night before, thanks to the pounding headache and the anxiety that had churned since her run-in with Bruce. Now that she had no work that afternoon, there was no reason to spend another moment at the trailer.

She greeted the young man who would spend the day on the property, climbed in her car, and headed toward town.

When she reached Nutfield, she parked on Crystal Avenue and stepped out of her car. Though it was early in the season for tourists, folks gazed in storefronts and wandered slowly, in no rush to leave the beautiful day. She could go home, but it was too lovely, too happy a day to spend alone. Just being in downtown Nutfield lifted her spirits. This place might not consider her a local yet, but it felt like home to her. The little souvenir shops with their post-cards of autumn foliage and their cheap T-shirts charmed her, as did the wrought iron benches spaced beneath the trees along the street. Of all the places she'd lived—from Louisiana to Texas to California and the many states in between—none of them had ever felt like home in the way New Hampshire did. She'd thought it was because her sister lived here, but Kathryn's leaving hadn't changed the way Ginny felt about Nutfield one bit.

She hoped nothing changed the way Nutfield felt about her.

Again, thoughts of Kade intruded. She wanted to call him, see if he might like to join her for an early lunch. She should have called him already to ask how the celebration went with his family. And she needed to tell him what Bruce had said. She hadn't told him before because she hadn't wanted to ruin his big day, but the longer she waited, the harder it would be. She pressed his number and waited for him to answer. After only one ring, the call went to voice mail.

She stopped walking and stared at the screen, waiting for a quick text to explain why he'd rejected the call, but she received nothing. How odd.

She crossed the street and entered McNeal's.

The restaurant was hopping with late Saturday morning diners. The scents of bacon and sausage wafted from the kitchen in the back. Most of the tables were occupied. The diners at the table closest to her turned. She recognized the older gentleman as a regular and smiled at him. His eyebrows lifted as if she'd surprised him.

Across the table, a woman about his age—his wife, probably—regarded Ginny through narrowed eyes and whispered something.

The man turned away.

At the table behind them, all four middle-aged women stared at her.

Anxiety bubbled in her stomach. What was going on?

Bonnie, the restaurant's manager, approached. "Table for one?"

She nodded as she caught sight of Kade in a booth on the far side of the room bent over a table with one of the men she'd met the day before. An investor. That explained why Kade hadn't answered her call.

Bonnie snatched a menu and led the way to a spot near the dark bar lining the back wall.

Was Ginny imagining it, or were people watching her?

And whispering?

She heard an under-the-breath, "That's her," from somewhere just behind her.

When she sat, she felt their stares.

"You want coffee?" Bonnie asked. "Something else to drink?"

"Um." She swallowed, kept her gaze lowered, afraid to meet anybody's eyes. "Just water, I guess."

Bonnie walked away, and Ginny forced a deep breath, then focused on the room.

At least two people's heads snapped away.

She pressed her back against the hard wooden chair. Seemed Bruce had already begun spreading his venom. Amazing how fast bad news traveled.

With the menu between herself and the room, she studied her choices. She didn't want to look at anybody else. She didn't want to see them looking at her.

She should leave. But the walk back to her table had been awkward enough. She'd hate to repeat it as she walked out.

The family at the table beside her stood. A dad, a mom, and three kids. The little girl reminded Ginny of her niece, and Ginny smiled at the child.

Her mother snatched her away and glared. "We don't need your kind in town."

Ginny was too stunned to reply before the family stalked away.

She should go. She should definitely go.

She set the menu down and pushed back from the table as she caught sight of friendly faces. Harper Cloud and Jack Rossi were headed her way. "Why don't you join us?" Harper asked.

Ginny stood. "I've lost my appetite. And based on the looks I'm getting, you probably don't want to be seen with me."

"I'm sure it's not true," Harper said.

Ginny stepped toward the door, then stopped. "What...?" She hated that she didn't know, hated that she had to ask. And she hated how much she feared the answer. "What are people saying? I mean, is there some rumor or...?"

Harper glanced at Jack, and he took Ginny's elbow. "Come sit with us, and we'll tell you what we heard."

It was the last thing she wanted to do, but she needed to know what people were saying. She allowed Jack to lead her across the room.

She caught the eyes of one of her clients. The woman averted her gaze.

Another client lost, no doubt.

When they passed Kade's table, he didn't look.

She felt his companion's eyes on her. Or maybe it was someone else's—she wasn't about to turn around to look. McNeal's had always seemed such a welcoming place, but today, the words *hostile environment* flitted through her mind.

Jack led her to a table by the window. A cheeseburger was on one side of the table, a gigantic salad on the other. Both meals looked about half eaten. He indicated the bench where she should sit, but she stepped back and let Harper sit first. She needed to be able to escape fast.

Who knew where the next attack would come from?

Harper slid in and pulled the salad in front of her, but she didn't eat.

As soon as they were settled, Bonnie brought her a glass of water. "Do you know what you want, hon?"

Ginny shook her head. "Seems I'm not that hungry after all."

"Bring her a plate of fish and chips," Jack said. "With extra tartar sauce."

It was one of Ginny's favorite choices. Jack would know that—they'd met here often enough when she'd been helping him find his rental properties.

Bonnie left, and Jack glanced at Harper.

She brushed her pretty blond hair behind her ear. "There was an article in today's *Gazette*. Red pointed it out to me."

Red was the elderly man Harper cared for. Ginny had found him his house. She'd sat in the hospital by his bedside when Harper had returned to Maryland the previous fall. Ginny and Red had become friends.

Maybe that was over, too.

"What did it say?"

"I suspect Bruce Collier was the one who dug into your past," Jack said. "He was heavily quoted in the article. He claims to have evidence that shows your parents owned a number of strip clubs."

Ginny closed her eyes, took a deep breath, and opened them again. "I only knew of one."

"According to the newspaper," Harper said, "they owned four. Two in San Francisco, one in Reno, and one near"—she glanced at Jack—"was it LA?"

He nodded.

Okay. Ginny could deal with that. "My parents owned a lot of businesses. I knew about the restaurants. I learned about one of the strip clubs accidentally. It's conceivable they owned others they never told me about."

"That makes perfect sense," Harper said.

"And even if you did know about them," Jack said, "it doesn't mean you're looking to open a place like that here."

"Of course not!" The very idea of sullying this quaint little town was unthinkable.

Jack was nodding slowly.

Harper's lips were closed in a tight line as if she were trying to keep something in.

Obviously, there was more. "What else did the article say?"

Harper looked at Jack, who said, "That you've wormed your way into a local development." He glanced across the room toward Kade. "There was no proof, just a lot of innuendo about"—he made air quotes with his fingers—"'the things that go on in private clubs.'"

"What? There's no... It's a golf course."

"I know," Jack said. "And I know you, and I know Kade."

Harper said, "Obviously you're not planning anything like what that Collier guy suggested."

Ginny sat back. "Great. You two believe me, but everyone else in the restaurant seems to think I'm some kind of a..." *Smut broker.*

That's what Bruce had called her.

Bonnie brought the plate of fish and chips. "You need anything else?"

"No." Her voice was rough, and she cleared her throat. "Thank you."

Bonnie eyed her a moment, then bent down and lowered her voice. "Bruce Collier is a piece of work. I went to grade school with that guy. Even back then he was an arrogant know-it-all."

Ginny tried to stretch her lips into something resembling a smile.

"Don't let him get to you."

But Bruce wasn't the problem. It was all the people who'd stared at her when she'd come in, the woman who'd insisted they didn't need *her kind* in town.

How was a salesperson supposed to make a living when half the town thought she was trying to destroy the very place they called home?

Worse than that, what would this mean for Kade and his development?

"I think you need to eat something," Harper said. "You're pale as a ghost."

But she just shook her head. What she needed was to leave McNeal's. Maybe leave Nutfield.

She thought of Kade—sitting across the room but not acknowledging her, not responding to her phone call—and knew he had already come to the same conclusion.

She'd done enough damage.

## CHAPTER TWELVE

From the corner of his eye, Kade watched Ginny push out the door of McNeal's.

It took all his self-control not to follow her, wrap her in his arms, and promise her everything would be all right.

But it wouldn't be all right until he managed his investors. A day before, he'd have called most of them friends.

Across from him, one of his biggest investors drummed his fingers on the table. "What assurances do I have that your club will be family friendly?"

Kade tamped down the rising fury and leveled his voice. "I don't know what I can say that I haven't already said. The restaurant will be open to the public, a place for families to gather, for golfers to relax after a round."

"But the private rooms?" Tom lowered his voice on the last two words as if they were curses.

"Meeting rooms. A ballroom to host wedding receptions and retirement parties and baby showers."

"Your girlfriend might have something to say about that."

Kade blew out a long breath. He'd had this conversation three times already that morning, and he was tired of it.

"First, Ginny Lamont is not my girlfriend." He'd said the words too loudly. He needed to get his temper under control.

Behind him, two people slid out of their booth and headed toward the door.

Tom's eyebrows lifted. "You two seemed pretty close yesterday."

"We are close, Tom. The word *girlfriend* doesn't begin to describe how I feel about her. I hope that by this time next year, she'll be more than a girlfriend. I hope we'll be engaged, maybe even married."

"If I were you—"

"Second, Ginny has zero control over my project. She's not an investor. She has no ruling shares. So even if everything that sick jerk Collier implied about her were true, she couldn't do anything to influence my development."

"So you say."

"You know me better than that." Kade forced a breath and sat back. "Come on, Tom, we've gone to church together for years. I can't believe we're even having this conversation."

Tom looked around the room, at the people who kept glancing their way, leaning closer to overhear. When he faced Kade again, the tight set of his mouth had relaxed.

Maybe Tom was starting to see reason. Maybe he'd stand by Kade, stand by his promises.

"You're a friend, Kade. I'm just saying you should distance yourself from Ginny Lamont, or your dreams are going to fall apart."

Some friend.

Kade slid out of the booth and dropped a twenty on the table. "Do what you have to do. I'm going to build the nicest country club in New Hampshire. You can be a part of it, or you can let the likes of Bruce Collier scare you off."

He stomped out of the restaurant, ignoring the looks and whispers that followed him out.

He was yanking open the door of his Mercedes when Jack and Harper caught up with him. Jack had a white Styrofoam container in his hand. "Are you going to see Ginny?"

"What did you two say to her?" When Harper stepped back,

eyes wide, he realized how harsh he'd sounded. He ran his fingers through his hair, told himself to calm down. "I'm sorry. I'm not mad at you. I just want to know what she knows."

Jack said, "We told her what the article said."

"She hadn't seen it?"

"You think she would have come here alone if she had?" Jack held out the to-go container.

"She was pale and shaky," Harper said, "but she refused to eat. We were going to take this to her house."

Kade snatched it. "I'll take it." He focused on Harper. "Sorry I snapped at you."

She patted his arm. "We believe in you, Kade."

"And we believe in Ginny, too," Jack added.

After they walked away, Kade sat in his Mercedes.

Jack and Harper believed in him and Ginny, but they weren't investors. Their faith wasn't going to pay the construction company.

Two of his investors—old friends, good friends—had already pulled their funding, and if the conversation he'd just had was any indication, Kade was about to lose a third. Their excuses still rang in his ears.

*It's not that I don't believe in you, but I have a reputation to uphold.*

*If Ginny leaves town, call me.*

His investors wanted Kade to dump Ginny, run her out of town. No chance.

He'd have to stop construction until he could find more funding.

Everything he'd worked for was slipping away, and it seemed there was nothing he could do to stop it.

He navigated along the narrow streets of the oldest part of town until he reached Ginny's home. He parked, snatched the take-out container, and headed for her front door.

No answer to his knock.

He rang the bell and faintly heard the scratchy sound on the far side.

How had he still not replaced that doorbell for her?

Surely she was here. He walked to the backyard and looked through the window on the garage door. Her car was parked inside.

She walked all over town. But without her car—and with the rumors and whispers following her—she wouldn't stay gone long.

He sat on her front porch step and dialed her number.

It rang once, then went to voice mail.

Maybe this was payback for when he'd rejected her call that morning, though she'd never seemed petty. Not answering was the last thing he'd wanted to do, but he'd been in the midst of a very difficult conversation. He'd been awakened by a phone call from one investor who'd read the newspaper article, and he'd been trying to hold his development together ever since. If she'd known, she'd have understood.

He should have made time to call her.

He was calling now, and she was ignoring him. Maybe she was on the phone. Or maybe she didn't want to see him.

Could he blame her? The only reason Bruce had searched for dirt on her past was because Kade had asked her to join him at the planning committee meeting back in April. Now, the whole town suspected her of wrongdoing, and it was Kade's fault.

Of course she didn't want to talk to him.

He settled in beside the take-out container that was filling the air with the scents of fried fish and potatoes and dialed her again.

It rang in his ear, once, twice...

He heard something, moved the phone away from his ear and stood.

Inside the house, he could hear her phone ringing.

She was home, just ignoring him.

Excellent.

He banged on the door, then rang the bell repeatedly.

He wasn't leaving until she answered. Eventually, the sound of that bell would send her to the door or to the crazy farm.

Finally, her door swung open. "Do you mind?" She stood on the other side of the screen, her dark hair cascading over her shoulders. Her eyes were as red as they were blue, and her cheeks were blotchy.

He forced a smile. "Oh, good." He snatched the take-out container from the stoop. "You are here. Jack and Harper wanted me to bring your lunch." He grabbed the screen's handle but found it locked.

"I think you should go."

He stepped back. "Look, I get it. This is all my fault. If I hadn't brought you to that planning committee meeting—"

"Bruce's actions aren't your responsibility."

Okay. But then... "Can I come in?"

She crossed her arms. "Why, when I'm not your girlfriend?"

"Wait... What?"

"I just got off the phone with one of my clients. Former clients. Another one who suddenly found a more suitable Realtor."

"Oh, sweetie, I'm so—"

"She told me you made it clear to your lunch companion and everyone within a five-table radius that I'm not your girlfriend." Her voice hitched on the last word.

"What? No, no. That's not what I said."

"I don't blame you for distancing yourself from me. I was going to suggest you do just that. I had the weird idea that you might take some convincing." She scoffed. "Seemed an easy decision, but the least you could have done was tell me first."

"I'm not..." The words came out too loudly. He forced a deep breath, lowered his voice to sound reasonable. "I'm not distancing myself from you, Ginny. Obviously, considering I'm standing on your doorstep."

"So now we're supposed to sneak around, pretend—"

"No. I wasn't saying... Look, I told Tom you were more than a girlfriend. That you were—"

"Save it. It doesn't matter." She stepped back.

"Wait. It matters to me. You matter to me."

She nodded slowly. "I can tell by the way you warned me today. By the way you went out of your way to tell me what was going on, to protect me from that scene I just endured at McNeal's. By the way you ignored me."

"I'm trying to save my development."

"Well, it'll be easier without me in the picture."

"Please don't do this."

But she closed the door in his face.

TEN MINUTES after he left Ginny's house, Kade parked in the long driveway in front of one of the oldest homes in Nutfield. The house had been expanded from its original construction, additions having been added through the years. The old barn had been repainted a pretty red that stood in bright contrast to the pines that surrounded the property. He'd never been here, but the stories about the McAdams family had abounded since he was a kid— stories of infidelity and mental illness and even a kidnapping years before. More recently, there'd been some drama involving Reagan's ex-husband. Kade never knew the details and found the rumors hard to believe. How could that much hardship surround one family?

Whatever had happened with Rae and Brady, they were happy now and settled into her family's home.

The front door opened, and a little boy of seven or eight bounded outside and bolted toward the barn. He was dark-skinned with straight black hair. A little girl with strawberry blond hair followed him, running to catch her big brother.

Then Rae stepped onto the porch. She wore a green T-shirt with jeans that stopped mid-calf and flip-flops. She lifted her hand to shield her eyes.

"I should have called." He started toward her.

When he reached her, she stepped inside and held the door open. "Come on in. I was hoping Ginny was with you. I've been trying to call her, but she's not answering."

Kade entered the foyer of the old farmhouse. The rooms were small and closed off, as had been the style when the house was built. He didn't know for sure, but he thought it dated back to the late nineteenth century, a good fifty years older than Ginny's house. The developer in him imagined tearing down walls and adding newer, larger windows. But there was something charming about the space just as it was.

Rae led them to the living room and called, "Brady, Kade's here."

Brady stepped into the opening between the living space and the kitchen. Kade had gotten to know the couple better since Ginny introduced them back in April. The chief of police was wearing joggers and a T-shirt this morning, and he still looked just as imposing as he did when a gun was strapped to his hip. "I wondered who you were talking to." He stepped forward and shook Kade's hand. Brady had the newspaper tucked beneath his left arm. "I was just getting up to speed."

"Have a seat and tell us what's going on." Rae sat on the sofa against the back wall, and Brady joined her. "How's Ginny doing?"

Kade settled in the club chair and angled to face them. "Not great, and I made it worse. I should have called her right away." He'd been so stupid, so focused on his own project, he'd hardly thought of her. He gave the condensed version of the conversation they'd just had, ending with, "I blew it."

Rae tilted her head to the side, brushing her light red hair behind her ear. "You aren't planning to distance yourself from her, then?"

"Of course not. Why would I?"

Brady cleared his throat. "I'm not saying you should, but a lot of people would tell you to do just that. This article—"

"Is filled with baseless accusations and innuendo." Kade stood and pointed to the newspaper Brady had tossed on the coffee table. "Her parents owned strip clubs. So what? That doesn't mean she wants to."

"I know that." Brady's voice was level, and he showed no annoyance at Kade's tone.

Rae said, "We're on your side, Kade."

He sat and forced a deep breath. "I'm not mad at you. I'm mad at everyone else in this stuffy town, myself included, but not you."

Rae clasped her hands together. "How can we help?"

Kade hated to ask, but he didn't have anyone else who could do what Rae could. "I thought maybe you could write an article about her combatting the one that ran this morning, something showing the kind of person she really is."

Rae was nodding as he spoke. "Yesterday, I would have told you she wasn't newsworthy, but after this, I think the town would devour it."

"I'm sure," Kade said. "But it seems there are people at the *Nutfield Gazette* who want to ruin her just because they can. Are they against her or me or the development or what?" Until then, all the news coverage about his development had been fair.

Rae smiled. "It's a pretty small operation, and Larry, my editor, has no beef with Ginny or you or progress."

"He printed that article."

She shrugged. "I wonder what today's circulation numbers will be. Pretty high, I imagine."

"Anything for a buck," Kade said.

Rae sat back against the couch. "Playing devil's advocate, there was nothing in the article that wasn't true. I guarantee Larry did his homework."

"But the accusations—"

"I know," Rae said. "I understand there's no proof that Ginny has any evil intentions. My biggest beef is that Larry didn't wait to speak to her, get her side of the story. When I talked to him a few minutes ago, he said he tried to call her yesterday all afternoon and evening, but she couldn't be reached."

"She had a headache," Kade said. "She went home and went to bed."

"And he was in a rush," Rae said. "We only publish Wednesdays and Saturdays. I'm sure Bruce convinced him to run with it—and threatened to go to the Manchester paper with the story if he didn't."

"The perfect storm." Brady said. "Bruce knew exactly what he was doing. The question is, why now?"

"What do you mean?" Kade asked. "He'll do anything to halt progress."

"I know that." Brady shifted against the couch. "Bruce came to me weeks ago asking me to help him learn more about Ginny and your investor from Massachusetts. I refused, of course. We don't investigate *people* in America. We don't dig into private lives—or even public figures' lives—in hopes of finding a crime. Our job in law enforcement is to investigate *crimes*. I told him that. I think he thought, since my family's been here forever, that I'd want to stop you like he does."

"Do you?"

Brady's smirk answered the question before he spoke. "I'll admit, I wish Nutfield would stop growing so fast. I like the idea of it staying hidden from the world, but that's not an option. Houses are being built, people are moving in, tourists are finding us. So our job"—he nodded toward Kade—"your job as a developer is to find a way to bring growth that'll be good for the town. What you're doing will be good for Nutfield."

"The point is," Rae said, "we're with you."

"Even if we weren't," Brady added, "it's not okay for one citizen to... to—"

"To excoriate another citizen for his own personal gain," Rae said.

"Not the word I'd have used." Brady gave his wife a quick smile. "Mostly because I have no idea how to spell it."

Kade hadn't been sure about coming here, but now he knew this had been the right decision. "Thank you both. Even if you can't help, I really appreciate your support."

Rae stood. "I'll call Ginny to see if I can make an appointment with her. Maybe she'll answer this time."

"Thank you." Kade stood as well, but Brady didn't.

"I have a couple of questions for you," he said.

Kade sat back down.

After Rae had stepped into the other room, Brady clasped his hands and rested his forearms on his knees. "Has there been any more trouble at Ginny's house? Any more signs of intruders?"

"No. Nothing."

Brady narrowed his eyes. "People who own strip clubs aren't the most upstanding citizens."

"Ginny is not her parents."

"We've already covered that ground." Again, Brady sounded as impartial and relaxed as he ever did. "I just wonder if maybe the people who broke into her house back in April are connected to her parents' business."

"Oh." Kade looked at the floor, unsure how much he should tell Brady of what he and Ginny had uncovered. The debate in his head was short, though. "It's not my story to tell."

"There is a story, though."

"She's already angry with me. I can't risk—"

"You think telling the police the truth in order to protect her is a risk?"

An excellent point. And even if she never forgave him, he needed to keep her safe. "I don't know any details, but let's just say, you're right about her parents. They were far from upstanding citizens."

Rae stepped out of the kitchen. "Still no answer." She focused on Brady. "You mind if I go over there to talk to her in person?"

"Not at all. The kids have any plans today?"

"Nope. They'll probably need lunch pretty soon."

"I can manage lunch."

After Rae left, Brady said, "So maybe it's all related."

Kade struggled to catch his meaning. "What all?"

"The break in at her house, the timing of the article."

"Why do you think that?"

"Collier has been trying to find dirt on your girlfriend since April. If he'd known, he'd have gotten that article out there weeks ago, long before you broke ground."

"On the other hand, if the investors pull out now, he'll destroy me." Kade tried not to think about that, though it hadn't been far from his mind. "I've sunk every penny I have into this project, not to mention years of work. If development stops, I'll have no way to pay back the loans I've taken out. I'll be ruined."

Brady was shaking his head. "I know Collier *seems* vindictive, but I don't think he is. He thinks he's protecting Nutfield, and that's all this is about." A beat passed before he focused on Kade again. "I think, if he'd had this information weeks ago, he'd have released it. Say what you want about Rae's editor, but there've been a lot of favorable articles in the *Gazette* about Clearwater Heights. Your project has only gained momentum."

"So Bruce just got the information," Kade said.

"But why? The kinds of businesses her parents owned wouldn't be that hard to find, unless someone was trying to keep it hidden. And if so, then how did he find it at all? Would he have spent the money to hire an investigator? And if the information hadn't been hidden, then why didn't Collier find it weeks ago?"

"Maybe it's just dumb luck."

"Maybe." Brady held his gaze. "But I wouldn't bet on it."

"So what does that mean?"

Brady shrugged. "I don't know, but with the break-in, with the fact that her parents weren't model citizens, and with this information coming out now, I'm worried there are bigger forces at play here. And if we don't know what they are, then we can't fight them."

Kade thought of Ginny, how he'd left her home alone. And Rae hadn't been able to reach her. "You're saying Ginny could be in danger?"

Brady's eyebrows lifted. "That's your first thought, that Ginny might be in danger? Not that someone's plotting against you and trying to ruin you?"

There was that, too, but... "She's more important to me than any real estate development."

Brady's smile was knowing and fleeting. "I want to help. See if you can get her to talk to me."

"First, I'll have to get her to talk to me."

# CHAPTER THIRTEEN

Ginny sat on the floor of her living room surrounded by boxes.

Boxes of every size and shape. Some of them she'd brought with her from California. Most of them she'd collected from clients who'd unpacked them and moved into their new homes. She usually passed them along to other clients who were selling their houses, but lately, she'd had a lot more boxes incoming than outgoing. Maybe that Higher Power she wanted so much to believe in knew she'd need them. Or maybe, on some level, she'd known.

Now that she looked at them, she realized the truth. She'd never really believed this could be home. She'd always known that, eventually, she'd have to leave.

As soon as she'd sent Kade away that morning, she'd grabbed as many boxes from her garage as she could handle and carried them into the house.

Then, she'd painstakingly unfolded them and taped them open. She'd continued that pattern until every single box was open and stacked—some four and five high—in her living room.

And now she sat in the middle of them, legs folded, and looked at the ugly brown walls all around her.

She should be packing, but she couldn't seem to make herself move.

Why, why had she let herself hope? When would she learn she didn't get to have a home? Dorothy's mantra in Oz had been *There's no place like home.* At least Dorothy had known a home. And she'd even come to appreciate it, that black-and-white Kansas world. Ginny's mantra had always been and, apparently, would always be, *There's no such thing as home.*

Home was a place where a person felt loved and valued and protected and trusted. Ginny had never known such a place. Nutfield was as close as she'd gotten.

Probably as close as she'd ever get.

She pulled a blanket from her couch, a soft, fuzzy thing she used in the winter and kept out for show in the summer. She curled on the floor beneath it.

Maybe after a nap, she'd have the energy to pack. Maybe, if she focused, she could be on the road by Monday. She'd rent a U-Haul trailer. Whatever she couldn't haul herself, she'd sell with the house. What difference would it make? It was mostly new, anyway. It wasn't as if she'd grown attached to the things she'd surrounded herself with.

It was the people she'd miss.

Someone knocked on the front door, but she didn't move.

They rang the bell, and the sound had her covering her ears. She couldn't handle that noise right now.

Whoever it was rang again, then banged. Probably Kade. She wasn't talking to him.

The thought of him brought tears to her eyes, as if she hadn't cried enough for that man today.

How humiliated she'd been that morning when her client had called to fire her. And to share the juicy tidbit that Kade was denying they were in a relationship.

She'd disconnected from the client and dissolved into stomach-clenching sobs.

More pounding on the door, then a woman's voice. "Ginny, open the door. It's Rae."

Hope, that useless bubbling thing she never could quite suppress, rose like fizz from a jostled can of Coke.

Ginny stood and headed toward the door. If she had half a brain, she wouldn't open it, she wouldn't allow herself to believe in anything. But she'd never been the smart one.

She pulled the door open. Rae Thomas stood on her porch.

Rae tried the screen, but it was locked. "I'm coming in."

Ginny unlocked it.

Rae passed her, walked into the living room, and stared at the boxes. "What are you doing?"

Ginny said nothing, and Rae peeked into a few. "They're empty. Are they all empty?"

She nodded. "I was packing."

Rae crossed back to where Ginny stood and rested a hand on Ginny's arm. "You can't leave."

*I have to.* But she didn't want to.

Could she make a living here if the whole town hated her?

Except Rae was here, so maybe one person didn't hate her. Jack and Harper were on her side. Red would never reject her. Four people. And Kade...

He'd denied she was his girlfriend.

She wouldn't think about Kade.

Rae took Ginny in her arms. "You're not running away. We won't let you."

Ginny stepped back. "Who's we?"

"Brady and I, of course. And I talked to Sam earlier. She would have come with me, but the baby's sick. I can get her over here if you need more convincing."

"I don't want to be any trouble."

Rae sighed. "You're not trouble, Ginny. You're a friend. The rest of the ladies from Bible study will stand by you. Marisa, Kelsey, Harper... You have to trust your friends to have your back."

Ginny wasn't sure what to say, so she just nodded. She so desperately wanted to stay. Hadn't she told herself she would fight for this home?

The boxes proved she hadn't won that battle yet. Wasn't sure she had what it would take.

Rae led her to the dining room and sat at the table. "Let's talk."

"You want something to drink?" Ginny asked. "You hungry?"

"Just sit, please."

When Ginny did, Rae said, "I want to interview you. I talked to my editor on the way over, and he's given me the okay to do an article on you, to get your side of the story."

"There is no story. I'm just... I haven't done anything wrong. My parents were... They owned those places. I didn't even know about them before. I mean, I found out about one not long before my dad died, but the rest... Sheesh, at this point, it seems like this town knows more about my past than I do."

Rae reached into her gigantic purse and pulled out a notepad and pen. "We don't know anything. We only know what Bruce learned. And I don't care about your parents. I want to do a story on you."

Ginny glanced at the paper and pen. "I'm not that interesting."

Rae smiled. "Everyone has a story, Ginny. And everyone's story is fascinating in its own way. I want to know yours, and thanks to Bruce Collier, so do the people of Nutfield."

Ginny glanced at the walls of boxes in the next room. She would probably still need to leave, but at least she could defend herself first. Who knew? Maybe God would perform a miracle.

She swallowed, nodded. "What do you want to know?"

GINNY ANSWERED Rae's questions for an hour. At first, she was reluctant, unsure how much to share. Her parents never outright told her not to tell anybody about their lifestyle, about all their moves from place to place, about the fact that they usually left in the middle of the night with nothing but what they could fit in the van. They never told Ginny not to tell classmates or teachers or friends how many different schools she'd attended, how sometimes she didn't attend school at all. Ginny's parents had never needed to remind her to keep quiet about how they'd eat beans and rice for weeks, and then suddenly have the money for steak—usually enjoyed at some truck stop on the road between one temporary home and the next.

They'd never had to tell Ginny to keep quiet. But the unspoken rule might as well have been painted like graffiti on the outside of their vehicle.

When the family had moved to San Francisco and her parents had settled down, started the restaurants, and bought the house, even then Ginny never told the truth about her past. When she enrolled in high school in California, when her parents were settled and seemed legitimate, she still kept quiet.

Only in the last year had she started to tell people. But even the version of her past that she'd shared with Kade on their first date had been whitewashed.

In retrospect, she could admit the truth. She'd been ashamed. Part of her still was. And there was still that unspoken rule that boomed through her consciousness right now.

*Keep your mouth shut.*

All those years, she'd complied to protect herself and to protect her family.

But there was nobody left to protect. Kathryn had disappeared. Mom had moved to who knew where, and Daddy was dead.

What would telling the truth hurt?

Besides, Rae was an excellent interviewer. Even when Ginny might have protected herself, protected her family, Rae managed to pull the truth out of her.

The only thing Ginny didn't share was the little she knew about her parents laundering money. She had no direct knowledge of that, only theories and conjecture. And that had nothing to do with what was going on right now.

So Ginny talked, and Rae took notes and asked questions. Every once in a while, she received and sent text messages, but Ginny understood that. The woman was a mother. She probably had other things to do on a Saturday than spend the day with Ginny.

They'd been at it more than an hour when a knock sounded at the door.

Ginny pushed back in her chair, but Rae was faster. "I'll get it."

Ginny called after her, "I don't want to talk to Kade," while she wiped her tears and tried to make herself presentable.

"I know," Rae called back.

A moment later, Ginny heard voices—Rae and Brady and... Kade.

She stepped into the foyer, crossed her arms, and leveled a look at Rae. "I just said—"

"I know." Rae closed the distance between them and whispered in Ginny's ear. "Just hear him out, okay?"

"Why should I?"

Rae shrugged and took her husband's hand. Ginny watched them as they walked down the hall and into the dining room. Then she turned to face the man in the doorway.

The look he gave her... if he'd had a hat, it would have been in his hands.

She was exhausted from digging into her past, emotionally wrung out from the events of the morning. She didn't have the energy to deal with Kade. "Why are you here?"

"I *did* say you weren't my girlfriend. What your client *didn't* hear was what I said after—that you're more than just a girlfriend. That I care very deeply for you. That I hope someday we'll be much more than just dating."

Oh. Could that be true?

Ginny wanted to believe him. With everything in her, she wanted to believe him. But her client's words still rang in her ears. *Even he doesn't believe in you.*

Kade took one step forward. "I lost my biggest investor today and a few of my smaller ones. It's more than even my family could raise. Unless some miracle occurs, I'm going to lose everything. But I'm not going to lose you."

"Just tell them all we're not together anymore. Then I'm sure—"

"No." His lips flattened in a line. "I won't do that. I had no intention of *distancing myself* from you, as you put it. And I won't now. If I don't have the development to focus on, I'll have nothing better to do than pester you until you take me back."

"That's not logical, Kade. Just... just build the country club. I'll be fine."

He closed the distance between them and took her hands. "I won't be fine, Ginny. I won't be fine without you. You're the reason I've gotten this far." He swallowed, closed his eyes. When he opened them, he said, "I love you, Ginny Lamont. Nothing matters to me as much as you do."

She tried to clear the emotion from her throat. His words were like soothing aloe on a sunburn. To know he loved her, to know he would lose everything for her... She'd heard of that kind of love. She'd even seen glimpses of it in other families. But she'd never experienced it.

It was a sacrificial love. And though she'd never felt it from another person, she thought she understood it. Which was why she stepped back until she bumped into the wall. Because right now, she was the one who needed to sacrifice. She should let Kade go so he could pursue his dream. "I'll ruin your life."

"What happened today is not your fault. If anything, I'm ruining yours. Bruce only targeted you because of me."

"My past is my past. I can't fix it or change it."

He approached as if she were a frightened kitten. "I don't care about any of that." He placed his hands against her cheeks. His skin was warm, his palms rough and familiar.

"It's a bad idea."

But her words dissipated into nothingness as he pressed his lips to hers.

The world that had been off-kilter since she'd walked into McNeal's settled back into place. She wrapped her arms around his neck and melted against the length of him. There she found the security that her past kept trying to strip from her future.

After not nearly enough time, Kade pulled away and rested his forehead against hers. "Thank God."

She felt the silly smile on her face. "It's not like I took that much convincing."

His expression wasn't at all amused. "I thought you were done with me."

"I thought you were done with me."

"I should have called you first thing this morning, the moment I heard about the article. That was stupid and selfish. I was so focused—"

"On saving the development, on salvaging your dream." She swallowed and made a decision. She would stay in Nutfield and fight. No matter what the people of this town thought about her right now, no matter what happened to her business, as long as she had Kade, she had a home worth fighting for. "You and I—we're going to save it."

His lips pulled higher at the edges, and the corners of his eyes crinkled with his grin. "I love that word—we."

From the hallway, someone cleared a throat.

Kade stepped back and faced Brady, who stood with his arms crossed. "If you two are finished..."

"Sorry." Kade took her hand. "Brady wanted to ask you a couple of questions, if you and Rae are done."

"We're done." Rae approached from behind Brady. "I have enough to get started. If I have any more questions, I'll call you."

Ginny turned to Kade. "She thought she'd write an article—"

"Kade knows," Rae said. "It was his idea."

"Oh." She looked at Kade.

He shrugged. "Fight fire with fire, right?"

"Words with words," Rae said. "This article should make a big difference in how the town sees you. I'm not going to paint you as a victim but as a survivor of a very difficult childhood. People are not only *not* going to judge you for your past, they're going to respect you for what you've overcome."

Ginny let out a short chuckle. "You can do all that?"

Rae winked at her. "Just watch me." She focused on her husband. "The kids are at Marisa's?"

He nodded, and she turned to Ginny. "I'm going to get the kids. I'll call you soon."

After Rae left, Brady said, "Now it's my turn."

The way Brady looked at Ginny, if she hadn't already been against the wall, she might have stepped back.

"You and I need to talk."

# CHAPTER FOURTEEN

hank God.

Kade let the relief fill him as Ginny led the way through the house. After a deep breath, he followed.

And froze in the living room.

The space was filled with cardboard boxes. They were piled floor to ceiling, blocking the light from the back windows. There was barely enough space to walk through to the dining room.

She'd been planning to leave. If he hadn't come, if he'd waited a day or two, would he have arrived to find her gone?

Ginny stepped back into the room, her eyes wide as she regarded him.

"You don't waste any time." His voice was flat.

She walked to the tallest tower of boxes and bumped it with her hip. They tumbled, hit the pile beside them, and sent them tumbling, too. "It's all show and no go."

He nudged one with his shoe, just to be sure. The empty box offered no resistance. "So they're all—?"

"I couldn't make myself do it."

He blew out a long breath, tried to settle his pounding heart. "I'll help you break them down later." And then load them in his truck and take them away, just in case she had any more wild ideas.

In the kitchen, Ginny got drinks for everyone and filled a bowl with popcorn, which she set in the middle of the table before taking a few pieces.

"Did you ever eat?" Kade asked.

"This is the first time I've felt like eating all day." She popped the salty treat in her mouth.

Brady pulled a small pad and pen from his shirt pocket. "It's time to tell me everything."

Ginny set the few remaining popcorn pieces that had been in her hand on a napkin. She glanced at Kade, who nodded his encouragement.

Brady said, "Now that I know what your parents did for a living—"

"They were restaurant owners." Her voice carried a twinge of defensiveness.

"And strip club owners," Brady said. "I'm just wondering if their work has anything to do with why your house was searched that day."

She crossed her arms. "How would I know?"

Brady set the pen down, folded his hands on the pad. "I'm going to have a chat with Bruce next, but I'd like to go in armed with facts. I'm wondering how he found all that information about you, and why now. He's been trying to find something to use against you since April. If he'd gotten it before now, he'd have shared it before now."

Ginny looked at Kade, who said, "Brady thinks someone slipped him the info."

"He could have been trying to find information on me this whole time." Ginny focused on Brady. "Maybe he just got it yesterday."

Brady said, "Maybe. Maybe not. But if someone slipped it to him, don't you want to know who it was—and why?"

Kade rested his hand palm up on the table, and she slipped hers into it. "Brady asked me if I knew anything about your parents' businesses. I haven't told him anything, but I think it's time to trust him."

"But, my mother..."

Kade gave her a moment to finish, but her gaze cut to Brady, and she said nothing else.

After a moment, Kade said, "It was her job to protect you, not the other way around."

"I know, but—"

"I'm not after your mother," Brady said. "If she broke the law in California, the authorities in California will have to deal with it. Right now, I just want to keep you safe."

"But will you tell them?"

Brady didn't shrug, didn't blink. "Depends on what you tell me."

At least he was honest.

"I don't really know anything," Ginny said.

"Then I won't have any information to pass along."

And even if he did pass something along, that was Ginny's mother's problem, not Ginny's.

Brady sighed. "Look, maybe they're not related at all. Maybe, like you said, Bruce has been trying for weeks to find something to use against you, and he just found it. That feels... unlikely to me. He's persistent, but what he learned isn't that hard to find. It's just... it's weird, that's all. I'm here as your friend, not as the chief of police. I'm not here to investigate you or anybody else. I just want to know if there are people I should be on the lookout for."

After a quick glance at Kade, her shoulders slumped. "It's just a guess. After Dad died, Mom sold all the businesses. At least the ones I knew about. Those other strip clubs... I had no idea about them, so I don't know. I called the restaurants, a few of the new owners gave me the impression Mom and Dad had been..." She paused, shrugged. "Maybe they weren't exactly living life on the up and up."

"They were involved in some sort of criminal activity," Brady clarified. "Any idea what?"

Kade gave her a go-ahead nod.

"We think maybe money laundering."

"That makes sense. All those cash businesses, that would be my guess. Do you know who they were working for?"

"How could I? I knew nothing about it."

"I understand that." Brady tapped his pen on the table. "But maybe you have some names, some—"

"I know nothing."

"Okay." Brady wrote something on his pad. "Can you tell me the names of the people they worked with?"

When she said nothing, Brady set the pen down again. "I know you're scared. Whoever searched your house in April was looking for something. You still claim you don't know what?"

"It was months ago. They're long gone."

"We hope," Brady said. "But what if these things are related?"

"How could they be? I don't even know why you'd think that."

"Call it a hunch," he said.

Her lips were clamped shut. Kade was about to tell Brady what he knew, even though it would likely infuriate Ginny, when she pushed back in her chair, stood, and headed for her office.

They said nothing while they waited.

A few minutes later, she returned with a piece of paper. Kade glimpsed the list she'd typed, but he couldn't make out any of the words. He guessed, though, that she was sharing the information she'd collected this spring. She'd kept notes when she'd called the businesses her parents owned. In the last few weeks, she'd been adding the names of her parents' friends, their lawyer, a few other people Ginny had heard her parents mention in passing. With Kade by her side, she'd called a few of them, but nobody had given her any information she hadn't already had. Either they'd known nothing or they hadn't been willing to share.

She stood beside the table, the paper dangling from her fingers. "I don't want my mother going to prison."

Brady nodded. "I understand."

Not a promise. Not even the hint of one. Brady would do what he'd promised to do, what the good citizens of Nutfield had hired him to do, even if it meant reporting Ginny's mother.

After a long sigh, she held out the paper.

"Thank you for trusting me." Brady set the paper on the table.

Kade tried to read the paperwork upside down while Brady studied it. Sure enough, he saw names, phone numbers, addresses, and how they were associated with her parents.

Brady asked about most of the names on the list, looking for what, Kade couldn't guess. After a few minutes of going through a whole slew of names, Brady tapped the paper on a particular one. "This person, Yuri Petrovich. How do you know him?"

"I don't really. He was at Dad's funeral. I met him at the house afterward."

"That was the only time you'd ever met him?"

"Why? Who is he?"

Brady's expression indicated nothing.

She closed her eyes. When she opened them again, she said, "That was the only time I met him, yes. But I'd seen him once before. I met Dad for lunch about a week before his accident. It was the day Dad gave me this necklace." She touched the pendant resting on her collarbone. "He got a call, and then said he had to go. We weren't even finished with our meals—it was weird he left as fast as he did. As he walked out, a car pulled to the curb, and the back window rolled down. It was weird, like something you'd see on TV. I mean, who has a driver these days?"

Brady said nothing.

Kade nodded his encouragement, but she didn't see. She was focused on Brady.

"Anyway," she said, "Dad walked around to get in the other side of the car. When he stepped away, I saw the guy's face. It was Petrovich. He has a birthmark, you know like..." She tapped her forehead. "I can't think. What's the name of the Russian leader, the guy who was in charge when Reagan was president?"

"Gorbachev?" Brady supplied.

"Yeah, that guy. The birthmark wasn't as big as Gorbachev's, but I remembered it. When I met him a couple of weeks later, I thought it was funny that he was Russian, too, and had a similar birthmark. I think that's why I remember his name."

"And how did you come to meet him?"

"I told you, he was at our house."

Brady's smile was kind. "What I mean is, did your mother introduce you to him? Or did you introduce yourself?"

Ginny looked at the ceiling. "I was talking to some neighbors when he approached me." She focused on Brady. "He shook my hand, told me his name, and said he was sorry for my loss. Nothing noteworthy."

"But he introduced himself."

"What difference does that make?" Kade asked.

Brady wrote something on his notepad, then glanced at Kade before focusing on Ginny again. "Probably none." He looked over the paper she'd given him. "No other Russian names." He tapped the paper with his pen. "Now that we're thinking about Russian names, do any others come to mind? Maybe people you met in passing but didn't think to add to the list?"

She shook her head. "I don't remember any others."

"Okay. This was your dad's funeral, right? When was that?" Brady asked.

"He died a year ago. July second. The funeral was a couple of days later."

Kade hadn't known the anniversary was near. He tried to catch Ginny's eye to offer solace or comfort or something, but she remained focused on Brady.

"What happened to him?" Brady asked.

"It was a car accident. We don't know exactly what happened, but Mom said he'd not slept well the night before. Maybe he fell asleep. He went off the road, flipped the car, and crashed into a concrete barrier. He died instantly."

"In San Francisco?"

"Oakland."

He wrote that on his notepad. "What was he doing there?"

"He had businesses there. I assume something to do with that. What does all this have to do with the guy who broke into my house and the newspaper article?"

Brady shrugged. "Maybe nothing. I'm just trying to put some pieces together. And where's your mother?"

Ginny shrugged as if it were no big deal that she didn't know the answer to that. "She sold all the restaurants and the house. I don't know where she went."

"She didn't tell you?" Brady asked.

"I didn't ask. When I spoke to her, I'd assumed she was still in San Francisco, but now I know she'd sold the house before that."

"When was the last time you talked to her?"

"The day of the break-in," Ginny said.

"You told her what happened?"

Ginny nodded. "And that Kathryn had moved away."

"Wait. Kathryn?" Brady studied his notes, then looked at her.

Ginny ran her hands through her hair. She looked so tired, so worn. Kade would give anything to make this easier for her.

"My sister and her family lived here in Nutfield for years. The day before the break-in, Kathryn left." She gave Brady a quick rundown on what happened.

Brady made a few notes. "Did your sister say why she was leaving?"

She closed her eyes. A long moment passed, but she said nothing else.

"Ginny?" Brady's voice was kind but insistent.

"She said I was in danger." Ginny opened her eyes and met Brady's gaze. "Kathryn said that I led people here, and that I should leave, change my name, and never look back."

"You don't scare easily."

Her eyes filled with tears. "I should have left." She turned to Kade. "If I'm the reason you lose your development—"

"Don't do that." He reached for her hand, and she let him take it. "I want you to stay. This is your home. You should fight for it."

"But at what cost?"

"That doesn't matter," Kade said. "Your safety matters."

Ginny shifted to face Brady again. "That's all she told me."

"She gave you no names, no details?"

She shook her head.

"I take it you two weren't close."

Sadness crossed over Ginny's face, but she said nothing.

"When did she move away from California?" Brady asked.

"Not long after we moved there, Kathryn transferred to Boston University. She met a guy, got married."

Brady looked at his notes, tapped his pen on the table. "Did she go home for the funeral?"

"Yes, but she left immediately. She didn't even stick around long enough to go to the house afterward."

Brady's gaze was far away. After a moment, he said, "So how would she know...?"

"She said she saw someone in town who'd been at the funeral."

Brady made a note on his pad, then tapped the pen against it, staring at nothing.

Ginny felt Kade's gaze on her but didn't meet it. All the shame about her past, the worry about her future, came back. What was she doing sitting here with these men? Brady couldn't protect her, and Kade would destroy his life standing by her. "I'm an idiot for still being here." Her words were whispered.

Kade stiffened beside her.

"Nobody thinks that." Brady shook his head. "I can't help but wonder why your sister wouldn't have given you more information. Where is she now?"

Ginny just shrugged, and Brady made another note.

"Back to your mother," he said. "You told her about Kathryn leaving and the break-in?"

"I hoped Mom would tell me what was going on, maybe who was after me."

"I take it she didn't?"

"She told me to run."

Kade scooted close, rested his hand against Ginny's back, and focused on Brady. "I told her to stay."

"Good. I'm glad you did." Brady set his pen down. "Is there anything else you think I need to know?"

"I'm not sure you needed to know all of that," she said.

Brady slid the pen in his breast pocket. "If you think of anything else, even if it seems inconsequential, call me."

"You know as much as I do now."

He stood. "I should go. I'll do some digging, see what I can find out. And then I'll pay Bruce Collier a visit, see if he can shed any light on how he came by the information about you."

They walked Brady to the door.

With his hand on the doorknob, Brady turned. "If I learn anything, I'll let you know." He pressed his lips together, shook his head. "Make sure you keep your doors locked and continue using your alarm. Maybe the newspaper article and your prowler aren't related at all, but it never hurts to stay vigilant."

Monday morning, after he'd read his Bible and prayed, Kade settled at the kitchen counter with his laptop. He usually preferred to work where he was surrounded by people, but he didn't need anybody eavesdropping on today's conversations.

He liked his condo, but he'd not made it home. It was supposed to be temporary, a place to live until he could build in Clearwater Heights. Since he'd graduated from college, he'd been working on this project. Every deal he'd made, every extra dollar he'd earned, he'd earmarked for developing his land. For a decade he'd been working, investing, working more, living on next to nothing in this tiny two-bedroom place. He'd foregone vacations, shopped sales, skimped on meals out, all so he could achieve his dream.

Now, everything he'd worked for was slipping away.

He closed his eyes and prayed for God's help. God could fix it. God could redeem all of this, make it work out for his good, for Ginny's good. Kade had to trust that God would do His part.

Today, Kade would do his.

After Brady had left Ginny's house on Saturday afternoon, Kade stayed as long as he could to comfort her. But one glance at his silenced phone and the many missed messages, and he'd known he'd been out of reach too long.

He'd gone home and returned calls. By bedtime Saturday night, all those he'd spoken to were demanding their money back.

Sunday, he'd turned off his phone completely and asked Ginny to do the same. They found a church in Manchester and worshipped among people who didn't know them. He hadn't been trying to protect himself—he'd have been much better off going to his home church, facing down his accusers. But Ginny's faith was new and fragile, and he'd feared putting her in a situation where people might treat her as badly as the people at McNeal's had.

After church, they'd driven north to Lake Winnipesaukee, waded in the clear water, eaten burgers and fries and ice cream, and purposely avoided talking about the issues that had bombarded them on Saturday.

But now it was Monday, and Kade needed to face it.

He powered on his phone and groaned as the messages loaded. He had... Could that be right? Twenty-five phone messages?

Even more texts.

He started with voicemail, put his phone on speaker, and prepared to take notes.

There wasn't much to record, though.

Investor after investor calling to demand repayment. Friends, people he'd known for years, suddenly didn't believe in him. Or if they did, they weren't willing to risk losing their money because nobody else believed in him.

Technically, he didn't have to give the invested money back. He wasn't legally obligated to pay them anything until the project was complete. But that didn't matter, and the investors knew it. They could get attorneys—some had already threatened to—and draw Kade into a legal battle that could last for years.

Either way, the result would be the same.

Kade would be ruined financially.

But with the article coming out on Wednesday, there was hope.

He called Tom first. On Saturday, Tom had demanded his investment back, but now that Kade felt he could share what he knew about Ginny's past—much of it, anyway—he thought Tom would be the most likely investor to change his mind. They'd been friends and gone to church together for years. If anybody was going to trust him, Tom would.

If Tom stuck by him, then Kade could use his faith to bolster the faith of others.

His friend answered on the first ring. "How you doing, brother."

*Brother.* Strong word, all things considered. "On Wednesday, the *Gazette* is printing a feature article on Ginny that will dig into her life and her family. It'll turn public sentiment back to her and the country club. I thought I'd give you a heads' up on what it's going to say, give you the chance to change your mind about pulling out of the development. I'd hate for you to miss this opportunity."

The words had sounded canned, unnatural. They'd been delivered too fast with an inauthentic cheerfulness. Kade should have practiced more.

On the other hand, he shouldn't have had to practice telling a friend the truth.

"I look forward to reading it," Tom said. "I guess we'll talk on Wednesday. Still, I'd like my money back today."

"Don't you want to know—?"

"I have a business in this town," Tom said. "I have a family to feed. I can't risk my livelihood. If you're wrong about that woman—"

"Her name is Ginny."

"Yeah. I met her. She's got the body for it. Did she ever work in any of those—?"

"Of course not!" Kade pushed back in his chair and stood. The suggestion had his hands clenching into fists, his adrenaline pumping.

"People do, you know. It's not that shocking. And if she didn't, that means she just profited from them."

"Her parents profited. She was a child."

"A decade ago, yeah, but now... Look, God can redeem anything. But the fact that she kept quiet about what she was involved in tells us a lot, doesn't it? Repentance—"

"She doesn't have anything to repent for."

A short laugh was followed by, "I know you care about her. I know you believe in her. But a woman like that... I'm just saying you should keep your distance."

A million responses filled his mind, most peppered with words that would only make things worse.

So he ended the call and banged the phone down on his granite countertop.

Took a deep breath.

Lifted the phone.

Excellent. He'd cracked the screen.

He dropped his head into his hands. If Tom didn't believe in him, nobody would.

It rang, and he lifted it, looked through the crack at the name.

His bank. Could things get any worse?

He swiped the call to connect. "Kade Powers."

"Kade, it's Donald. After the news this weekend, where does your development stand?"

Kade spent twenty minutes giving his loan officer a rundown on what had happened and on the article that would be printed in Wednesday's newspaper. He considered glossing over the details, but Donald wasn't stupid. He had access to all the same information that Kade's other investors did, and because he was local, he knew many of the same people. Glossing over the details would only serve to make things look worse.

Still, Kade focused on the article about Ginny. "When that comes out, people will see her differently. They'll understand that she had nothing whatsoever to do with her parents' businesses. She didn't even know about the strip clubs until recently. She's a kind, generous Christian woman who only wants what's best for this town."

"I hope that's true. I know you believe it is."

"I do. Unequivocally."

"Good." Donald was not much older than Kade, a successful banker who understood real estate and risk. They'd known each other for years. "I hope you're right about Ginny, so I'm willing to wait until the article on Wednesday."

"Wait? For what?"

Donald blew out a long breath. "Yours is a demand loan, a short-term loan."

"Right. Just to get us through until next year. When the lots are sold, I'll have the money to pay it back."

"Except nobody's going to buy lots right now, Kade. Not unless—"

"It's all going to turn around."

"I hope you're right," Donald said. "But my boss is very nervous. We're a small bank. We can't absorb the loss if you default."

"I'm not going to—"

"Demand loans are callable."

Callable. That word ricocheted in his brain like a ping pong ball. Had Kade known that when he'd signed the papers? He could vaguely remember Donald explaining it along with some flippant remark like, *but no need to worry about that. We only call loans if you miss your payments or suddenly become a bad risk.*

Kade swallowed. "Don, you can't—"

"We'll be making a final determination on Friday." Don's friendly tone had disappeared. He was all business now. "Pull together all your financials, along with any other information you think might be relevant, and let's plan to meet Thursday morning."

"So much for friendship."

"It's out of my hands, Kade. This crazy story will blow over, but if you lose your investors before it does, then we'll have no choice. I'm sorry."

Two hours later, Kade spotted his father on the sidewalk at the airport in Manchester. His hair was nearly white, his slender build marked by a little paunch and stooped a bit, but he still seemed like the biggest man in the world to Kade.

He parked against the curb and climbed out of the car.

His father opened his arms, and Kade stepped into them.

"Good to see you, son." Dad slapped his back a couple of times.

"I can't believe you're here."

"Just for the day," Dad said. "Darren called and told me what's going on."

Kade had been in the middle of calling more investors that morning—and getting more bad news—when his mom had phoned to tell him Dad was flying in and that Kade would need to get him from the airport.

"When is your flight back?"

"I need to be here by seven tonight."

They settled in the car. "Where to?"

"Amazingly, the peanuts and coffee on the plane didn't satisfy me. How about we find a place to eat?"

Kade glanced at the dashboard clock—just after eleven. "The Backroom?"

"Perfect."

Twenty minutes later, they were seated and ordering at a restaurant that had been a family favorite as long as Kade could remember. The place, with its wood paneling and exposed overhead beams, its red carpet and brass accessories, had been in Manchester forever. Being here with his father, knowing Dad had flown from Florida to talk to him, made Kade feel loved. It also added a gnawing in his gut, the kind he'd gotten as a kid whenever he thought he was in trouble.

He hated letting his father down. He hated being in this position, hated the failure that probably smelled stronger than the meals at adjacent tables. Part of him wanted to tell Dad everything was fine, skim over the details so he wouldn't know the truth. But what foolishness would that be? Dad was the wisest man Kade knew. No doubt Dad would be disappointed in him when he found out everything that had happened. Heck, Kade was disappointed in himself.

Maybe Bruce had been right. Maybe Kade had aimed too high, too soon. Maybe he'd let his own pride and arrogance lead him to this place. The Bible said pride would come before the fall, and Kade was keeling headfirst toward a splat.

But, as embarrassing, as shameful as the truth was, Kade had to face Dad's disappointment in order to get to the advice that would surely come on the other side.

They made small talk until their lunches came—fried haddock for Dad and a pastrami sandwich for Kade. After the waitress left their meals, Dad nodded toward him. "Darren gave me just enough information to convince me to get on a plane. Tell me what's going on."

While Dad cut his fish, Kade sipped his drink and steeled his courage. He launched into the story of everything that had happened over the weekend, beginning with the call that woke him Saturday morning and ending with the call he'd gotten from the bank that morning.

Dad listened, offering little more than an occasional *hmm* as he ate his lunch. When Kade was finished, he waited through a long silence. He tried a potato chip, then followed that with a sip of Coke to settle his stomach.

Finally, Dad said, "You're in a heckuva pickle. I'm disappointed that—"

"I know, I know." Kade put his glass down. "I should have anticipated this. I should have had a plan. Maybe I should have waited longer, waited until I could invest more of my own money. Now, I'm not only going to lose everything, but I'll probably have to sell the land you gave me just to survive. You built something amazing, and I'm ruining it. Ruining your legacy. I should have..." But he didn't know what he should have done differently. Maybe that was his problem. He just wasn't good enough, wasn't smart enough. He couldn't look his father in the eye, so he focused on his untouched sandwich.

His father pressed his back against the bench seat. "Are you finished?"

Kade forced himself to meet his eyes. "I'm sorry I disappointed you."

"That's not what I was going to say at all." Frustration etched lines on his forehead and turned the corners of his mouth down.

It took all of Kade's concentration not to let his shoulders slump, his head drop. He needed to look strong and confident, even if he didn't feel it. The last thing he'd ever wanted to do was disappoint his father. Dad opened his mouth, and Kade braced himself.

"Son, how could I ever be disappointed in you?"

Kade blinked. What was that?

"You've made me proud every single day of your life. I brag about you to everyone I know."

"But you just said—"

"I'm disappointed in your investors. In your friends and mine who jumped ship so fast. People have no backbone anymore." Dad closed his lips, shook his head. "They're so worried about perception, they've forgotten about loyalty. I'm disappointed that the people you thought you could count on have let you down. But you?"

When Dad met his gaze, Kade had to blink through the tingling feeling in his eyes.

"Son, there's one man in a hundred, maybe in a thousand, who would stick by a girlfriend who brought him so much hardship."

Wait... That's not what Kade had expected. What was Dad saying, that he should throw Ginny over? That he should dump her?

"She's not your wife," Dad continued. "You've made her no promises as far as I know. You owe her nothing. And yet—"

"Dad, I can't—"

"Don't interrupt me. Please." Dad took a deep breath. "You obviously care about her. She matters to you, and you're not willing to sacrifice that relationship for anything—not money, not reputation, not pride. I don't think I've ever been prouder."

*Proud?* Could that be true?

"I only wish I had more time so that I could meet this woman who's so captivated you."

Kade swallowed. "Me, too."

"I hate that you didn't already know how I'd feel." Dad sipped his iced tea. His hands trembled slightly as he set the glass down. "I'm sorry I wasn't better about... You know, telling you stuff like that. I was always so consumed with business. Raising you was your mother's job. The way you're standing up against this attack proves she did it well."

"You're a great dad. I've admired you my whole life. I always wanted to be just like you. I just thought... You wouldn't have gotten yourself into this mess. Or if you had, you'd see a way out."

His father chuckled. "When I was your age, I'm not sure I'd have made the choice you're making. The right choice. You're a good man, Kade. Whatever happens now, if the development weathers this storm or if you lose everything, it doesn't matter to me. I know you'll find your way. And the land..." He waved the words away like he would a pesky fly. "That's not my legacy. If I'm leaving any legacy, it's you and your brothers and sister. The money, the land—those don't matter."

Fear, worry, and shame lifted like a fog. And when they did, what settled was determination. Kade hadn't been defeated yet. He wouldn't be defeated. "Do you have any advice for me?"

"I wish I could fund it for you, but it would be some time before I could get the cash. Most of our investments aren't liquid. And even then... I don't know—"

"I would never ask you."

"Yeah." Dad adjusted his napkin. "I kept waiting for you to ask us to invest. But you never did."

"I wanted to do it on my own, to make you proud."

"You think I wouldn't have been proud?" Dad shook his head. "Just so you know, I am proud of you, I was proud of you before, and I'll always be proud of you. And I would have been honored to invest."

Kade wasn't sure what to say. All he managed was, "I'm sorry."

Dad lifted an onion ring and waved it his direction. "None of that. Your mom and I will pray that the article on Wednesday will do the trick. If it doesn't, call me, and we'll figure out a plan."

With that, Dad changed the subject, and they enjoyed their lunches. Even though nothing was solved, nothing had changed, Kade felt stronger after talking to his father. He'd known all along that his father would be willing to help him. But Kade wasn't going to risk his parents' retirement on this project. What had seemed like a sure thing a week before suddenly felt risky. And even if his dad did want to help him, Kade needed more money than even Dad could gather.

Which meant Rae's article in the *Gazette* would have to shift sentiment about the development and put Ginny back in their favor, or no amount of planning and strategizing with Dad would make any difference at all.

# CHAPTER FIFTEEN

Ginny's parents hadn't made it to a single parent-teacher conference in all of her childhood. They'd been late to her high school graduation and had skipped her college graduation altogether.

Kade's father had flown to New Hampshire from Florida for a single day because he'd heard Kade was in trouble.

She couldn't imagine having that kind of father. Having the kind of parents who would drop everything because their kid needed them.

Someday, if she ever had the opportunity, Ginny wanted to be a parent like that. She didn't have the first idea how to love that way, but she wanted to. She certainly would like to have met the amazing man who'd made a one-day round-trip flight to comfort and advise his son.

It was fine, though, that Ginny hadn't been included. It made sense. Kade had explained when he'd called the evening before that, after lunch in Manchester, they'd headed south to Salem so his dad could spend the afternoon with Andrea and her kids. The other brothers had come for an early dinner before Kade had taken his dad back to the airport.

Ginny had spent Monday morning at the food bank helping to unload crates of donated food, and she'd had an inspection yesterday afternoon. So she couldn't have joined Kade and his father even if she'd been invited.

Kade knew her schedule. That's why he hadn't invited her. Logically, that made perfect sense. But what if his father had spent the day trying to convince Kade to dump her?

What if the whole family had spent the evening talking sense into him?

If Kade ended things with Ginny, his dreams would be back on track. His family had to know that. If they had his best interests at heart, then of course they'd advise Kade to dump her.

Except when he'd called her the night before, he'd seemed as devoted as ever.

Maybe she was being ridiculous.

And she didn't want to think about what it meant to Kade's business that he was standing by her. Her very existence was ruining his life.

Tuesday morning, Ginny was working in the trailer at Clearwater Heights. Her assistant had been there all day Sunday and Monday and reported that not a single prospective buyer had walked through the doors. Even on their slowest days, they'd had people who wanted to see the show homes. Ginny refused to believe it was due to Saturday's article. Everybody in southern New Hampshire couldn't have read the article in Saturday's *Nutfield Gazette*. Right?

Except when she typed *Clearwater Heights* into the search bar on her laptop, the article was the first thing that came up, even above the website she and Kade had developed to showcase the property.

*Scandal Surrounds Clearwater Heights.*

Excellent.

Ginny had already accomplished everything she'd planned for the day, and it wasn't even noon yet. Normally, she'd be interrupted by potential buyers. Not today, though. She'd blame the weather, except the sun was shining. It was a perfect June day.

It was Tuesday. People worked on Tuesdays. All was not lost.

It just felt that way.

She'd been inside the cramped office too long, and the walls were closing in. She stepped outside and locked the door behind her. It was hot—mid-eighties, at least—and humid. She'd probably regret this, probably return covered in sweat, but she had to get out of there for a few minutes. At least she'd worn capris and sandals instead of her usual slacks and heels. With no scheduled meetings, she'd dressed to walk around the property, planning to show people the land to help them envision all Kade had planned.

All around, men hammered and drilled, working on the few houses already under construction. Their talk and laughter carried on the wind.

In front of her, the partially constructed clubhouse stood empty. Construction had been halted after Saturday's article.

Ginny turned right, passed the two show homes she'd helped decorate, and continued down the hill along the recently paved asphalt road, little flags waving from the plotted-off land on either side. For Sale signs marked each one. She couldn't bear to look. They wouldn't ever sell if she continued on as the agent. She'd lost nearly all of her residential clients already. Only the investors, like Jack Rossi, had stuck with her so far. They didn't care if her reputation was sullied. They only cared that she was good at finding deals.

That wasn't fair, though. Jack and Harper were friends. At least Ginny still had some of those.

This was all going to blow over.

Rae had told Ginny the article about her would come out the next day. Rae had offered to send Ginny an early copy, but Ginny hadn't wanted to see it. It felt weird having someone write about her life. It hadn't even come out yet, and Ginny felt like a circus attraction.

Like a victim.

She hated it. She wasn't a victim, not of her past, not of her parents. Something Kade had said months ago came to mind. He'd said maybe she'd become who she was not because of her parents but despite them.

Now she'd be using her ugly past to garner sympathy, to… ugh, she hated thinking about it, but it felt like she was using it to manipulate people into liking her, into supporting her. Yes, everything she'd said to Rae was true. But still...

Ginny hadn't left California because she'd wanted to escape her past. Her mom had forced her to leave, had shoved a bag of money at her and told her to run.

At the time, it had felt like the worst betrayal, as if she'd lost everything. But then, when she'd achieved some distance from her parents, she realized her mother's insistence that she leave had been a gift—even if Mom hadn't meant it that way. When Ginny had gotten settled in Nutfield, when she'd made friends and started building her business, she'd realized the freedom that came from being far from her mother, from the darkness that had always hovered over their family, from the pressure of trying to get them to love her.

Now she was trying to get the townspeople to love her. The article coming out in tomorrow's newspaper made her feel uncomfortable, exposed. But she'd already been exposed. Thanks to Bruce Collier, the town already knew all her dirty secrets.

Ginny reached the lake and peered across the sparkling blue surface. The inlet surrounded on three sides by Kade's land was quiet, but beyond that, motorboats buzzed by. Every so often, Ginny could hear the squeal of a child playing somewhere on the far shore, where vacation homes dotted the landscape.

A car door slammed in the distance, and she swiveled toward the sound.

Beside an old red pickup truck, a man stood on the road in dingy jeans, boots, and a dirty T-shirt. Ginny expected him to turn away, to head toward one of the construction sites nearby, but instead, he lifted his hand to shield his eyes and looked toward the water.

No, toward her.

She recognized him. She'd seen him at the groundbreaking Friday. He must have been one of the construction workers. He had blond hair and wide shoulders. Even from this distance, she could see the muscles bulging beneath his T-shirt.

He was familiar, and not just from Friday.

She'd seen him before.

An image of her father's burial came to mind. It had been a cold, drizzly day. She and her mother and sister had sat in the front row beneath a tent arranged for the occasion. A few others had come out for the burial, had listened to the short ceremony. When it was over, when Ginny was thanking friends and inviting them back to the house, she'd seen someone standing near the line of cars, watching.

The same man who was watching her right now.

A chill slithered down her back despite the sunshine beating down on her.

He lifted his hand as if in greeting, then climbed in his truck and drove away.

Ginny waited until he was out of sight before she rushed up the hill.

It couldn't have been the same person. Except something told her it had been.

Maybe he'd been the one who'd searched her house.

Maybe he'd been watching her all along.

GINNY RUSHED TOWARD THE TRAILER. At every noise in the distance, she turned, certain she was about to see that red truck barreling toward her.

She tried to tell herself the man had just been a construction worker. Maybe he was just a creepy guy who didn't understand it wasn't okay to stare at women. Maybe he'd waved because she'd caught him.

She wanted to believe her fear was unfounded. She wanted to believe she had nothing to worry about. But he'd been too familiar.

Kathryn's words came back to her. Kathryn had seen someone in town who'd been at the funeral.

Saturday, Brady had said he believed that the timing of the

newspaper article didn't make sense. That perhaps the timing had been planned, the information planted by someone.

The man in the red truck?

Though the hill that led back to the trailer wasn't a steep incline, the weather and her speed had sweat dripping down her back. She longed for the air-conditioned comfort of the trailer. And the safety of the door she could lock.

And the handgun she'd left in her purse, despite Kade's effort to get her to carry it on her wherever she went.

When she rounded the wide curve and saw the trailer in the distance, she exhaled in relief. Almost there.

There were two cars in the driveway. One a minivan she recognized as Rae's. The other was Kade's Mercedes.

She was still ten yards away when Kade stepped outside, a phone pressed to his ear. He spied her and spoke. "Never mind. She's here." He met Ginny's eyes, no smile. After a moment, he spoke again to whomever was on the other end of his call. "Believe me, I'll tell her."

When he disconnected, she tried for a bright smile. "Am I in trouble?"

Kade slipped his cell into his jeans' pocket. "Where've you been?" His words were harsh, and the look he gave her was no kinder.

"I took a walk."

"I've been trying to reach you." His cheeks were flushed, the corners of his mouth tight. "Why didn't you take your phone?"

She checked her pockets. "I didn't realize I'd left it."

A moment passed while he glared at her. She resisted the urge to step back.

Then, he took a deep breath and approached, his arms outstretched.

She stepped into them. She was too hot to hug, but when she was in his arms, she forgot about the heat.

"I'm sorry," he said. "When you weren't here…"

He didn't finish. After a minute, she said, "I'm fine." And then she remembered. "When you were driving in, did you happen to see a red pickup truck?"

He stepped back, narrowed his eyes. "No. Why?"

She glanced around the area, but even in the distance where the construction workers were busy at their tasks, she didn't see the vehicle.

"Let's go inside," she said. "I'm melting."

He held the door open, and Ginny stepped inside to find Rae sitting in one of the chairs on the guest side of the desk.

The cool air hit her moist skin, and she shivered.

Rae stood when she entered. "I thought I heard your voice out there." She approached, gave Ginny a quick hug. She had the grace not to mention how sweaty Ginny must have been. "Glad you're here. I thought Kade was going to have a stroke when he dialed your number and it rang on the desk."

"I forgot to take it."

Behind her, Kade said, "What's the deal with the red truck?"

Ginny related what had happened at the lake shore.

"Had you seen him before?" Rae asked.

"I saw him at the groundbreaking on Friday. He reminded me of someone."

"Who?" Rae asked.

Rae looked curious, mildly worried with her lips pressed together, her head tilted to the side.

Kade's eyes were narrowed, his hands on his hips.

"Um..." It was going to sound stupid, and Kade was already furious. "It's probably nothing."

Kade continued glaring.

"There was a guy at my father's funeral." She explained that she thought perhaps it was the same person. "Except, really, I didn't get a good look at him then. Or today. Maybe it was just the moment that was familiar, the feeling of being watched from afar."

"Did you get a license plate number?" Rae snatched her phone from her purse.

"The angle was wrong. I couldn't read it from where I stood." And it hadn't occurred to her.

"Was it a New Hampshire license?" Rae asked.

Kade's shoulders were bunched as if he'd just taken on a great weight.

She closed her eyes, tried to picture the plate. New Hampshire plates were bluish-gray with an image of the Old Man on the Mountain. They had green lettering.

The plate had been white with red lettering. "Massachusetts, I think."

Phone pressed to her ear, Rae stepped out of the trailer. "Brady, there was a red truck..." The words were lost when the door closed behind her.

Kade said, "I'm just going to drive around, see if I see him." He left, too.

Ginny grabbed a bottle of water from the mini-fridge and sipped it. She checked her phone for missed messages. Aside from the ones from Kade and Rae, there were none. She sat and perused her email, finding nothing that needed responding to immediately.

Ten minutes that felt like an hour passed before Kade returned. "Rae's still on the phone out there."

"Did you see him?"

"No sign of the truck. Guess he's long gone." He looked so serious, almost angry, as he approached her. "You left your phone, your purse, and your gun here."

"I just went—"

"It's not safe. I understand it's been months since the break-in at your house, but after what Brady said the other day, I'd think you'd be more careful."

"I needed to get out of here for a minute."

He closed his eyes, took a deep breath. When he opened his eyes again, he stepped closer and wrapped her in his arms. "I'm not angry with you. It just scared me when you weren't here. And then that man—"

"That was probably nothing." Ginny let herself enjoy the moment. "That man probably works here for one of the construction companies, don't you think?"

"If he did, then I'd have seen his truck when I drove around."

Good point. She stepped out of his arms. "Why is Rae here?"

Kade shrugged. "No idea. I came to see if you wanted to get lunch. I wish you could have joined us yesterday."

"Me, too."

"Dad wanted to meet you, but he and Mom are coming back in August, and they've already made me promise they can meet you then."

"Your parents want to meet me?" She hated the uncertainty in her voice, the fear.

"Of course. My siblings told Dad all about you. And Mom's been grilling Andrea for months. They can't wait."

"Oh." She couldn't think of a thing to say, so relieved at the words. Relieved and concerned. "I want to meet them, too. But we haven't had a person stop by to look at the lots in days. I just think maybe—"

"We're not talking about ending this." Kade stepped away.

"But maybe we should."

"The article is going to come out tomorrow, and when it does, everyone in this town is going to love you as much as I do." His lips quirked with a smile. "Well, maybe not quite as much." He brushed her hair back from her face. "Stop trying to talk me into dumping you. It's not going to happen."

The door opened, and Rae stepped back inside. "Brady's got his men on the lookout for that truck."

"It was probably nothing," Ginny said.

"I'm glad you're both here. I have some news." By the look on her face, it wasn't good.

Kade slid his arm around Ginny's back, and they faced Rae. "What's wrong?" he asked.

"Why don't we sit?"

Uh-oh. This wasn't starting well, and the look on Rae's face brought no comfort.

Ginny slipped into one of the guest chairs. Kade rounded the desk and sat in the rolling chair on the far side.

Rae sat beside Ginny and focused on her. "My editor called me this morning. He's not going to run our article tomorrow."

Kade stood. "What? Why?"

"I don't know. He just said the timing wasn't right."

"The timing is perfect," Kade said. "Everybody in town is talking about her right now."

*Her.* As if Ginny weren't there.

"People will devour it," he added.

Rae said, "I'm sorry. I can't force him—"

"Take it to the *Union Leader*, then. Maybe they'll—"

"I work for the *Gazette*. I can't write an article for another newspaper. It doesn't work that way."

Kade ran his fingers through his hair. "If that article doesn't come out..."

But the words trailed off.

Ginny didn't need him to end the sentence. She stood. "It's over, then."

Kade faced her. "We'll figure something out."

"You will. Without me." She kept her voice emotionless, forced out words she knew nobody in the room would believe. Not right away, anyway. "You're a nice guy, Kade. But this is more trouble than it's worth, for both of us. It's been fun, but, seriously, I can't handle any more drama."

He blinked once, twice. "What are you talking about?"

"I'm sorry. I'm done." She waved around the room at the messy files and paperwork, at the poster propped on the easel beside her. "Thanks to your development, I've lost my business. I have to try to salvage it, either here or elsewhere. And you'll have to salvage this." She snatched her purse from the table. "We're done."

She didn't meet Rae's eyes as she passed. She pushed open the trailer door and stepped into the blazing sun.

She hurried to her Toyota, but she needn't have. Kade didn't follow her out.

# CHAPTER SIXTEEN

Kade had spent half the day Saturday trying to get Ginny not to break things off with him. Hours he should have spent reassuring his investors instead of dealing with her drama.

And at the first sign of trouble, she'd dumped him.

Fine, then.

He wasn't going to try to talk her out of it. He couldn't be the only one fighting for their relationship. If she was so willing to let him go, then he'd let her.

Kade didn't subscribe to the newspaper. He read most of his news online, including the *Gazette's*. But this morning, despite the rain that had moved in the night before, hope had bloomed. Maybe Rae's editor had changed his mind and run the feature article. It made no sense that he'd decided not to. He had nothing to gain by seeing Clearwater Heights fail, and the paper had been supportive of the development for months.

So after Kade dressed and read his Bible, he hurried to the closest gas station and bought a newspaper. Just a glance at the front page told him his hopes had been in vain.

Back home, he fixed his coffee, sat at his kitchen table, and read the headline.

*Construction Halted as Investors Run from Clearwater Heights.*

The headline over the sidebar story above the fold read *Local Real Estate Agent Linked to Scandal.*

Already sick to his stomach, Kade skimmed the articles. In the first, he saw the names of two investors, friends, who'd been interviewed, who'd explained in detail why they'd decided to demand their money back. One implied an attorney had been consulted to represent them all in a lawsuit. Other investors had commented anonymously.

The article about Ginny was more of the same of what had been printed in Saturday's paper. Rae's editor, Larry, had the byline on both stories. He'd tracked down an old neighbor of Ginny's family, who'd been quoted as saying she wasn't surprised that the Lamonts were *"into strip clubs and that sort of thing."*

*"You could tell there was something not quite right about that family,"* the woman had been quoted as saying. *"And the girl, Ginny, always played herself off as innocent, but those are always the guiltiest ones."*

More digging on Larry's part—or somebody's—had revealed that all of Ginny's parents' businesses had been sold, and her mother was wanted for questioning in the murder investigation of one of her previous employees.

*Darlene Lamont disappeared right after the murder. Investigators believe she fled the country.*

And then there was the expected final line: *Ginny Lamont couldn't be reached for comment.*

Kade slammed the newspaper on the kitchen table. He couldn't prove that anything in the article was inaccurate, but it was filled with half-truths and innuendo. And once again, Larry hadn't bothered to get Ginny's side of the story.

Kade stood, snatched his phone and keys from the kitchen counter, and then froze.

What was he going to do, rush to Ginny's side? Bang on the door to convince her to let him in? He'd already gone that route once.

He set the keys down. He folded the newspaper and shoved it in the rubbish bin.

He wanted to talk to his father, but he knew what Dad would do. He'd cash out of his investments—paying a hefty penalty to do so—in order to keep Kade afloat. It wouldn't be enough, and then Dad would lose everything, too.

Kade wouldn't let that happen.

He could call all his investors right now, tell them he and Ginny were over. He could tell them she was no longer working for him as the selling agent on the lots and assure them that he had no intention of getting involved with her again. The problem was, the words would be a lie. Because as frustrated as he was with Ginny, he loved her.

And he wasn't sure he believed her.

Had she left him because he was causing her too much trouble? Or had she done it for his sake?

Either way, it was irrelevant. With today's newspaper article, he doubted any of his investors would be eager to dive back in. A few of them had not only pulled out of the project, they'd sabotaged it. And those who'd been quoted in today's article? There was no way Kade would let them back in. He certainly didn't need friends like that. He needed people he could count on.

There was only one investor who hadn't demanded his money back yet. Kade hadn't reached out to Mike Sokolov, hoping the man hadn't heard about Saturday's article. No need to poke the bear, as it were. But now, Kade had no choice. Sokolov was his only option.

He sank into his chair and dialed.

The man answered on the second ring.

"It's Kade Powers."

"I was wondering when you were going to call." Sokolov's accent seemed stronger today.

"There's been some drama surrounding the development."

"I am aware," Sokolov said. "I have just finished reading the newspaper articles on the computer. According to this, most of your investors have pulled their funding."

If Mike did the same, the bank would surely call the loan. Kade would have to put the land on the market in order to pay back his debtors. And he'd probably declare bankruptcy anyway. "They have."

"And your girlfriend, Ginny Lamont." His voice was gruff and no-nonsense, as always. "Is she still in the picture?"

Kade blew out a long breath and prayed for wisdom. "She and I broke up, but it wasn't my idea, and though she seemed pretty certain of her decision, I hope we'll get back together."

"You care for her."

"She hasn't done anything wrong, Mike. She's a good person whose parents were monsters. I'm not one to punish a child for her parents' crimes."

The gruff, "Hmph" through the line didn't raise Kade's hopes. And then Sokolov chuckled. "My wife has not always been an asset to my business. She is not so good at keeping her opinions to herself. Sometimes, her opinions are strong. Always, they are loud. Even though she's cost me some business, her wisdom has made me much money. I wouldn't trade her for any business deal."

Kade stood, paced toward the back slider on his condo, and stared out at the rain. He thought of Ginny, of everything he knew about her. Right now, being associated with her was making his life difficult. But in the long run... In the long run, a man didn't choose who to love based on how much money she might make him or cost him.

Ginny was the woman for Kade. He'd known it for weeks, maybe ever since that first date. Every prayer he'd lifted for her, he'd felt confident that the Lord would bless their relationship. Right now, Ginny had run away, maybe for her sake, though he suspected she'd done it for his.

He didn't know for sure. What he knew was that his decision not to continue to pursue her was a mistake. He needed to find her today, to beg her to reconsider. If he lost everything... Well, Jesus had sacrificed much more than a business for the sake of love.

Ginny was worth his business and more.

"Are you still there?" Sokolov asked.

"Yeah." Kade ran his fingers through his hair. "I'm not done with Ginny, so if it makes you want your money back—"

"On the contrary. It makes me want to invest more. How much do you need to get construction started again?"

~

IT TOOK a couple of hours for Kade to settle the details with Sokolov and get the construction back on track. The rain was supposed to stop that afternoon, so they would begin work on the clubhouse the following day.

After the money had been deposited in his account, Kade called his banker, who assured him that they would not call the loan *at this time*. Kade wasn't going to worry about that last remark right now. Right now, it seemed everything would work out.

That evening when Kade neared Ginny's house, her car was in the driveway, and the door to the detached garage was open. He parked, approached the garage thinking he'd find her there, and stopped just inside the space.

Many of the boxes the two of them had painstakingly broken down on Saturday evening were open again. There were four stacks of them along one wall. He crossed to the first stack and tapped it with his finger.

Unlike Saturday, the boxes didn't topple. Because, unlike Saturday, these boxes were full.

She was packing.

The back screen door slammed. Kade stood beside the boxes and waited.

She didn't see him when she entered the dark space carrying a small box, the size a person would choose to pack books. Her hair was pulled back in a ponytail, and she wore jeans and a T-shirt. She lifted the box to rest on the top of the shortest pile, uttering a quiet *oomph* when she dropped it.

The stack was a bit too high, and the box didn't settle properly. The boxes leaned precariously toward her.

Kade moved forward and steadied them with his palms.

She gasped, stepped back. "You scared the tar... What are you doing skulking around out here?"

He straightened the boxes so they wouldn't topple, taking his time to rein in his anger. "Am I skulking? I thought I was coming to see the woman I loved."

Ginny backed up a step. "Now's not a good time."

He made a show of looking around the garage. "I see that."

She swiveled and headed toward the back door. Over her shoulder, she called, "Go home, Kade."

Red hot fury rose in his middle. He followed her out of the garage and caught her in two steps. He grabbed her arm, not tight but not so loose she could pull away easily. "You're leaving, just like that?"

She glanced his way, but her eye contact wouldn't hold.

Raindrops landed on his arms and clothes, but he didn't care.

"What did you think I was going to do? Of course I'm leaving."

"You don't have to." He forced kindness he didn't feel into his tone. "Listen, it's all going to work out. Sokolov invested the difference."

Her eyes widened, and her jaw dropped, a look of... fear?

"It's okay," he said. "I've paid back all my other investors, and Sokolov and I are in this together."

"That's a bad idea."

"It's perfect. He's made up the money that the other investors demanded back. He's with me in this, and he supports you, too."

"He doesn't even know me."

"Right, but... I mean, he supports that we're together."

"We're not together."

Kade took a breath. He wasn't sure if he was not being clear or if she was being intentionally obtuse. "He understands how I feel about you, and, like my father, he supports me. Supports us."

Finally, she met his eyes, and he had a flash of hope. And then she spoke. "First of all, there is no *us*. Second, doesn't it seem odd that he's willing to fund your project when everyone else is pulling out?"

"He sees the value of what I'm trying to build. He's an investor. It makes perfect sense."

She stared past him, eyes narrowed. Then, she shook her head. "If I were you, I'd avoid that guy. But it's your business, not mine."

"But that's just it. If you'll just—"

"You don't need Sokolov. Just tell the rest of your investors that you and I are over. I'm sure they'll line up to get back in on the development."

"After the way they betrayed me in the newspaper today, you think I want those people back?" He shook his head, tried to keep the frustration out of his words. "They don't matter anymore. Sokolov—"

"I don't trust him."

Kade let his head fall back, let the rain cool his heating temper. He prayed for patience, for help, then faced her again. "He's going to save the development. Clearwater Heights is going to happen, and you can stay on as the listing agent for the properties. Nothing has to change."

She laughed, though the sound was anything but amused. "You're kidding, right? You think everything can go back to the way it was before? Maybe if Rae's article had been printed, but not now."

"Look, I get that your business is going through a rough patch, but I can help—"

"I don't want your help or your charity," she snapped. "I can make my own way."

He stepped back. "I'm not offering charity, Ginny. I love you. People who love each other help each other."

"I guess that's the problem."

He blinked. What was she saying?

"You need to go."

"You can't be serious." he said. "How can you throw away—?"

"Oh, stop it." Her words were harsh, her tone scornful. "It's not like we're married. We've only known each other a couple of months. It's not that big a deal."

*Not that big...?*

He released her arm.

But just before she turned away, he saw the tears that filled her eyes.

If she didn't care, then why the tears?

Why the red-rimmed eyes, the blotchy cheeks that he was only now noticing?

She started toward her door, moving faster this time. He kept pace. "So you don't care about me?"

She kept walking. "Not enough to weather this."

"Then why are you in such a hurry to get rid of me?"

"Because I have packing to do."

"Ginny, please."

She climbed the steps to the back door and reached for the screen, but he propped his foot in front of it to keep it from opening. "I think, after everything, I deserve at least a conversation."

She kept her gaze forward. "Get out of my way."

He placed his hand on her back and leaned in closer. "Please?"

She rested her forehead against the door. "You need to go." The words were void of the vehemence she'd spoken with before. He was breaking through.

He slid his hand around to her hip and, pressing his shoulder against the screen, turned to face her. He was so close, he could see the tears hovering in her eyes. Wisps of her hair had escaped the ponytail and, thanks to the moisture in the air, stuck to her face. He brushed them back.

If she didn't care for him, she'd have stiffened at his touch. But she didn't. She shivered.

He left his hand on her cheek and lowered his voice to nearly a whisper. "Don't do this, Ginny."

"You need to go."

"Ginny, I love you."

She sniffed, turned her head just enough to meet his eyes. "I know, and I'm sorry about that. It was a mistake. All of it. Please, get out of my way."

She might as well have slapped him.

He dropped his hands and stepped back.

She went inside and closed the door behind her.

# CHAPTER SEVENTEEN

Ginny snatched the blanket from the back of her sofa, wrapped it around her shoulders, and stood a few feet back from the front window.

And there was Kade, trudging through the rain to his car. He climbed in and started the engine. The lights came on, but he didn't move.

He needed to leave before she changed her mind. He sat there, stared at the house. Maybe he was waiting for her to rush outside and stop him.

The urge was strong. She had no choice but to resist. The floodwaters were already pulling her under. It was too late for her. Kade had to save himself.

Because she'd learned something in the last twenty-four hours, something Kade knew nothing about.

The conversation she'd had with Brady Thomas the night before came back.

She'd walked to town for dinner, desperate for human companionship, but the looks she received from the few people who recognized her had sent her back home empty-handed. She'd just turned onto her street, watching the clouds roll in and trying to figure out her next move, when the chief of police's unmarked sedan stopped on the road beside her. He rolled down his passenger window.

"I saw you in town and wanted to talk."

"Something wrong?"

"Stay there." He parked his car and climbed out.

She joined him beside it. "We could go back to my house."

Brady looked at the sky. The air had cooled, and the sun was hiding behind clouds that were just rolling in. "I don't mind getting some air. Let's walk."

He started down the street toward her house, and she fell into step beside him. He was a good foot taller than she was, but he walked slowly so she didn't have to rush to keep pace. "I talked to Collier about where he got his information. He admitted to having done some digging on you but said most of what he learned came from a letter that was mailed to him anonymously."

"What'd it say?"

"It had a list of all the businesses your parents owned and implied that you were involved with the strip clubs. There was no proof, just a lot of innuendo. But it was enough to get Larry to investigate."

"Who would do that to me?"

"Good question." Brady walked a few paces while the information settled. Then, he said, "One of my officers spotted the truck with the Massachusetts plates Rae called me about. It was clocked going over the speed limit, so she wrote him a ticket. I got the driver's name."

The red pickup truck. Right. That moment at the lake the day before seemed like a lifetime ago. It was funny how big events in a person's life could feel like one-way portals. That stranger at the lake had frightened her *before*. Everything before she'd ended things with Kade seemed irrelevant now. The only thing that mattered was getting as far from Nutfield and Kade as possible, as soon as possible, so she wouldn't turn around to see if that portal might swing back open.

"He's a foreman with NEB. His name is Kristopher Pavlo."

She pushed aside thoughts of Kade. "Pavlo. Any chance that's Russian?"

"Technically Ukrainian, but he was born in California. With a little more digging, I discovered he has ties to the Russian mob out there."

The Russian mob. Was that who her parents had worked for?

"The Russian mob specializes in high-tech crimes—fuel fraud, insurance fraud, things like that," Brady said, "But according to my sources, Petrovich, the guy you saw with your dad before he died, has branched out into some other things. Drug trafficking, which isn't unusual for Russian mobsters. But also smuggling people over the border. And human trafficking."

The words were as painful as physical blows. Her parents had worked for those people? Her own flesh and blood had been involved in such horrendous crimes?

"Rumor has it that he's gone rogue, that he's so far off the reservation that even the Russians in California want nothing to do with him. Russian mobsters aren't like the guys in *The Godfather*. They won't kill a man and then send flowers to his widow. I've never had any dealings with them, but I understand they're ruthless. They'll kill a man, then slaughter his whole family... and they won't think twice about it."

She stumbled off the road to a pretty birch tree and steadied herself against the papery white bark.

"I'm not trying to scare you, Ginny," Brady said. "But you need to know this. Because this guy is so bad that even the *offi-cial*"—he made air quotes around the word—"Russian mob, if there is such a thing, won't work with Petrovich. That's how evil he is."

She breathed through the nausea that rolled through her stomach.

"You're in serious danger."

She swallowed twice, tried to straighten, but the nausea was as real as the rest of the nightmare she was living.

She sat on the grass, her back against the tree.

Brady sat beside her, said nothing.

When she got her voice back, her words sounded flat. "He was watching me, that Pavlo guy?"

"Rae said you thought you'd seen him before?"

"At Dad's burial. He didn't join the guests at the gravesite. He stood by the cars."

"Why would he follow you all the way here?"

She thought of the duffel bag full of cash her mother had given her—shoved into her arms, more like—the day she'd demanded Ginny run. Why hadn't the man just asked her for it? She'd hand it over in a heartbeat if he'd only ask. "I don't know."

Brady studied her with narrowed eyes. "It's just you and me now, Ginny. I don't know what you're hiding, but it's time you told me everything."

Maybe Brady had been right. Maybe she should have told him about the money, but she hadn't. Instead, she'd assured him she knew nothing more, then forced herself to stand and finish the walk back to her house. When they reached her property, she could barely force herself to wave to the old man across the street before she made her way inside and started packing.

She would run just like her sister had told her to. Like her mother had told her to. She couldn't stay in Nutfield any longer. When she was gone, Kade would be able to rebuild his life, the Russian mobsters would clear out, and everything in this sweet little town would go back to normal. That had been her plan. That was still her plan.

Now, she watched Kade watching the house and prayed he'd hurry and leave.

Another few minutes passed before his car finally backed out of the driveway and he sped off.

She should just get in her car and drive away. She had no idea what would become of her home or her property, but staying to gather her things suddenly seemed foolhardy. She was making things worse for Kade. And what did she care about her furniture and decorations? She'd come with no more than a few boxes. She could leave with just the same. The sooner she was gone, the sooner everybody could go back to their normal lives.

The sooner Kade could get his dreams back on track. Construction could start again...

Construction.

She swiped the tears that wouldn't stop falling and tried to focus. Her mind was trying to tell her something.

The weekend before, when Brady had asked her about other Russian names she'd heard from her parents, she hadn't thought of Sokolov. He wasn't someone from her past, nor was he from California—at least as far as she knew.

But Brady had said Pavlo worked for the construction company at Clearwater Heights. The construction company had come with the deal Sokolov had made. The company had ties to Sokolov.

Sokolov, who was also Russian.

She was searching for Brady's contact information when her phone rang. She didn't recognize the number, but after years in real estate sales, she was conditioned to answer every call. She swiped to connect. "Ginny Lamont."

"Ah, Miss Lamont." The voice was familiar, as was the accent.

She settled on the sofa in the living room. She'd been right. Only her epiphany had come too late. "This is she."

"You have something I need," Sokolov said. "Something your father gave you."

All her talk about handing over what Mom had given her seemed like big words just now. Was she really going to do business with a Russian mobster? She fingered the pendant hanging from her neck and prayed for wisdom. All she could think to say was, "Okay."

"We're going to make this simple. You are going to take the item with you, get in your car, and drive to your boyfriend's new development."

"He's not my boyfriend."

"Ah, yes. You two aren't together anymore. I heard all about it. I also know he's still quite devoted to you. I suspect you're devoted to him, too. Am I correct?"

"Kade has nothing to do with this."

"I disagree. Now that his future is entirely in my hands, he has everything to do with it. If you give me what I ask for, I will continue to fund his development. If you do not, I will pull my funding, and he will lose everything."

"You don't have to do that," Ginny said. "I don't even want it. You never had to... to destroy my entire life."

"Ah, well, perhaps it was overkill, telling that politician Collier about your past, but I needed you vulnerable."

He'd definitely made her that.

"And you seem the type who'll do more to protect the people you care about than you'll do to protect yourself. The fact that you didn't run away when your sister told you to tells me that much."

"How do you know—?"

"I know much more about you than you can fathom, Ginny."

That was no doubt true. "Let's say I do what you ask," Ginny said. "Then what happens?"

"When I have confirmed I have what I need, then nothing. Your boyfriend will build his development, and I will remain his biggest investor. You will say nothing, Clearwater Heights will be built, and we will all make a lot of money."

And then Kade would be in deep with the Russian mob. And it would be her fault. She closed her eyes, swallowed a sob. "You won't hurt him?"

"Why would I hurt him? I stand to profit from his development. I want only good things for your boyfriend."

"And you won't ask anything else from me?"

"If you keep quiet, nobody ever needs to know. The money I invested has been washed clean, thanks to your parents. There's no reason this should ever come back to haunt any of us."

All this for a small duffel bag full of cash? She couldn't imagine it would be enough to warrant the investment Sokolov and his cohorts had poured into getting it back.

She didn't understand.

"Ginny," he said. "I sense some hesitation on your part. I suppose it would be wise for me to tell you what happens if you decide *not* to do as I've asked. If you refuse to turn over what's mine, I will not only pull the funding on your boyfriend's project so that he'll lose everything, I will also arrange it so that it seems

Kade is guilty of fraud. I will make it seem as if the money was only ever intended to be a short-term loan to convince the bank not to call his loan. And then, I will make it look as though he came by the money through less than honorable means. He will likely land in prison, though, with the American justice system, one never knows."

"Kade hasn't done anything to you."

Sokolov continued. "I will also tell your friend Bruce Collier—who will, no doubt, tell the editor of the *Gazette*—exactly what your parents did for a living, and I will ensure that they uncover evidence that shows you were not only aware but involved in their illegal activity."

"I wasn't."

"I know," he said. "It's all so unfair. At that point, if you still refuse to give me what's mine, your boyfriend will die. Which won't hurt me at all, actually, because everything he owns will become mine." He exhaled a short laugh. "Actually, I think I've worked this out quite well."

She closed her eyes, swallowed hard.

"If you call your police office friend, Chief Thomas, or any law enforcement, you and your boyfriend will both die. And it won't be an easy death. It will be slow and painful. I think I'll start with Kade, so you can watch exactly what—"

"Stop. Please." She bent over, hugged her stomach. "Just tell me where to meet you."

"You will go to the lakeshore on your boyfriend's property. It should be quiet there today with this rain. Park where you saw my associate yesterday. He will meet you there."

"When?"

"You have what I need at the house?"

"It's in a safe deposit box."

"Okay, your bank is right around the corner."

"How do you know where I do my banking?"

His laugh was light, as if he were chatting with his grand-daughter, not a woman whose life he'd just threatened. "I know everything, Ginny. I know how you like your coffee. I know what you eat for breakfast—toast with avocado? I couldn't stomach it."

She looked around her living room as if he might be watching her at that very moment.

"I also know everybody you speak to on the phone, so don't make the mistake of trying to call anyone for help. You understand?"

She nodded as if he could see her. Maybe he could.

"Go to the bank now," he said. "When you have the item, drive to Clearwater Heights. My man will be there."

THIRTY MINUTES LATER, Ginny inched past the trailer on Kade's property. This had been a good choice of meeting places on Sokolov's part. Thanks to the rain that was coming down hard, the property was empty of construction workers. The state highway that led here had only a smattering of small businesses and old homes along it, but on a day like this, it was largely deserted. And with visibility so low, even if someone did see her pass, they wouldn't get a good look at her car—or anybody else's.

Ginny's assistant was supposed to be at the trailer, but his car wasn't there. No surprise. Nobody would be dropping by to tour the show homes today. Ginny had the wild impulse to stop and run inside the office and lock the doors. She could use the landline to call the police. But at the memory of Sokolov's words—*I know everything*—she quashed it.

The rain that had slowed to a drizzle that morning now pounded her car with renewed force, bouncing off the windshield. The sky, the land, and the road were varying shades of gray, making it hard for her to see where she was going. Slowly, she headed down the hill and rounded the curve. She pulled to a stop where she'd seen the man watching her the day before.

Just beyond the beach, the lake water churned in the storm.

Her passenger door opened. The suddenness of it jolted her.

A man slid into her car. He wore a Yankees baseball cap, which was pulled down to conceal his eyes. The little hair she could see beneath the cap was blond. His skin was pale. His T-shirt bulged at the biceps, and when he turned toward her, the muscles in his neck pulled taught.

"You have it?"

It was as if her entire being were vibrating with fear and tension as she reached in the backseat, yanked the duffel forward, and shoved it into his lap.

He glanced at the bag. "What is this?"

"That's it." Her voice was high, near panic. "That's everything my mother gave me."

He opened the duffel, revealing the cash, then closed it again. "This is everything?"

"Yes."

"We'll find what we need in here?"

What was he talking about? "Yes, yes. That's all I have."

The man sat there another moment, facing her. She couldn't see his eyes beneath the cap, so she didn't know what he was looking at. Suddenly, she felt warm, stifled, as if the air in the car were being sucked out by this person beside her. She wanted to turn on the A/C, but she was afraid to move, afraid to breathe.

What did he expect from her?

Why wouldn't he leave?

"It's your fault I was pulled over yesterday, right?" Unlike Sokolov, this man didn't have an accent.

"I didn't... I told Kade I saw somebody watching me. My friend Rae was there. Rae's—"

"The chief of police's wife. We know. And now they know my name."

"Nothing else, though. Just your name."

"You won't tell them anything about this little meeting." Not a question, a command.

"I won't say a word."

He lifted his cap.

She averted her gaze. She didn't want to see him. She didn't want him to have reason to hurt her.

"Look at me, Ginny."

With effort, she lifted her eyes.

He was her age, maybe younger. His eyes were grayish-green, pale. His skin looked freshly shaved.

He reached toward her, and she shrunk away, pressed her back against the cold door. He grabbed her chin and squeezed hard. "Get a good look at me."

She did.

"If you tell anybody anything about this..." He leaned closer, close enough that, for a moment, she feared he might kiss her. "If you betray us, this face will be the last thing you see before you die. Do you understand?"

"Yes."

His eyebrows rose.

"I won't tell anybody. It's over now. You have what you want. I'll never say a word."

If anything, he leaned in a little closer.

Lightning flashed in the distance.

Thunder rumbled.

Finally, he released her chin, patted her face a little too hard, and backed away. "We understand each other." He grabbed the duffel, opened the door, and stepped out into the rain. "Be careful out there."

The door slammed. He jogged up the hill beside the car and disappeared over the top.

Ginny pressed down on the accelerator and sped along the circle that would eventually drop her near the entrance to the development. Her stomach was roiling, and she swallowed two times, three , trying to settle it. She couldn't stop the car, she wouldn't, not until she was far, far from this place, from that man.

Her hands were clenched so tightly on the steering wheel they ached, but she couldn't relax them. Finally, she reached the development's entrance. This was the spot where, months before, Kade had brought her target shooting. This was the spot where he'd told her his plans for the land. Here, together, they'd shared their dreams.

She wouldn't look as she passed, couldn't think about all she'd lost and all she had yet to lose.

Because no matter what Sokolov had told her, this would never be over for her.

She could never undo what she'd just done. She'd handed cash to mobsters—to thugs who imported drugs, who smuggled people across the border in conditions so bad, many didn't survive the trip. These were the kinds of people who sold children into slavery.

And she'd just handed them a bagful of cash.

She turned onto the state highway, hit the gas, and sped toward town, her stomach lurching with every bump.

She wasn't going to make it.

It would be stupid to stop in the storm, but her nausea didn't care about the storm. She turned the car into the breakdown lane, slammed on the brake, and yanked it into park. She all but fell out, then stumbled to the grass, where she landed on her knees and retched.

## CHAPTER EIGHTEEN

______

By the time Ginny reached her driveway, it was dark outside. Thunder rumbled, and lightning flashed all around. Her little house was right in the middle of it.

Ginny let herself inside, where she disengaged the alarm and set it again. A quick look around told her nothing had changed. Boxes were still stacked, some empty, some full. She wouldn't continue that project, though. She'd leave everything behind, leave a note for Kade to take it all. She'd give him the house, too. He could sell it and keep the little equity she'd built. It wouldn't atone for what she'd done to his life. It would be no more than a token of her remorse.

She had to get out of Nutfield. She'd leave right now if not for the storm.

She dreaded storms. That had been the best thing about San Francisco. In the years she'd lived there, there hadn't been a single thunderstorm. Not like when they'd lived in Kansas and Texas and eastern Colorado, where thunder and lightning were as common in the spring as blooming trees and budding flowers. Those storms brought winds so strong she'd worried her whole life might just blow away. But it wasn't the wind she feared, nor the thunder and the lightning. It was the rain, always the rain.

New Hampshire could handle the rainfall. This marshy land

would absorb it, and, except on a few low-lying roads, there would be no flooding. On this hill where she'd bought her house, she was safe from rising waters.

But she hurried to the second floor just the same. She stripped out of her wet clothes, slipped on her nightgown, and crawled into bed. She covered herself with the blankets and curled into a ball, suddenly seven years old again.

Thunder cracked outside. All the memories of that horrible night, memories she'd refused to think of for years, came crashing down like the floodwaters that breached the levees.

Ginny had been just old enough to know something bad was going on, but not nearly old enough to understand. She'd heard snatches of conversation everywhere she went. Folks were boarding their windows, gathering supplies, muttering prayers and talking about things she didn't understand, like levees and evacuations. The name *Katrina* was never far from anyone's lips.

While the neighbors packed their cars and drove away, Ginny's parents were nowhere to be found.

When the storm hit, Ginny and Kathryn huddled in their shared bed as thunder rumbled and lightning struck. They reassured each other that Mama and Daddy would be back soon.

Outside, water sloshed against the side of the house. It seeped beneath the doors. When Ginny made the mistake of looking, she saw it was ankle-deep on the floor.

Kathryn found the ladder, propped it against the opening in the ceiling in her parents' bedroom, and coaxed Ginny into the attic. They huddled next to the tiny window and watched the world float away.

After a while, boats motored down the street, taking people to safety.

"Maybe we should flag one of 'em down," Ginny said.

"Daddy said to stay here."

Daddy and Mama were long gone, but Ginny didn't say that out loud. Sayin' it out loud might make it true.

Every once in a while, they'd see something that looked like a head, maybe hair splayed beside it. Hands, feet. When they saw that, Kathryn would pull Ginny close so she couldn't look.

The water kept rising, rising. Ginny and Kathryn stayed close and didn't talk about the fact that their bottoms were sitting in the water now. They didn't talk about how they were gonna drown and be just like those floating bodies.

Maybe that's where Mama and Daddy were already. Maybe they were floating facedown and weren't ever coming back.

And then, a boat motored toward them.

Mama's voice carried over the storm, "Kathryn? Oh, my God, Tommy, we're too late. Kathryn!"

Kathryn and Ginny pounded on the glass. "We're here. We're right here."

The glass broke, and Daddy climbed in. He took both Kathryn and Ginny in his arms and hugged them tight.

Everything they'd ever owned was gone. Somehow, Mama and Daddy had collected other stuff during that storm, expensive stuff like jewelry and cell phones still in their boxes. Days later, they arrived in Houston with a wad of cash bigger than Ginny'd ever seen before.

Her family never returned to Louisiana. When Ginny asked about her Granny and PawPaw one time too many, Mama had blurted, "They're dead. Katrina killed them all."

Ginny wondered now if her mother had lied to her that day about the rest of their family the way she'd lied about everything else. Maybe, all these years, Ginny had had grandparents and aunts and uncles and cousins still living in Louisiana, family who loved her. Maybe Mama and Daddy had forfeited their family and their home and their sense of right and wrong when they'd spent the hurricane looting their neighbors' homes and businesses instead of protecting their children. Because after that, everything changed. Her old life had floated away in that flood.

As today's storm raged outside, Ginny knew her life was about to float away again.

~

THE STORM HAD PASSED, and, somehow, Ginny had slept. It was dark outside, and rain pattered against the roof.

Beside her, a shadow moved.

She gasped and reached for her nightstand. The drawer was empty.

The shadow closed in.

A scream caught in her throat.

A hand pressed over her mouth, pushed her against the pillow. "Let's have none of that." Sokolov's voice, cool and collected as if it were a conversation between friends over dinner. "There's no need to panic. It's just you and me."

As if that should calm her.

"Just breathe," he said.

She did what he commanded, pulled in a deep breath through her nose, pushed it out. How had they gotten past her alarm system? All the safeguards she'd put into place had been useless.

"You're not going to scream?"

She shook her head.

"Not that anybody would rescue you." He removed his hand from her mouth and stood beside her bed. He lifted his other hand, and in the dim light, she saw the shape of a gun. "I assume you were looking for this."

She couldn't think of a word to say and couldn't have forced her voice to operate anyway.

His shadow moved. "I thought we had a deal."

"How did you get in? The alarm—?"

"Easy to disable. Maybe not for your common everyday burglar, but there's nothing common about us."

"What do you want? I gave you everything my mother gave me. I never touched—"

"My dear, you can't believe I went to all this trouble for the cash in that bag."

She hadn't understood, but she'd hoped. "That's all they gave me."

There was a bang and a door slammed downstairs. She turned toward her doorway.

"Pay no attention to the noises. My friend is bringing in boxes from the garage."

Someone else was there? Probably Pavlo. She shuddered at the thought of that man in her house.

"Your mother gave you that money the day of your father's memorial. She intended for you to use it to start your new life." The shadow shifted, and a moment later, something plopped on the bed.

She sat to see the duffel bag by her feet. The shock of his words —and the presence of the bag—surprised words from her mouth. "How could you possibly know why she gave it to me?"

"She told me when we spoke to her the day after the funeral. She said she'd given you money and told you to hide. She was trying to protect you. But there was no need for you to run away. I'm not here to steal your future, not if you give me what I came for. Before he died, your father gave you something. A journal, perhaps, a letter? It has instructions on it. You see, your father was holding onto our money. He was in the process of getting it laundered when he was killed."

"Daddy didn't give me anything," she said. "He never—"

"If I were you, I wouldn't speak just now." Sokolov blew out the sigh of a disappointed parent. "I'm going to tell you everything my associates and I have gone through to get to this point. I want you to listen carefully, and I don't want you to speak. You understand?"

Keep quiet. She could do that. She'd been practicing keeping her mouth shut all her life.

"After your father's accident, our associates had a chat with your mother. You see, your father and our organization hadn't worked together for very long, so we weren't well acquainted with how he worked. When we first began our acquaintance, though, your father assured us that he always had a backup plan, somebody who would have the information we would need should anything happen to him. When he died, we assumed your mother would be able to locate our money for us."

That made sense. Mom and Dad had always worked together. Surely Mom could have given them what they needed.

"Unfortunately, your mother claimed she knew nothing about the money. With a little persuasion, we convinced her to tell us in whom your father might have confided. Your father had been making frequent trips to China. You knew about those?"

Sokolov had told her not to speak, so she nodded. In the two years or so prior to his death, Dad had gone to China many times on business.

"Your mother believed that he was connected with the relatives of a man who worked for them. She further believed that he'd become involved with a woman in China. According to your mother, your father and this woman had quite the love affair."

"My father would never—"

"I told you not to speak."

She swallowed the rest of her protest. Daddy had always been loyal to Mom. All their other sins aside, her parents had loved each other.

Was even that a lie?

"This woman was the sister of the manager of one of his restaurants, a man named Wang Lei Chen."

Wang Lei had managed *Tammy Jean's*. He'd been murdered in September.

Sokolov continued. "Wang Lei's family owned a factory in China. They manufacture cheap trinkets—souvenir items, costume jewelry, that sort of thing. That's how he met the woman, Li Min.

"It was very difficult to find Li Min. After your father died and her brother was murdered, she went into hiding. Fortunately for us —not so for her, I'm afraid—she is like most people, like you yourself. People cannot fathom the idea of being alone. They flock to places or people they know. You came here to be near Kathryn. Li Min went into the countryside to stay with her grandparents. She stayed out of sight for some time, but eventually, she felt confident enough to show her face. That was when we found her."

Ginny tried to imagine her, this Chinese beauty who'd lured her father away.

"Like your mother, though, Li Min did not have the information. She told us your father gave it to you."

"What?" Panic had her voice rising. "No, he never gave me anything. She must have it. She must have it, and she sent you after me so she could keep it. I swear, Daddy never gave me anything." She pushed herself to a seated position. "You have to believe me. I don't care about any of that. I don't care about the money. I'd give it to you, I'd do anything to protect Kade right now. But I don't have it."

"Are you through?"

"I'm just saying—"

"Like you," Sokolov went on, "Li Min had people she loved. Her beloved grandparents, her aunties and uncles. Only when she knew my associate would kill each and every one of them did she tell him about you. Only when she thought all was lost."

"But I don't—"

"But you do. And I know you do because after we killed Li Min, we found your mother again."

They'd killed that woman, Dad's friend. They'd murdered her.

And then the rest of what he said penetrated.

"You found Mom?" Ginny tried to shake off the panic. "Mom sold the house and... How did you find her?"

"You remember the day you and I met in the restaurant?"

The day Kathryn had left, the day Sokolov had bumped into her at McNeal's. Of course she remembered.

"I was only in town to keep tabs on you," he said. "I originally invested in Kade's property because I needed a good excuse to be in town—and I'm always looking for legitimate places to invest my money. When you and Kade started dating, it made my job of watching you that much easier. The day we met, I downloaded an app on your phone."

"You bumped into me on purpose. I didn't drop my phone. You stole it."

"But I gave it back." His voice sounded amused. "And when you called your mother the following day, I got her phone number. Then it was just a matter of bribing someone at the phone company to tell me her location, and voila, there she was. She was in Baton Rouge when we found her. She had rented a house, changed her name."

Mom had gone home to Louisiana after all those years.

"Your mother said it made sense that your father would have given you the information. He trusted you, trusted your innocence."

Her mother had told them that? Why would she do that, unless she'd been trying to protect herself?

Was this her mother's latest betrayal?

"I need you to understand this, Ginny. Everyone you love is in danger. Your friends, your sister—"

"You know where Kathryn is?"

"Of course. She can't escape any more than you can or your mother could. We will kill her. And your precious Kade... They will all die if I don't get what I want."

"I don't know—"

"I'm not going to listen to your protests any longer. We are searching your house right now. If it's here, we'll find it. It would go better for you if you simply told us where it is."

"I don't know what you're looking for."

She could smell his breath. "Maybe you aren't aware of what you possess. When you handed over that silly bag, I was almost convinced that you truly are innocent. That's why I'm giving you another chance. But make no mistake, we will get the information we need from you today, or Kade will be the first to die. And then your sister and her family. We will keep killing people until you turn over what we need."

Face after face flitted before her eyes. Kade, Kathryn, her husband, their children. There weren't many, but they were all precious. She squeezed her eyes shut.

Sokolov stood over her and put his hand on top of her head. It was hot and heavy, and she resisted the urge to duck away. "Of course, if we don't get what we want, you will die, too. And I'd hate for that to happen. I've grown to like you. If you get me what I want, then the deal we made earlier will stand. Your boyfriend can build his little community, and nobody ever needs to know about any of this. So, where is it?"

~

ALL OF GINNY'S protests meant nothing to the man. He questioned her for ten, maybe fifteen minutes, and then lost his patience and yanked Ginny from the bed.

She shivered before him in nothing but her flimsy summer nightgown.

He turned her to face the bed and bound her hands behind her back with plastic zip ties, which he tightened until the sharp plastic bit into her skin.

Then he pushed her back onto the bed. She tried to slide under the covers, but with no hands to pull them over her, she could only get her legs covered.

Sokolov walked to the door and called, "Come here."

A moment later, Pavlo stepped into the room. He saw her, and his lips stretched into an evil smile.

Sokolov said, "We'll search each room together, and we'll keep her with us."

Pavlo approached the bed.

Ginny pushed back against her headboard, but there was no escape as the man sat beside her. He placed his hands on either side of her face and closed in. "Just tell us where it is, Ginny, and we'll get out of your hair."

"I don't know. I swear I don't."

Pavlo's hands slid down to her shoulders, her arms. Then they shifted to her hips. "You and I could have some fun together."

"Focus," Sokolov said. "We need to search."

Pavlo didn't move, didn't take his eyes off her. "She knows where it is. Let's just get it out of her."

She said, "I don't know—"

His hand closed over her mouth and muffled her words. He pressed harder, shifted until he covered her nose as well. She couldn't breathe. She struggled to take in a breath, to get away from him.

His other hand slid around her back, pulled her against him.

"Oh, yeah, you and I could—"

"Let her go," Sokolov said.

Pavlo stood and stepped away.

She sucked in a deep breath and tried again to scoot beneath the covers. All that accomplished was sliding her nightgown higher. She gave up and rested against the headboard and prayed.

"If we don't find the information"—Sokolov looked at her through narrowed eyes—"you can do whatever you want to her."

Pavlo smiled. "Well, now I don't know what to hope for."

Sokolov turned his irritation on his partner. "Hope we find that money. Now."

"Right, boss." He nodded, then headed for her bureau. With his back to her, she saw a handgun shoved in the waistband of his jeans.

Sokolov had shoved her gun into his waistband. He had another in a holster on his side.

She prayed the guns would stay where they were.

Sokolov started pulling artwork off the walls while Pavlo yanked every drawer from the furniture, emptied it on the floor, and pawed through her belongings.

Ginny was taken from room to room with them, forced to sit and watch them demolish her home. Sokolov mostly ignored her. Pavlo turned to her with a leer whenever he'd hit another dead end.

She watched them and prayed for help, for guidance. For a miracle. God could save her if He wanted to. God could rescue her.

Unfortunately, she didn't think He would.

That spring, her Bible study group had been reading Genesis, and she'd heard the story of Abram and Sarai and Hagar for the first time. The rest of the ladies in the study focused on how Abram and Sarai had tried to make God's promise come to pass by themselves.

But Ginny had thought more about Hagar. She was a slave, unloved in her own household and forced to sleep with her master and carry his child. Had they consulted her? Had she mattered to them at all?

When she became pregnant and Sarai mistreated her, she ran away, but she met an angel of God in the desert. The angel had told her that God would bless her and multiply her descendants. That's when Hagar had proclaimed that she had met the God who saw her.

Ginny had felt seen by God for the first time in her life during that Bible study. She'd felt He truly cared for her.

Where was God now? Did He see this?

Did He see how Sokolov destroyed the few photographs she had of her family in his quest for information?

Did He see the way Pavlo leered at her whenever Sokolov wasn't looking?

Did He see that she was trapped, broken, alone, and without help? Without hope?

Where was the God Who Sees now?

By the time the sun started to turn the black into gray outside, four hours had passed, and Sokolov and Pavlo had searched every square inch of her house. They'd pulled every drawer from every cabinet and bureau, searching for secret compartments. They'd gone through every box she'd packed.

They left her house in shambles, and still they hadn't found what they were looking for.

Now, the men stood over her in the living room, both glaring down at her.

"We're going to have to hurt her." Pavlo didn't seem too upset about his declaration.

Sokolov glanced at the man, then crouched in front of Ginny. He put a hand on either side of her neck.

This was it. They'd kill her now. Better her than everyone she loved. Maybe they'd stop with her. She closed her eyes and waited for the end to come.

"Open your eyes," Sokolov said.

She did, and he stared into them. "Do you know where the information is?"

"No. My father didn't give me anything."

"That would be very unfortunate for you. Very unfortunate indeed. Because Li Min didn't have it, and we killed her. Your mother didn't have it, and we killed her, too."

She gasped, and Sokolov shook his head. "You didn't think we left her alive, did you? I should have made that clear."

Mom was dead? Dead because Ginny had called her, had given her location away.

She was a fool. She'd always been a stupid fool. Tears filled her eyes, tears shed for the woman who'd never loved her. The woman who'd put her in this position.

"You understand that if we don't get what we want, you will die, too. But you're the end of the road for us. If you don't have it, then..." He shook his head. "We will have to consider the money lost."

Behind him, Pavlo said, "The sister was at the funeral, though. Maybe the mom gave the information to Kathryn."

Sokolov's eyebrows rose. "It is possible."

"No," Ginny said. "No, Kathryn wouldn't have it. She wanted nothing to do with my parents and their business."

"Ah, but maybe she doesn't know she has it."

"No. Kathryn wouldn't take anything from them, even if Mom or Dad had tried to give it to her. If either of us has it, it's me."

Sokolov smiled. "I agree. Though if we don't get what we need from you, we'll kill her anyway. Her and her whole family. It's only fair after what your father took from us that everyone he loved die."

Ginny closed her eyes again. He'd never loved her, and she was going to die anyway. There was truly no hope. She had no idea what they were seeking. *Lord, help! I need a way out of this.*

Sokolov stood. "What about the safe deposit box? Is there anything else in it?"

"It's empty," she said. "I closed it and turned in the key yesterday."

Pavlo smirked at her. "We're supposed to just believe that?"

"We can call later," Ginny said. "We can call and ask about it, if you want."

Sokolov bobbed his head and focused on Pavlo. "We will call when they open."

Pavlo glanced at her, licked his bottom lip. "What do we do 'til then?"

"She worked in that trailer on the property," Sokolov said. "Maybe the information is there."

They both looked at her. It seemed a waste of time to argue, and right now, she wanted nothing more than to waste time. Why rush the inevitable? So she said only, "Can I at least put on some clothes?"

Sokolov pulled her to her feet and marched her to her bedroom. Pavlo followed. When they were all three standing beside her bed, Sokolov cut the plastic ties holding her hands together. "You have two minutes."

Now? With both of them watching? She'd glanced at Pavlo, and Sokolov said, "Turn around, Kris."

The man huffed and turned.

Sokolov kept his eyes on her.

She dug through the clothes they'd strewn all over her floor, finally locating what she needed. She pulled on her jeans and slid into a roomy T-shirt—it snagged on her necklace, but she didn't break it—all without taking off her nightgown.

Sokolov seemed amused.

Then, she pulled the thin straps of her nightgown down her arms one by one and slid her arms out. She shimmied out of the gown and tossed it aside.

"Impressive." Sokolov pulled more zip ties from his pocket. "Turn around."

"I promise I won't run," Ginny said. "Can you please just leave them off?"

"Alas, no," Sokolov said.

"Can you bind them in front, then?" she asked. "How much damage could I do with my hands tied in front?"

His eyes narrowed to slits.

Pavlo swiveled and gazed at her. "She needs to stay bound." He closed the distance between them, stopped inches behind her. The heat from his body warmed her back, made her want to step forward. "I prefer her defenseless."

She swallowed and focused on Sokolov. "Please?"

The man looked over her shoulder at Kris, then back at her. "Okay." He silenced Pavlo's protest with a look.

A few minutes later, hands tied in front of her, Sokolov held her arm and waited at the front door while Pavlo went out the back. A few minutes passed, and then Pavlo pulled into the driveway in a big black sedan.

She glanced at the clock on the dashboard when Sokolov pushed her into the backseat. Six-fifty in the morning.

# CHAPTER NINETEEN

Kade glanced at the cloudy sky as he parked in front of McNeal's. It was drizzling still. He was going to lose another day of construction on the property.

He imagined workers looking out their windows and going back to sleep even now.

He grabbed his laptop bag, slammed the door too hard, and made his way into the restaurant. He'd come here to prepare for his meeting at the bank. He could have worked at home, but after getting dumped the day before, he craved a friendly conversation. Most of his friends had turned on him, though. At least at McNeal's, Bonnie would chat with him when she delivered his coffee, and strangers would smile, would make him feel welcome.

But when he walked inside, the glances from the patrons were anything but friendly. Suddenly, everyone in town was a local news aficionado. He decided to order his breakfast to go.

After he snatched the sack from Bonnie, who gave him an encouraging smile, he dashed through the rain to his pickup.

What now? He didn't want to go home. He had hours before his meeting. This meeting that could shift the course of his life. Maybe he should drive to Manchester and find a place to work there. On Sunday, he and Ginny had been able to relax in

Manchester despite everything that had happened. It had been a good day. Their last good day together.

It was all wrong. Her family, this mess they'd put her in... it was all so weird and crazy. So unlike his normal, ordered life.

Maybe it would be for the best to let Ginny go.

Even as he had the thought, he took a left toward her house. He'd just drive by, see if there was a moving truck outside yet.

As he turned onto her street, he tried to decide if he was behaving like a jilted boyfriend or a creepy stalker. Hopefully, if she caught him on her street, she'd think the former.

But when he neared her house, something didn't seem right. He slowed the car to a crawl and studied the sight.

Her car was parked in the garage, which made sense. But the door on the detached garage was open. He glanced at the clock—not quite seven in the morning. How strange. Maybe she'd gotten an early start. Except that the blinds were all closed. If she was still asleep, then that would make sense, but he'd never been here after the sun had risen that the blinds were closed, even on rainy days. She liked natural light.

Had she been too busy to open the blinds? Or perhaps too depressed?

With everything in him, he wanted to walk to the door. He wanted to hear that awful doorbell screech, then see her beautiful face. He desperately wanted to see her smile at him as she had before the story came out on Saturday.

It was a stupid decision, but he couldn't seem to help himself as he pulled over to the side of the road and jogged through the wet grass to her house. He would just check on her, make sure she was okay, see if she needed help. He'd be a friend. If he couldn't be more, then he'd just be a friend.

He hit the doorbell and listened to the screech inside.

No answer.

He knocked, but she didn't answer that, either.

He dialed her number, then pressed his ear against her screen door to listen for her ring.

Faintly, he heard it.

She was there.

Ignoring him, of course.

He backed into the yard and stared at her bedroom window. Had she looked out, seen his car? He should have hidden it.

Nope. That would have put him squarely in the *stalker* camp.

He waited another minute, then took the walkway to avoid getting his shoes any wetter than they already were. When he reached the driveway, he glanced at the garage.

The boxes that had been stacked there the day before were gone.

Had she already had someone take them to... wherever it was she was moving? Why would she send the boxes if she weren't ready to go?

He peered in the garage. It was empty except for the lawn mower and other garden tools. How strange. Why wouldn't she have had them taken, too?

And why did he think it was any of his business?

If she came out and caught him in her garage again, she'd have every right to call the police. And wouldn't that be a nice addition for Larry to put in his newspaper. *Sleazy Real Estate Developer Caught Stalking.*

He was losing his mind. He stormed down the driveway and back to his car. He refused to look back as he drove away.

# CHAPTER TWENTY

T he drive was silent except for the sound of tires on the wet streets and the rhythmic hum of windshield wipers. The constant stream of prayers Ginny sent made no noise in the car, but she hoped Someone in heaven was hearing them.

Twenty minutes later, they arrived at Clearwater Heights. Pavlo let her and Sokolov out in front of the trailer.

"Hide the car and hurry back," Sokolov said.

Pavlo nodded, and Sokolov pushed her toward the door. "Are you expecting anybody today?"

The associate she'd hired to help her with the properties had resigned, apologizing and explaining he had to protect his reputation. She shook her head.

Sokolov used her keys to open the trailer door, and they stepped inside.

Another place for them to leave in shambles, and this one wasn't hers. *I'm so sorry, Kade. So sorry.*

But whatever state they left the trailer in would be the least of Kade's worries if Sokolov made good on his threats.

Sokolov pushed Ginny into one of the metal-and-fabric guest chairs. "Don't move."

He started the search at the file cabinet, opening every file and tossing papers on the floor after he looked at them.

Pavlo returned a few minutes later, and, together, they tore the space apart.

It took a couple of hours for them to look at everything. When they were finished, Sokolov's lips were set in an angry line.

Pavlo's face was red, his eyes bulging.

He stalked behind her and grabbed a handful of her hair and yanked. Her head snapped back, and she pushed on her toes to try to relieve the pressure. But he pushed her shoulder down with his other hand. "Where is it?"

"I swear, I have no idea. I told you, I don't know."

Pavlo dug his fingers into her flesh.

She gasped, tried to duck away, but with his grip on her hair, she couldn't move.

Sokolov stepped in front of her, looked down at her, and shook his head. "We don't want to kill her yet."

"I'm not going to kill her." Pavlo squeezed harder. "I'm just going to hurt her."

"Stop," the older man said.

Pavlo let her go, and she pulled in a deep breath, closed her eyes. She couldn't do this anymore. She couldn't take another minute of it.

*Please, Lord...*

Pavlo said, "You told me if we didn't find it—"

"I know what I told you."

She kept her eyes closed. She didn't want to see what was coming. She wanted to float away.

There was a bang, a whoosh of air, and then Sokolov said, "Open your eyes."

She did and found him seated in front of her.

"I do not want to let my friend violate you. I've seen what he does to women, and it is not pretty. However, you will tell us anything we want to know when he's done with you. So please, make it easier on yourself. Just tell us now."

She said nothing. There was nothing else to say. She had no idea what he was looking for. She had no idea what her father had given her.

Nothing. He'd given her nothing.

Dad had spared her a few moments of conversation now and then when she was a kid. He'd smiled at her, he'd asked about her days sometimes, and she'd called his casual concern love.

No father who loved his child would put her in this position.

Her mother had betrayed her. Her sister had abandoned her. Her father was about to get her killed.

And the God she'd desperately wanted to believe in was nowhere to be found.

There were no words for any of that.

~

WHILE PAVLO WAS GONE to get the car, Sokolov stared at her. "I am very disappointed."

"Me, too," she said. "I'd love nothing more than to give you what you want and send you on your way."

Which wasn't true. What she wanted was for these men to pay for what they'd done to her mother. And she wanted to protect Kade. And she didn't want to die. Not like this, not now.

"Your father gave it to you," he said.

She shook her head and looked away. Her gaze snagged on the poster-sized artist's rending of Clearwater Heights, which had been tossed on the floor and stepped on.

What a beautiful dream. She hoped and prayed Kade would live to see it come true. These men had no reason to kill Kade or anybody else. They would kill her, no doubt, but why would they risk murdering a bunch of other people who had nothing to do with any of this? Maybe, if Sokolov could stay out of prison, he'd let Kade use his money and develop this property. Maybe it would be built and Kade would never know his business partner had murdered the woman he loved.

The thought brought tears to her eyes. Funny, she hadn't cried all morning. Not while she'd witnessed Pavlo and Sokolov destroy her home. Not when Sokolov had watched her change her clothes. But now, at the thought of Kade's love, tears dripped from her eyes.

"Your father gave you nothing?" Sokolov said. "In those final few months before he died, he handed over nothing to you."

"I already told you," she said, "he gave me no papers, no books, nothing he could have written instructions on."

"Not even a birthday present?"

She shook her head, lifted her bound hands, and touched her fingertips to the pendant hanging from her neck. It had been a gift from Dad.

The door banged open. Pavlo said, "Let's go."

Sokolov was watching her closely. He nodded, and they both stood.

They were settled in the car when he said, "That pendant... Did your father give you that?"

She sighed. Of course he would take her last connection to her family. He'd destroyed everything else. Why not that, too? They would strip her of everything that mattered before she died. She nodded. "He gave it to me a few days before he died."

Pavlo backed away from the trailer and angled the car toward the highway.

"Wait," Sokolov said.

Pavlo braked hard.

Sokolov reached out, grabbed the pendant hanging from the thin chain, and yanked.

It broke easily, and he held the black crystal—or glass, probably —up to the dim light outside. "Go to the clubhouse."

"Boss, we gotta get—"

"Nobody is coming here today. We are all alone."

Pavlo parked on the far side of the partially constructed structure so that if anybody did go to the trailer, they wouldn't see the car.

Usually, Sokolov managed her, but as soon as the vehicle stopped, he opened the car door and rushed inside.

Pavlo came around and pulled her from the backseat. He pushed her through the mud to what would eventually be oversize French doors. Right now it was simply a gaping hole framed by two-by-fours. They stepped onto the concrete slab.

The roof and exterior walls had been built. Inside, it was dark and dreary and creepy.

Sokolov was on the far side of the room looking at his phone. What was that about?

But no. When her eyes adjusted to the darkness, she was able to see better. He was holding his phone in one hand and the pendant in the other. He had the camera app on and pointed at the pendant.

The flash went off.

"I need it..." Sokolov's voice trailed as he messed with his phone.

"Whatcha looking for, boss?"

"I need your flashlight," Sokolov snapped. "It's too dark in here."

Pavlo pushed her to the floor. "Don't move." Then he crossed to Sokolov. "What's going—?"

"Just get your flashlight and don't ask any questions."

She'd never heard Sokolov be so short with anybody. But it wasn't anger in his voice. It was eagerness.

Which made no sense.

Pavlo lifted the flashlight to shine on the pendant.

Sokolov grinned. "And there it is."

"What?" Pavlo angled to look.

Sokolov slipped the pendant into his pocket. "When we were in China, I saw them in souvenir shops. They weren't as nice as hers. That's why I didn't realize they were the same."

"What are you talking about?"

"Necklaces. The ones in China, when you looked into the crystal with a light, they had *I love you* written in all different languages. Typical foolishness aimed at tourists. Hers was different."

They both glanced at Ginny, who hadn't moved. Who should have moved, should have run. Except both Pavlo and Sokolov were armed. Now that they had what they wanted, they had no reason to shoot her.

Now that they had what they wanted, they had no reason not to.

She couldn't seem to get herself to move. Moving meant getting shot in the back. Staying meant... Would Pavlo get his way, or would Sokolov make it simple?

This was it. This was when she'd die. This was where she'd die. And nobody was here to stop it.

She needed to run.

Pavlo focused on Sokolov. "What did you see?"

Ginny shifted slowly forward and set her hands on the concrete.

"The instructions, of course," Sokolov said. "Just like I told you."

She very slowly turned her toes beneath her so she was on her hands and feet.

Pavlo glanced at the man's pocket. "I don't get to see?"

She looked around. She'd go out the door and around the building. Her best shot would be the woods, but they were a good fifty yards from here. She'd head in that direction. Maybe if she caught them off guard...

There was no way she'd make it, but she had to try.

"Of course you do. But right now, we must take care of her."

She pushed to her feet.

Pavlo glanced her way.

She sat back down, but it was too late. He walked over to her and kicked her in the side.

The force knocked her sideways. She landed on her shoulder on the concrete.

"I told you to stay put."

# CHAPTER TWENTY-ONE

Kade had gone home to work, typed a document with details about his investors to take with him to his meeting at the bank. He'd sent it to the printer and then remembered... He'd taken his printer to the trailer weeks before.

He could send the documents to the office store in town. He used them for big print jobs. They could have this ready in minutes.

And then he had a thought. Ginny had things at the trailer. Maybe she'd go there before she left town. Maybe he could accidentally run into her. Accidentally on purpose, now that the thought had occurred to him. But she didn't need to know that.

He'd snatched his laptop and headed to the property. He was just about to go down the hill when he'd seen a big black sedan backing away from the trailer. A prospective buyer? On a day like this?

And this early in the morning? It wasn't even ten o'clock.

The black car turned toward him, then angled into the mud in front of the clubhouse. Weird. Were they vandals? There was no piping in the building yet, so they couldn't steal any copper. And why would they have been at the trailer?

That made no sense. Too nice a car. It had to be people who

were interested in building on the property. He should catch up with them, talk to them about it.

But when he'd neared, he'd seen a bright light shining through one of the clubhouse windows. They'd gone in.

His heartbeat thudded in his chest, and adrenaline flooded his veins.

Despite how he tried to tell himself it was nothing, his body disagreed. And his spirit. Something was wrong.

He reversed his truck and parked near the entrance to the development. Then, he called the police.

# CHAPTER TWENTY-TWO

At Pavlo's words, Ginny opened her eyes and saw the business end of Pavlo's handgun aimed at her face.

She squeezed her eyes shut.

A gunshot split the silence.

Ginny waited for the pain, prayed she'd die quickly.

She heard a thud.

"Idiot." Pavlo's voice.

She dared to peek. Pavlo was still standing over her. She turned and found herself staring into Sokolov's lifeless eyes. His body lay just a few feet from her. Blood dripped from a hole in his forehead.

She sucked in a breath, then another, then another.

"Oh, my God. Oh, God, you shot him." She squeezed her eyes closed. *God, please, please...* She didn't want to die like that. She didn't want to die here. *Oh, Lord, please...*

Pavlo searched the body, came out with the pendant, and stuck it in his pocket. Then he turned to her, and that evil grin stretched across his face. "I warned you, Ginny. I told you if you didn't give us what we wanted, mine would be the last face you ever saw."

"You have it now." Her words rushed out, high and panicked. "I didn't know. I didn't..."

Her words trailed as he walked toward her. She tried to scoot away, but he reached her in a second and kicked her in the side again.

She gasped for breath, curled into the pain.

He worked his foot between her shoulder and her head until it rested on her neck. "I recommend you don't give me any reason to shoot you. I will eventually kill you, of course, but maybe the cavalry will come." He threw the words out there with the undertone of hope. "Maybe you'll be rescued. So if you want any chance to survive, you better hold real still. Understand?"

She said nothing until he pressed his shoe harder. Her face pressed into the concrete. The tread of his heel dug into her windpipe. "I won't move." She rasped out the words.

"Good start." He released the pressure and stood beside her.

She closed her eyes and prayed. *Are You the God who sees me? Do You see this, Lord? Please, please save me.*

She heard the clicking of a cell phone, then the faint sound of ringing.

"It's me," Pavlo said. "I got it. It's like a little fake rock thingy. I'll show you how it works."

She could just make out the sound of the voice through the phone.

"He's dead, like you ordered," Pavlo said.

A pause, and then, "Just the girl. I'll take care of her and meet—"

The voice on the other end rose. Pavlo paced as he listened.

"It's fine, man. There's nobody anywhere near here. The place is deserted."

More yelling from the other person. Finally, Pavlo said, "Whatever you say." She heard the faint beep-beep-beep telling her the other person had disconnected.

Pavlo fell to his knees beside her. "It's your lucky day. I gotta meet the old man post haste, so we're gonna have to do this fast." He straddled her.

She tried to hit him with her bound hands, but he grabbed them and held them in one of his. With the other, he worked the button on her jeans.

# CHAPTER TWENTY-THREE

"**S**teer clear, sir. Help is on the way."

"I'm getting closer." Kade silenced the phone and slid it into his back pocket. No way was he sitting in his car, not after that gunshot. They'd spared a few trees in the development, but not nearly enough. As he crossed empty lots toward the clubhouse, he wished desperately for something, anything, to hide behind. Because that gunshot hadn't come from a rifle or a shotgun. He'd done enough hunting to recognize those sounds.

He thought of Ginny. Surely she wasn't here. Surely she was home safe. But now, the missing boxes from her garage seemed very odd. The closed blinds on her house seemed sinister. He should have kept pounding until she opened the door.

He should have called the police hours earlier.

If Ginny was here, if this had anything to do with her, he'd never forgive himself.

He made it to the edge of the building and peeked inside.

There was a body on the floor, blood beneath the head. *God, no...*

He forced himself to focus.

He saw a business suit. It was a man. A huge man. He studied the face, tried not to look at the bullet hole.

*Oh, no.* It was Mike Sokolov.

Ginny had been right not to trust him. Which meant…

The sound of a scuffle had him shifting to see the other side of the space.

Another man was on the floor, very much alive. Beneath him, a woman was squirming, trying to get away. Kade couldn't see her face.

But he caught sight of the long dark brown hair.

Ginny.

He swallowed his fear and nausea and the overwhelming desire to burst in and stop this now. The man was armed. For all he knew, a gun was pointed at her right then. Kade could make things worse if he weren't careful.

He crept to the opening to what would someday be the rear floor-to-ceiling windows and stepped inside.

"Please don't," Ginny said. "Please, you don't have to—"

"Ah, but I want to."

There was the gun, lying a few feet from them.

Kade crept toward it.

Ginny caught sight of him, and her eyes widened.

A cell phone rang.

The man reached behind him to grab it from his back pocket. When he did, he saw Kade.

Kade lowered his shoulder and barreled toward him. He wrapped his arms around the attacker. They rolled off Ginny. "Run!"

She scrambled away.

He punched the man in the side of the head, twice, three times.

From the corner of his eye, he saw Ginny scoot toward the gun. But Kade couldn't focus on that. This man was strong.

He didn't know if he could best him.

"Run!" he shouted again. "Please!"

She stood, seemed unsure.

The man kneed him in the stomach. Kade ignored the pain and aimed punches at his back, his ribs.

He couldn't see Ginny now. She'd left, thank God.

But then, he saw movement.

Ginny kicked the man in the head.

The man reached toward her feet, but she danced away.

Kade landed a hard blow against his nose.

The man faltered, weakened.

Ginny kicked him in the back. Kade punched him again in the face. And again.

The man lifted his arm for another hit, but it went wide.

Kade punched him in the face again, then scrambled away. "Where's the gun."

"I have it."

He grabbed it from her and aimed at the man.

His eyes were closed, and he didn't move.

A new voice said, "Drop it or she dies first."

*No.* Whoever it was, Kade wanted to turn and fire, but he couldn't take a chance with Ginny's life. He stole a quick glance behind him and saw a weapon pointed at them.

He dropped the gun.

He and Ginny swiveled toward the voice.

"Now, kick it toward me." The stranger had an accent like Mike Sokolov's.

Kade did as he was told while he studied the face.

It was the old man who lived across the street from Ginny. The one who always waved. The one who always wore the hat. He bent down, grabbed the firearm, and slid it into the pocket of his jacket.

He had no hat on now. The birthmark on his head meant something, but Kade was too rattled to put it together.

Ginny said, "Yuri Petrovich. It's nice to see you again."

While Petrovich chuckled at Ginny's remark, Kade tried to figure a way out of this.

Where were the police? They should be here by now.

"I called to warn Pavlo you were here"—he nodded toward Kade—"but it seems he was busy." Petrovich pointed a look at Ginny's jeans.

Kade followed the gaze and saw her pants were unbuttoned and unzipped. He turned to face her, expecting a bullet any second. But he hated that invasion of her privacy. With her hands bound as tightly as hers were, she probably couldn't lift the zipper. "May I?" he asked.

She nodded, and he zipped and buttoned the jeans. This was as intimate as they'd ever been, as intimate as they would ever be. He met her eyes. "I love you."

"I love you, too."

Of course she did. The breakup had all been a ruse to send him away.

"Where's the information?" Petrovich said.

Ginny glanced at her attacker, who lay a few feet away. His eyes were closed, but Kade didn't think for a moment he was unconscious. "He has it. It's in his pocket."

Petrovich barely spared the man a glance, then focused on Ginny again. "Get it."

"I'll do it," Kade said. "There's no need for anybody to get hurt."

"You will stay still," Petrovich said, "and she will get it. She knows where it is and what it looks like."

Ginny met Kade's eyes as she turned. She seemed to be trying to communicate something to him. What, though?

She walked across the space slowly. "Are you going to kill us?"

Petrovich sighed. "I don't wish to hurt anybody, but I need to know how to access my money, and I need to know now."

Ginny stood above the stranger. "Did you order my mother killed?"

Her mother was dead?

"Your mother betrayed you," Petrovich said. "Why do you care?"

Ginny shrugged. "She was a lousy mother, but she was the only one I had."

"Get the information," Petrovich said.

"I don't think so," she said.

"Fine." He shifted his gun to aim at her and moved his finger to the trigger.

"No!" Kade didn't think of anything except saving Ginny. He rushed the man, ducking low to avoid the bullet that was sure to come.

Petrovich turned toward him, but he was too slow.

Kade reached for the weapon. The man lifted it high, backed away, tried to fight Kade off. Kade pushed him until they hit the framed wall.

Kade kept his left hand on the man's arm to keep the gun from coming down. He used his right arm to land a blow against Petrovich's ribs.

Another blast from a weapon.

Petrovich's gun clattered to the floor.

Blood spewed from the old man's hand.

Behind him, Ginny screamed.

And there was another gunshot.

## CHAPTER TWENTY-FOUR

Ginny didn't know what had happened.

A man climbed into the room from the window, and she lifted her gun toward him. But he wore a uniform. He was a cop.

Another rushed through the front door's opening.

"Lay the weapon down real slow," the first officer said. His gun was aimed at Kade.

A few feet away, Kade rested the gun he'd just snatched on the concrete.

The officer focused on her. "You, too, ma'am."

But she couldn't seem to do it.

She couldn't process what had happened.

She'd shot Petrovich's hand. Petrovich was on his butt, holding his bloody palm in his other hand. He was white as a sheet.

Somebody should help him.

But everybody in the room was looking at her.

More officers had stepped inside. A few guns were aimed her way.

"Ma'am, put the gun down."

She looked at the man at her feet. How had he gotten so close? She'd stepped away from him, hadn't she? She remembered... She'd run to get the gun from Sokolov's body. Sokolov was there, too. Pavlo was on top of him.

She was confused. She hadn't planned to shoot Pavlo. Had she shot him? He was staring at her, unseeing. Blood poured from his head.

She'd shot him? She'd killed him?

"Ginny."

She looked up at the name. Kade was walking toward her. His eyes were fixed on her.

"Can I have the gun please?" he asked.

The gun. She was still holding the gun?

She looked at her hands. And there it was.

She lowered the weapon, and Kade approached. He took it from her, set it on the concrete, and pulled her into his arms.

"It's over," he said. "It's all over."

She closed her eyes and wrapped her arms around Kade and held him and shivered. She had no idea what had happened, but Kade was here. Kade was safe.

Police officers and EMTs poured into the space. They ushered Ginny and Kade outside to a waiting ambulance. How had all these people gotten here?

One paramedic made her sit on a gurney while another wrapped a blanket around her shoulders. Kade was by her side, also wrapped in a blanket as if it were January and not June.

The rain had stopped, and the sun was trying to peek through the clouds. She and Kade watched as three gurneys were carried over the mud to the ambulances. Two were completely covered, the men beneath them dead. Petrovich was alive. His bloody hand was lying on his torso. His other hand was handcuffed to the gurney.

Brady spoke to a uniformed officer in the building and approached them. "Quite a mess you made here." He smiled to soften the words, then focused on Ginny. "What happened?"

She couldn't get it all straight in her head, just babbled about how they'd been at her house, at the trailer. How they'd been looking for her necklace.

Brady pattered her shoulder. "It's okay. Just relax right now. You can tell me the story later." He focused on Kade, and she turned to the man beside her.

His mouth was pressed in a tight line. "The young one... He had her pinned to the floor when I got here. He was working on getting her pants off."

Brady's grim expression turned grimmer still as he turned back to her. He said nothing, just waited.

She swallowed. "Kade got here in time. Another few minutes... He planned to kill me afterward. He told me that."

Brady nodded slowly. "Glad we shot him."

"What?"

"We were nearly here when we heard the gunshot—I assume when you shot Petrovich. My officer got there first. He saw that guy barreling toward you," Brady said. "He fired just in time, took him out before he could hurt you."

"Oh." That explained it. Tears filled her eyes.

Kade pulled her close. "What is it?"

"I thought I did it. I thought I shot him."

"It would have been good if you had," Kade said. "He had it coming."

"They killed my mother."

Brady's eyes narrowed. "You know about that?"

*What?* "You know? How do you know?"

"After our conversation Tuesday, I've been looking into things."

"Wait," Kade said. "What conversation?"

She shook her head. There was so much information to share, so much to learn. There was plenty of time for that, though.

It was really and truly over.

# CHAPTER TWENTY-FIVE

Kade needed to know what happened.

There were two dead bodies—one of them a man he'd thought a friend. Ginny had almost been raped, almost been killed.

He glanced at her as they sat together on the bed in the ER. Her eyes were glazed over, and she stared at the curtain separating them from the rest of the space. He hadn't been there for her exam, so he didn't know enough about how she'd been hurt. He did know she winced when he hugged her too tight. She'd rubbed her shoulder a few times. There were angry red marks on her wrists where she'd been bound.

It looked like she hadn't processed any of that.

He rested his hand, palm up, on his leg, and she slid hers into it and smiled at him.

"You okay?"

She nodded, looked away again. "Sorry. I'm so tired. I just want to go home and sleep."

"I'll stay at the house with you while you rest."

"I can't... I can't go back there. My house is in shambles. They tore it apart."

He processed that, tamped down the quick flash of anger at

everything those men had done to her. "You can come to my house. I'll stay with you. You'll be safe there."

After she refused a prescription for pain medication, they were released. They walked out of the hospital hand in hand to find a uniformed police officer leaning against his cruiser waiting for them. "Chief wants me to take you to the station."

Brady had told them to expect this. Kade didn't know if Ginny could handle it, but when he'd argued his point with Brady, the man had only shaken his head. "The sooner we get the details, the more she'll remember. It'll be hard, and then it'll be over."

So they slid into the backseat of the cruiser and rode to downtown Nutfield in silence, Ginny's head against his shoulder.

He'd do anything to make this easier for her.

They were taken to a conference room with a long table surrounded by cushy chairs. On one side sat a table with a coffee maker, cups, napkins, and a few plastic utensils. Beside it rested a small refrigerator.

They rounded the table and sat facing the door. Neither one of them could handle any more surprises today.

A moment after they arrived, Brady joined them and sat at the end of the table. He rested a file and a notepad on the table. He added a recorder beside it. "I know you guys are wrung out," Brady said, "but we need to know exactly what happened. And we're recording this. Okay?"

Ginny and Kade both said, "Okay."

Kade squeezed Ginny's hand. "She saved our lives."

Ginny shook her head and took her hand back. "No. Kade had it well in hand. I only grabbed the gun so Pavlo couldn't. But then... Petrovich still had a weapon, and Kade was in his line of fire. I thought I might be able to shoot the gun from Petrovich's hands. I tried, and it worked."

Kade smiled at her. "You were awesome."

"You taught me how to shoot. And before that, you saved me. You saved me from..."

"You're safe now." Kade wiped tears off her cheeks. Would she ever stop crying?

"Okay," Brady said. "Suffice it to say, you're both heroes. Ginny, you start. Tell us what happened. Leave nothing out."

Kade listened closely, tried to put all the pieces together. She mentioned Russian mobsters whom her father had worked for.

"Wait," Kade said. "How do you know they were Russian mobsters?"

Ginny looked at Brady, who said, "I'll have to fill you in. I did some digging, told Ginny what I'd learned."

Oh. He'd been way out of the loop.

She talked about a duffel bag full of cash that apparently her mother had given her. "I shouldn't have given it to them," she said. "I know what terrible people they are. But I was trying to save Kade. And myself. Honestly, I was trying to save us both. And they didn't give me any time to think. I handed it over. But it wasn't what they were after. They left the bag at my house."

"My officers found it," Brady said. "Your house is a crime scene, by the way. It'll be cleared soon."

"Any chance your men'll clean it?" she asked.

Brady smiled. "Probably not, but I bet we can find some friends to help." Brady asked question after question, and Ginny told the whole story. She told how Sokolov had threatened her, had gone into her home in the middle of the night, yanked her from her bed, and bound her hands. How they'd searched her house, then taken her to the trailer to search there. How Pavlo had murdered Sokolov, then turned his evil toward her.

Brady focused on Kade. "And how did you find out what was going on?"

"Pure luck," Kade said. "I happened to see the car when they went to the clubhouse."

"Not luck." Ginny swallowed hard. "Not luck. God. The God Who Sees."

Kade kissed her head. "Yes. He took me there."

While Kade and Ginny talked, people came in and out, gave Brady updates, handed him information. When they were both done, Brady said, "Petrovich is in surgery. When he gets out, we'll charge him. He'll spend the rest of his life in prison."

"Have you looked at the information on the pendant yet?" Kade asked.

"We've given it a cursory look. I have people getting it on paper. The Feds will be interested. To me, it's irrelevant. Petrovich ordered his men to kidnap you. He ordered them to kill you. Your testimony will put him in prison for life."

Kade said, "But if he's a mobster and she testifies against him, will she be in danger?"

Brady was shaking his head before Kade finished the question. "I told Ginny this the other day. Petrovich had gone rogue. He had a small operation. There were some underlings, low-level hired hands who've crawled back into their holes like the cockroaches they are. The top level of the organization was Petrovich, Sokolov, and Pavlo. Petrovich ordered Pavlo to take Sokolov out, and I wouldn't be surprised if he planned to do away with Pavlo when the opportunity arose. Although we can never know for sure, my guess is that he planned to get his money and get out of the country. Most of their operation in California had been shut down. The mafia out there was squeezing him out."

Ginny said, "So you're saying..."

"You're safe," Brady said. "It's over."

She closed her eyes, took a deep breath as if pulling the information in.

She opened her eyes and focused on Brady again. "And you found out about my mother how?"

"A detective in San Francisco called me this morning after I made some inquiries. Turns out, your mother was killed in Baton Rouge a few weeks back. Authorities there didn't know how to contact you."

"They murdered her," Ginny said. "She told them what they wanted to know—that I was the one holding the information—and they murdered her anyway."

Kade wrapped his arm around her shoulders, careful not to hurt her, and pulled her close.

"My father caused all of this," Ginny said. "He gave me that stupid necklace. I was so proud of it, so sure it meant he loved me.

It nearly got me killed. Why? Why would he do that and not even tell me?"

Brady shook his head. "How long before he died did he give it to you?"

"A week," Ginny said. "Not even... It was five days. He told me when he gave it to me that there was a story behind it, but..." She sat straighter. "Our lunch got cut short when his phone rang. That's when he went outside and got into the car with Petrovich."

"So he was going to tell you," Brady said.

Ginny nodded. "That makes sense. I never saw him again after that lunch. But what doesn't make sense is why he gave it to me instead of Mom."

The grim set of Brady's mouth warned him Ginny was about to hear more bad news. "You weren't living at home at that point, right?"

"I never moved home after college."

Brady took a piece of paper out of his folder and turned it to face her. It looked like a rental agreement. "I've been doing some digging. It looks like your parents had separated. Your father had leased an apartment in San Francisco a couple months before he died." He added another piece of paper to the pile. It had a mixture of Chinese writing and English. "He'd rented an apartment in Hong Kong as well. I made a call and found out he'd moved a few things in. A woman lived there with him. He'd only been there a few times before his death."

So Sokolov had been right. Dad had planned to leave Mom. And Mom had known. They'd been separated, probably planning to get a divorce, and they hadn't told her.

"My guess," Brady said, "is that your father didn't trust your mother, considering they were going to get a divorce, and didn't trust Li Min enough yet to give it to her. He trusted you. He gave you the information and intended to tell you what it was but was interrupted. And then he died."

"So he put me in danger and planned to leave me?" Ginny couldn't imagine.

Brady said, "We can't know what he was thinking."

Kade had a theory. He took a deep breath and swiveled her chair to face him. "I think he was trying to protect you. Once he told you about the information, you'd have been able to turn it over to Petrovich, and none of this would have happened. It was Petrovich's presence at the memorial that triggered all these events. He must have asked your mother for the information. She didn't know where it was, and she didn't think you would know, either, so she sent you away. She did it to protect you."

"That makes sense," Brady said.

Ginny's smile was forced, unconvinced. And why should she have any faith in her parents now? All she knew was that the two people who should have loved her and cherished her and protected her had lied to her and put her in danger.

And now, they were both dead.

"I guess I'll never really know." Ginny shook her head. "Some family I come from, huh?"

Kade started to speak, but Brady scoffed. "Ginny, your parents were liars and criminals. You're obviously nothing like them." He patted her hand and smiled. "You're a hero."

# CHAPTER TWENTY-SIX

Though Kade had offered to let her stay at his condo that night, Ginny had decided she'd be smarter to spend that night with Brady and Rae. Kade had stayed with her, though. He'd rescheduled a meeting at the bank that she'd known nothing about, and he'd sat beside her on the couch and watched funny movies until she couldn't keep her eyes open. Then he'd tucked her into bed in their guest room and kissed her forehead. If she'd been at her house or his, she might have asked him to climb right in beside her, to hold her until she fell asleep.

Which was why she'd chosen to stay at Rae and Brady's.

When she'd mustered the nerve to go home on Friday, she'd found her house set to rights. Her friends from Bible study and their husbands had apparently worked most of the night and into the morning to get it back to normal. Her photo frames had been broken, a few other things damaged. But all that stuff could be replaced.

It was early Saturday morning, and she was just drying off after her shower when she heard her doorbell making its horrid noise. She donned her bathrobe and looked out the window. Kade's car was in the driveway. After twisting her wet hair in a towel, she hurried down the stairs, anxiety kicking her heartbeat into overdrive. What could possibly have him at her house before sunrise?

When she swung open the door, Kade stood on the stoop with a huge smile on his face. "Good. I didn't wake you."

"What in the world are you doing here?"

He lifted a plastic bag with the hardware store's logo on it. "I bought you a present. I'll install it while you get ready."

"Install...? Wait, ready for what?"

"I have a surprise." He made a shooing motion with his hands. "Go on, hurry."

When he stepped into her house, she gave him a long kiss. "I love surprises."

He kissed her back, then groaned and stepped back. "Clothes... You need clothes."

She looked down at her thin bathrobe. "Oh, right."

"You have twenty minutes."

She rushed to her room, brushed out her wet hair, and threw on a T-shirt and jeans. Twenty minutes even gave her enough time to add some makeup. Throughout her rushed morning routine, she prayed. She couldn't keep the praises and thanksgiving in, not when Kade was downstairs even now with a surprise. Not when all the danger that had followed her for months—for years, really, considering her parents' business—was gone. She felt freer than she'd ever felt in her life.

And yes, her parents were both gone. She grieved for them. She'd spent the day before trying to find out what had become of her mother's body. When nobody had claimed it, Mom had been buried in Louisiana. Ginny would leave her there, near her home. She hoped she'd be able to locate Kathryn to tell her the news—Brady had promised to help, as had Sam's husband, Garrison, who had contacts in the FBI. Whether she succeeded or not didn't seem to matter anymore. Ginny would grieve, and she would go on with her life, make a fresh start in this wonderful little town. God willing, Kade would be by her side.

God was so good.

She slid into her sandals and went downstairs to find Kade standing at the front door as if he'd never moved. He opened the screen, reached out, and pressed the doorbell.

It ding-donged, just like a doorbell should.

"That's the loveliest sound I've ever heard."

"I was going to get one that whistled Dixie, seeing as how you're a Southern girl at heart, but they don't sell those in New Hampshire."

She laughed. "Glad you didn't. I don't really 'wish I was in the land of cotton.'" She pulled him inside and gave him a proper kiss. "Thank you for my surprise."

"The doorbell isn't the surprise. I was just tired of listening to that old screechy one. Let's go."

"Where are we going?"

He just shook his head.

A few minutes after they drove through Dunkin' Donuts for coffee, he pulled onto his property and parked where he had that first day of target practice. He walked around and opened her door. "M'lady?"

She stepped out. "What's going on?"

"I take it you haven't read the paper this morning?"

She shook her head. "When would I have done that? It's barely dawn."

He laughed. "I'd hoped, because I want to show you this myself." He reached in the backseat of his car and pulled out a newspaper.

Plastered across the front page was the headline, *Nutfield's Own Bring Down Russian Mobsters.*

She leaned against the car door. "So now I'm one of 'Nutfield's own'?"

He peered at the newspaper over her shoulder. "You think that's good, keep reading."

Seemed Brady had given Larry a whole lot of information, and all of it made Ginny and Kade out to be heroes. "There's nothing here about how everything Larry printed about us last week was wrong. What was his problem, anyway?"

"Bonnie told me yesterday that he and Collier went to school together. I guess he believed all the lies Collier fed him. But don't worry. This town won't let him get away with it. I'll be surprised if Rae's not the editor by next week."

"Does she want the job?"

Kade shrugged. "I hope so. Anybody would be better than Larry at this point."

Ginny continued reading, her heart thumping with joy at the words. Not only would she no longer be seen as a pariah, this article made her out like a saint, a woman who *threw off the trappings of her past and forged a life as an upstanding member of society*. She tapped the paper. "Look at this. Even Bruce Collier is quoted."

She glanced to see Kade nod, a big smile on his face. "That's my favorite part. '*Nutfield needs more people like Kade Powers and Ginny Lamont, people willing to fight to keep our citizens safe.*'"

"I wonder if it pained him to say it."

"I hope so," Kade said. "After the truth gets out about his involvement in all of this, he'll be finished as town manager."

"I hate to sound vindictive, but that's the least of what he deserves." She turned to face Kade, an idea coming to mind. "Maybe you should run in the next election. You'd be great for the town."

"I'm not going to have time for that." His smile told her he'd kept the best for last. He tossed the newspaper back in the truck. Hand in hand, they walked to the crest of the hill and looked down at his land. From here, they could see the houses in their various stages of construction. The clubhouse that had been the scene of their terror on Thursday now shone in the light of the rising sun. Beyond the land, the lake glittered gold.

"News got out Thursday afternoon about what happened," Kade said. "The bank manager let me know yesterday that they don't plan to call the loan, that I'm a good risk again. I started getting calls yesterday from investors. They're apologizing and wanting back in."

She turned from the beautiful view to see his face. "Oh, Kade, I'm so happy for you. But I thought you were angry with them for turning on you."

"I was. But there's no room in my life for bitterness." He shrugged. "They apologized. I forgave them. That's what God expects me to do."

She loved this man's faith.

Kade continued. "I thought when I learned Sokolov's money was tainted, my dream was dead, but apparently being a *hero*"—he made air quotes—"has been good for my reputation. It's all going to work out."

"You are a hero." She slid her arms around his waist and hugged him. "I'm so happy for you."

He kissed the top of her head, then backed away, threaded his hands into her hair, kissed her cheek, the corner of her mouth.

The sensation sent tingles through her body. She couldn't have moved away from him if she'd wanted to—and she never, ever wanted to.

"I love you."

"I love you, too."

He leaned back. "I should have a whole thing planned, or at least..." He shook his head. "I can't wait another minute."

"Can't wait for...?"

He fell to one knee.

She stepped back, covered her mouth.

"I know it's crazy. I don't even have a ring yet. And after the week we've had, I should let you process it. I should give you time and space. But two days ago, I thought I was going to lose you, and I knew then... I've never been so certain of anything. I never want to be apart from you. I love you, Ginny. Now that we've put the past behind us, I hope you'll make a future with me. Will you marry me?"

She was nodding, trying to force words past her tears. "Yes."

He stood, wrapped her in his arms, and spun her in a circle.

Her past was gone, her future secure. She'd never been more free.

# CHAPTER TWENTY-SEVEN

Ginny steeled her courage while she waited for her new husband to open the door of their rental car.

The wedding had been the stuff of dreams. The ceremony at their church had been followed by the reception in the clubhouse at Clearwater Heights. With the two-by-fours and concrete—and all the evidence of what had happened there—covered by walls and flooring and paint, it was a beautiful space. A space redeemed for good, the way Ginny's whole life had been redeemed.

Kade's family—which had quickly become her own—and all their friends had celebrated the day with them. For the first time, Ginny had felt like she belonged.

She did belong in Nutfield. But did she belong in front of this house? She couldn't believe they were doing this.

In the months after the incident, while they'd planned the wedding, while Kade had built his dream, Ginny had searched. With Brady's help, she'd found Kathryn, Matthew, and the kids in a little town in Florida. She'd called Kathryn, but her sister wouldn't talk to her. So she'd emailed and told her about their mother's murder. Then she'd explained that they no longer had reason to fear. She'd directed her sister to the special agent at the FBI who was handling the case. They'd communicated via email a little since then. Ginny had kept her sister informed on her life and all she'd discovered, but Kathryn never replied.

Then, Ginny had found the rest of her family.

Kade opened the door, and Ginny stepped into the Louisiana humidity. It was evening in early May, and the sun had warmed the air to the low nineties. Cicadas and tree frogs were practicing for their evening symphony.

She'd expected to find her family near New Orleans where she'd grown up, but after Katrina they'd moved north. She and Kade had flown into Shreveport, rented a car, and driven to a little town about a half hour off the interstate. They'd passed through the charming downtown area and stopped in front of a large plot of land. Cars were parked on the street and all along the windy driveway. A single-story house sat back behind tall trees that were as plentiful here as they were back in New Hampshire. But they were different here, the cypresses and oaks and pecan trees. The scent of them as she stood beside the car brought back memories she hadn't thought of in years. Happy memories of her childhood before Katrina, before her parents had chosen the path that had nearly gotten them all killed.

Kade took her hand. "You ready for this?"

"Not exactly the honeymoon of your dreams. We should have gone to Europe."

He laughed. "You're not chickening out on me, are you?"

She wasn't. Of course she wasn't. But so much time had passed. What would this be like? And who did all these cars belong to?

Beyond the trees, the front door opened, and a heavy-set white-haired woman stepped onto the porch, propped a hand over her eyes, and peered at them.

"We've been spotted," he said.

"Too late to back out now."

He kissed her forehead, took her hand. "You're far too brave for that, my love."

Together, they walked up the driveway.

The old woman gripped the handrails and stepped off the

porch, then walked along the gravel driveway toward them. When they were close, she held out her arms. "It really is you," she said.

Ginny stepped into Granny's arms. Emotion clogged her throat, but she didn't need words. Because this was her Granny.

"Ooh-ee, child," Granny whispered. "Ooh-ee, it's good to have you home."

Ginny stepped back, gazed into those familiar blue eyes framed in wrinkles. "I'm sorry I've been gone so long. I didn't know." Tears streamed down her cheeks, and she couldn't form any more words.

"No need for any of that," Granny said. "You told me all about that foolishness on the phone. I'm just sorry I never found you."

Ginny sniffed. "Did you look for us?"

"Surely we did. For years. We finally decided ol' Katrina'd washed you away." Granny looked past Ginny. "And this is your young man?"

"This is my husband, Kade."

Kade stepped forward, hand outstretched. But Granny was having none of that. She wrapped Kade in a hug as if he were her own. "It's good to know you, Kade." When she released him, she asked, "Any chance you're thinking of relocatin'? 'Cause this is a great place to live."

Kade glanced at Ginny, then shook his head. "We hadn't considered that."

Ginny started to say something, but Granny beat her to it. "I didn't figure. But PawPaw and I always did want to visit New England. I hear it's right pretty in the fall."

"Downright beautiful," Kade said. "You're welcome anytime."

Granny nodded once. "We'll be taking you up on that."

Behind her, the door opened. Ginny expected to see PawPaw, but it was another figure stepping onto the porch.

Kathryn made her way down the three stairs. She looked just as she had when Ginny'd seen her last. Short blond hair, pretty eyes that were so much like Ginny's. She halted a step behind Granny and offered a shy smile.

Ginny stepped around her grandmother and pulled her sister into a hug.

Kathryn hugged her back. "I got your emails. I'm sorry. I didn't know how to... Can you ever forgive me for leaving you?" She pulled away. "I should have stayed. I should have had your back like a true sister, but instead, I protected myself. I—"

"Stop," Ginny said. "You protected your family. It all worked out. God had my back. He protected us all."

"No thanks to me."

Ginny hugged her again. "I forgive you."

Kathryn broke down and wept.

When she and Kathryn had pulled themselves together, when Kathryn had greeted Kade, congratulated them both on their marriage and offered her apology all over again, when he'd assured her of his forgiveness and Granny had interrupted and said, "Stop all that sorry-ing. They said you were forgiven. Now you gotta believe 'em," only then did they turn to the house.

Faces peered through the windows and the glass door. Beloved cousins and aunts and uncles. There were little faces Ginny had never seen before, new relatives she hadn't known she had. There were Kathryn's four children and her husband, Matthew. And beside him, Ginny's grandfather, PawPaw, with a smile that reminded her of ham and black-eyed peas and cornbread and joy.

New Hampshire was her home now. But this was home, too, because these people were her family. Her past was more than just crime and deceit. It was love and laughter and faith.

That was her true legacy.

~

*Legacy Restored.*

IF YOU ENJOYED Ginny and Kade's story, you're going to love LEGACY RESTORED, Angel and Donovan's story.

**She's a new Christian working to take down a murderer. He's a grieving man who refuses to let another woman die needlessly. When their desires clash, will it lead to hostility...or fireworks?**

Turn the page for a sneak peek of

~

ONE MORE THING. I don't want you to miss a brand-new Nutfield novella, *Sleigh Bells and Stalkers*, featuring familiar friends from Nutfield—and some new ones as well. *Sleigh Bells and Stalkers* is just one of the novellas in the *Christmas in Nutfield* boxset. Little Daniel from *Innocent Lies* is all grown up, coming home from college, and bringing an unwanted guests along with him. It releases November 2024. Secure your copy now.

~

ONE MORE THING... Did you grab your free book? Visit my website at http://robinpatchen.com/subscribe to get a copy of *Escaping with You,* the edge-of-your-seat prequel to Robin Patchen's bestselling Wright Heroes of Maine series. You're going to love it!

# ABOUT LEGACY RESTORED

*She's a new Christian working to take down a murderer. He's a grieving man who refuses to let another woman die needlessly. When their desires clash, will it lead to hostility... or fireworks?*

Angelica Rossi deserves to be behind bars, but if secretly working with the police to take down an art thief will keep her out of prison, she's willing to take the deal—even when she discovers the target is also a brute and a murderer. As a former thief, she's learned to take care of herself.

Artist Donovan Gilcreast recently lost his sister. He blames himself for not protecting Katie, and he blames Angelica Rossi, Katie's old friend, for introducing her to drugs years before. When Angel moves into the house he's restoring, Donovan tries to keep his distance. But her bruises pull at his protective nature.

Donovan can't help but be enchanted by the injured woman who seems to have turned her life around. Angel can't help but feel comfortable with the brooding artist who seems so wounded. Their relationship might have a chance—if she can keep him from learning her secret.

Romance, danger, and intrigue. You're going to love LEGACY RESTORED. Buy it today.

The Nutfield Saga

Convenient Lies

Twisted Lies

Generous Lies

Innocent Lies

Beautiful Lies

Legacy Rejected

Legacy Restored

Legacy Reclaimed

Legacy Redeemed

Sleigh Bells & Stalkers

One Christmas Night


Amanda Series

Chasing Amanda

Finding Amanda

# ABOUT THE AUTHOR

Robin Patchen is a *USA Today* bestselling and award-winning author of Christian romantic suspense. She grew up in a small town in New Hampshire, the setting of her Nutfield Saga books, and then headed to Boston to earn a journalism degree. After college, working in marketing and public relations, she discovered how much she loathed the nine-to-five ball and chain. After relocating to the Southwest, she started writing her first novel while she homeschooled her three children. The novel was dreadful, but her passion for storytelling didn't wane. Thankfully, as her children grew, so did her writing ability. Now that her kids are adults, she has more time to play with the lives of fictional heroes and heroines, wreaking havoc and working magic to give her characters happy endings. When she's not writing, she's editing or reading, proving that most of her life revolves around the twenty-six letters of the alphabet. Visit robinpatchen.com/subscribe to receive a free book and stay informed about Robin's latest projects.